MINOTAUR

PHILLIP W. SIMPSON

Month9Books

Published by Month9Books
Cover designed by Najla Qamber Designs
Cover Copyright © 2015 Month9Books
Map of ancient Greece used with permission from greeka.com.

Month9Books

For Emeritus Professor Vivienne Gray. Emeritus Professor Geoffrey Irwin and Professor Tanya Fitzgerald. Thanks for instilling within me a sense of wonder and thirst for knowledge about the ancient world.

"With record of his deeds. When men shall have read of ... the mingled form of bull and man." **Ovid, Heroides 2. 67 ff**

"Krete rising out of the waves; Pasiphae, cruelly fated to lust after a bull, and privily covered; the hybrid fruit of that monstrous union - the Minotaurus, a memento of her unnatural love." **Virgil, Aeneid 6. 24**

"What Cretan bull [the Minotauros], fierce, two-formed monster, filling the labyrinth of Daedalus with his huge bellowings, has torn thee asunder with his horns?" **Seneca, Phaedra 1170**

"Theseus escaped the cruel bellowing and the wild son of Pasiphae, the Minotauros and the coiled habitation of the crooked labyrinth." **Callimachus, Hymn 4 to Delos 311**

CAST OF CHARACTERS

Cretan Royal family

King Minos: King of Crete. Stepfather of Minotaur.

Queen Pasiphae: Queen of Crete. Mother of Minotaur.

Princess Ariadne: Daughter of King Minos and Queen Pasiphae of Crete.

Prince Asterion: Also known as the Minotaur or just Minotaur. Sometimes as the 'starry one.' Son of Queen Pasiphae of Crete and the Greek god of the sea, Poseidon. Step-son of King Minos of Crete.

Prince Glaucus: Son of King Minos and Queen Pasiphae of Crete. Youngest sibling to Asterion.

Prince Androgeus: Eldest son of Minos and Pasiphae. Brother of Asterion.

Prince Catreus: Son of King Minos and Queen Pasiphae of Crete. Twin brother of Deucalion. Younger brother of Asterion.

Prince Deucalion: Son of King Minos and Queen Pasiphae of Crete. Twin brother of Catreus. Younger brother of Asterion.

Princess Phaedra: Illegitimate daughter of King Minos.

Cretan retainers

Daedalus: Master craftsman. Builder of the labyrinth with his son, Icarus.

Icarus: Master craftsman. Builder of the labyrinth with his father, Daedalus

Alcippe: Nursemaid for the King's children on Crete.

Paris: Martial trainer in the palace of King Minos of Crete.

Athenians

Prince Theseus: Prince of Athens. Son of King Aegeus and Poseidon.

Princess Aethra: Mother of Theseus

King Aegeus: King of Athens. Father of Theseus.

Queen Medea: Queen of Athens

Other

Publius Ovidius Naso: Also known as Ovid. Roman poet in 1st century BC.

Periphetes: An outlaw

Procrustes: An outlaw

Sciron: An outlaw

Sinis: An outlaw

MINOTAUR

PHILLIP W. SIMPSON

CHAPTER 1

The ship swept into port at Iraklion. Swaying slightly, Ovid stood at the rail and waited impatiently for it to dock, eager to see the sights and sounds of this island. Shipboard life, whilst vaguely entertaining, had begun to be a little monotonous.

Crete was a place he'd always been keen to visit, especially given his current work in progress. His most ambitious work to date. The *Metamorphoses*, his epic poem of Greek and Roman mythology, was almost complete. He considered it his *magnum opus*, his greatest work—something that he was immensely proud of. It would, he hoped, cement his place amongst the best Roman poets and live on long after his death. It was a monumental piece of work, comprising fifteen books and over two hundred and fifty Greek and Roman myths, painstakingly researched, rewritten and reinterpreted. It chronicled the history of the world from its creation all the way through to the reign of Julius Caesar. All that remained was a little editing and some fact checking and then it would be ready—he hoped. Ovid desperately needed it to be a success. Even poets with the Emperor's favor could not afford to waste years on an unpopular work.

After working for so long, he'd had a sudden desire to get out, to actually see some of the places he'd been writing about. To see where these events had taken place. Not that it was especially important—most of his work had taken a decidedly creative approach to historical events—but it was invigorating nonetheless. He was a poet after all, not an historian. That was why he was on Crete. To see for himself the fabled home of the Minotaur.

Ovid's thoughts turned for a moment to Rome. For once, he didn't miss the bustling metropolis. He wondered for a moment what his daughter was doing. No doubt busy with his three grandchildren. They would have liked this trip, but he had quickly discarded the idea of bringing them along as foolhardy. At fifty, he felt old. The grandchildren exhausted him.

He disembarked, unburdened by any baggage other than a wineskin. A sailor trailed in his wake, carrying bags that contained his few important items; his writing implements and a few changes of clothes.

The port was a bustling hive of activity; sailors and dock workers vying with each other for elbow room, loading and unloading crates, urns, and a bewildering array of other products, which included live animals and people like himself.

A nearby voice raised in anger drew his attention amongst

the chaos. A circle of bodies formed, incorporating Ovid into their midst. Within the circle, two figures stood. A shattered urn lay at their feet, shards of broken pottery lying in pools of what was clearly wine. Ovid drew a long breath in, savoring the delicious fumes even as he mourned the waste of good wine slowly evaporating.

One was an average sized man, unshaven with hair that looked like it had been chopped and sawn off with a clumsy blade. He wore a battered and torn tunic that appeared Roman in origin. Facing him was perhaps the largest man Ovid had ever seen. He stood head and shoulders above the other man and most of the others that gathered eagerly nearby. The simple tunic he wore could hardly contain his chest and arms, thick with corded muscle. Legs like seasoned oaks supported him.

The huge man's tunic marked him as Cretan. Ovid really didn't think Cretans were so, well, large.

"You clumsy fool," snarled the smaller man. "You'll pay for that."

"I'm sorry," said the huge man. "It was an accident." A breeze suddenly sprung up, wafting the man's long, greasy hair so that his face was suddenly revealed. His cheek bore evidence of ancient scars.

"Pay me now," said the other man, holding out his hand expectantly.

The giant shook his head. "I have no money to pay," he said, almost sadly.

The smaller man's face twisted in anger. "Then my fist will extract payment," he said, aiming a mighty blow at his opponent.

The huge man did nothing other than bring his hand up.

He caught the fist of his attacker, stopping it dead like it had impacted with a stone wall.

The other man's eyes went wide with surprise. He tried to wrestle his hand back from his opponent but found that it was stuck fast. The situation might've degenerated into something much worse then but for the intervention of the town's garrison.

Three legionaries were pushing their way through the crowd.

"Break it up," shouted one of them. The crowd grudgingly dispersed, grumbling. The two antagonists melted away with them.

The legionaries pushed through them until they were standing before Ovid.

"Publius Ovidius Naso?" said one of them.

Ovid sighed wearily. He was beginning to sober up, which didn't exactly improve his mood. "That is my name, yes, but most call me Ovid."

If the legionnaire was annoyed or disconcerted, he didn't show it. "The Emperor sent word you would be coming. You are here to see the palace at Knossos?"

"I am indeed," said Ovid.

The legionnaire nodded. "Please come with us, sir."

"Don't I get to put my bags down? Perhaps a small goblet of wine? Maybe rest my legs for a moment or two?" said Ovid irritably. Not that he needed any more wine. Or rest for that matter. He'd had ample on board the ship. But that wasn't the point. These legionnaires didn't seem to possess any manners. Perhaps, this far away from the center of Roman power, they'd forgotten what civility they had once possessed.

"The ship leaves again in three days' time, sir," said the legionnaire patiently. "If you really want to explore, you don't have much time. I thought you might want to make a start."

"Oh, very well," grumbled Ovid. More wine would evidentially have to wait.

The legionaries led him through the small town of Iraklion. It was a picturesque place with simple white washed cottages. Dotted amongst them were larger wooden and stone buildings with gabled roofs covered in terracotta tiles. Ovid's delicate nose knew exactly what most of them stored. The air was filled with the heady fumes of sweet, sweet wine, Crete's specialty. Ovid would've loved to have an opportunity to explore the contents of these buildings but it seemed he was to be denied.

They came to a stout structure that, in contrast to the buildings of indigenous design, was clearly of Roman origin. Its walls were tall, comprised mostly of large blocks of stone. Its fortified nature marked it for what it was—the local Roman barracks, home to the garrison.

He and the sailor were escorted inside. A stool was provided for Ovid and the sailor dropped the bags next to it, holding out a hand expectantly. Ovid fished around and produced a coin. The sailor bit it and, apparently satisfied with its authenticity, hastily departed. The legionaries told Ovid to make himself comfortable, promising to return shortly. Ovid complained loudly at this treatment to anyone who would listen but his complaints were largely ignored.

After waiting for an hour, Ovid, thoroughly irritated and more than a little thirsty, decided to take a more active approach. He stood and stalked over to a table where two legionaries were playing with dice.

"I demand to see someone in charge," said Ovid. "I wish to complain."

"We've noticed," said one of the legionaries dryly, looking up from his game of chance.

"I have been kept waiting for longer than even the most patient man could tolerate. I haven't even been offered some refreshment," said Ovid. He would've said more but was interrupted by a voice behind him. Ovid turned.

"My apologies," said the new arrival—a centurion by the looks of him. "There was an altercation down at the dock that I had to address. I'm sorry that we kept you waiting. Please follow me, sir." He eyed the two dicing legionaries critically. "You," he said, pointing to one of them, "get off your lazy ass and bring his bags."

Ovid, slightly mollified by this, nodded his head curtly. The centurion led him through the barracks toward the rear of the building. They exited through an ancient wooden door that appeared to belong to a much older structure and found themselves out in a large training yard. It was empty save for one man holding the reins of a donkey.

Ovid blinked in surprise. It was the giant that he'd seen earlier.

"Publius Ovidius Naso, this is Ast," said the centurion, introducing the giant. "He will guide you up the hill to the palace and show you around."

Ovid extended his hand. It disappeared into the palm of the larger man.

"Greetings," said Ast, his voice a low rumble reminiscent of boulders grinding against each other. He kept his head down and only met Ovid's eye for a moment. His long hair shadowed the rest of his face, almost as if he was embarrassed somehow.

"The pleasure is all mine," said Ovid easily. This, he

decided, would be an interesting trip. Ast was clearly a local. Who knew what tales this man had? Perhaps some Ovid had never heard before. He felt his scholar's intuition and thirst for good, well told stories flare up.

Even if Ast were lacking in conversation, the donkey would ensure an easy climb. Ovid's wine skin was full. The sky was bright and clear. The sun was shining. Already, his irritation over his treatment by the legionaries was starting to subside.

The legionnaire dropped Ovid's belongings at his feet. The poet fumbled around in his toga for his purse and extracted another coin. He held it out and then had second thoughts.

"You'll get triple if you undertake another little task for me," said Ovid, addressing the legionnaire. "See that warehouse in the distance over there? The one that smells of wine?"

Ω

Riding on the donkey was not as comfortable as Ovid had imagined. The roughly paved path that wound gently up the hill was not well maintained. This, Ovid mused, is what you got in the backwaters of the Empire.

The path followed the river Kairatos, which was pleasant enough. The cool air from the rushing waters kept the worst of the heat from stifling the two men as they ascended. The path was shaded in parts by large cypress and oak trees.

"I take it you live around here?" asked Ovid, more to pass the time than any great urge for conversation.

Beside him, Ast nodded his great head. "Yes. I live in a

cottage not far from the ruins."

"And what is it you do? I mean other than get into fights at the docks and act as guide to drunken poets?"

Ast looked surprised for a moment. "I'm sorry you had to see that," he said slowly. "It was—as I said at the time—an accident. The aggrieved party didn't concur with my worldview and decided to take his complaint to the garrison commander. The only reason I am not currently residing in one of their cells is because I agreed to guide you. As for what I do—I tend goats. I grow olives. I maintain the gardens of the palace. It is enough."

"Why didn't you hit that man?" asked Ovid. "He had it coming."

Ast shook his head. "I have discovered that violence rarely solves problems. Years ago, I might've responded differently, but not now."

"And what were you doing down at the docks?" asked Ovid.

Ast turned to stare at Ovid for a moment and the poet felt a little intimidated by the intensity in that stare. "You ask a lot of questions, poet, but if you must know, I was picking up supplies. And waiting," said Ast, somewhat mysteriously.

"Waiting for what?" asked Ovid. Ast did not respond.

Ovid decided to change tack. "Was it the Romans who built this road?" he asked.

"No," said Ast. "This is the remains of the royal road which led from the port to the palace itself."

"Ah," said Ovid. Maybe he couldn't blame Roman engineers after all.

It was clear that the huge man was not inclined toward

conversation. Ovid was content to let the remainder of the voyage pass in silence, guessing that Ast preferred to be alone with his thoughts.

It was over a league from Iraklion's port to the top of Kephala Hill—where the ancient ruins of the palace of Knossos sat. It took the two men almost two hours to reach it, by which time Ovid had had enough. His body ached. The donkey, although well fed, was bony enough to cause his rear great discomfort.

He dismounted with a sigh of relief.

"Here you are," said Ast, without preamble.

Ovid was surprised. He knew he would find ruins but he hadn't quite expected this. The palace, scattered over a huge arca, had well-tended gardens. Clearly, it wasn't as neglected as he'd been led to believe. Ast must have been busy.

They tied the donkey to a nearby cypress and Ast led the way into the ruins. They passed under a covered stairway, which led them into the palace proper. Entering a massive courtyard, Ovid followed the giant, picking their way over fallen columns, some blackened by ancient fire. A shattered wall offered a vista over the valley.

"To the south there is the ancient site of the Caravanserai," said Ast, pointing. "Further south, there used to be many houses. Once, a bridge crossed the river Vlychia. It collapsed during the last earthquake." Ast pointed at the opposite shore. "That is Gypsades Hill," he said. "The limestone for this palace and what lies beneath was quarried there."

"And what exactly lies beneath?" asked Ovid. "Are you referring to the labyrinth, the home of the mythical Minotaur?"

Ovid saw Ast stiffen for a moment and wondered what he had said to offend.

"Yes," said Ast. "We stand above the labyrinth."

"Can I see it?"

Ast hesitated for a moment. "Why would you want to see it?" he asked.

"I am a scholar and a poet," said Ovid. "Myths and legends of all sorts interest me. I am particularly interested in the tale of the Minotaur. You've heard of him, of course?"

Ast nodded. "Yes. Every Cretan has." Without another word, he turned and began making his way through the myriad ruined rooms of the palace. Ovid had to confess that it was all very confusing. The palace itself contained over a thousand rooms. If he hadn't had Ast along, he surely would've become lost.

Eventually, they came to the lowest floor of the palace. A large part of it had collapsed, tumbling massive limestone blocks down into the darkness below.

"This is the way into the labyrinth," said Ast. "Come."

"Don't we need a torch?" asked Ovid. He'd always been a little scared of the dark.

"There is no need," said Ast. "I know the way better than any other. Inside, other parts of the roof have collapsed allowing light to enter."

Sighing theatrically, Ovid gingerly picked his way over the tumbled blocks and down into the darkness of the labyrinth. The things he did for his muse, he reflected.

Ω

"So, this is where it all happened, is it?" asked Ovid, squinting in the gloom. As promised by Ast, the destruction wrought by the earthquake over a thousand years earlier had opened up enough of the ceiling to see. Just. "Not much to look upon, is there?"

"This was the home of the Minotaur," said Ast, leading the way into the darkened depths. Amazingly, the huge man seemed utterly confident and at ease within the ruins, picking his way through the rubble as if born to it.

"How much time do you actually spend down here?" asked Ovid.

"More than I should," said Ast. "Less than I used to."

"You're not being terribly helpful," complained Ovid, puffing as he struggled to keep up. Ahead of him, Ast simply shrugged his great shoulders.

True to Ast's word, there was just enough light to see by. The labyrinth was made of massive limestone blocks, which seemed to glow ever so slightly. Many of the blocks lay toppled on the ground before them, shattered and broken. Ovid suspected it was more a maze now than it had ever been.

Ast paused at a branch in one of the corridors. A spear of light, produced by a rift in the smashed palace above, illuminated what appeared to be ancient scratches on the blocks. Ast regarded them thoughtfully, almost sadly.

"What are those?" asked Ovid, squinting at the marks.

At first, it appeared that Ast had not heard him, lost in his own thoughts. Finally, he spoke.

"Marks left by the old inhabitant. Marks he used to count the passing of days."

"You mean the Minotaur?" asked Ovid.

Ast nodded once. "Yes," he said.

"And how exactly do you know that?" asked Ovid scornfully. "All this," he said, indicating the ruins around him, "happened long, long ago. How could you possibly know what transpired here?"

"I know more than you think, poet," said Ast. "More than you would dare to ask. Even if you did know the truth, I doubt whether you would believe it."

"You'd be surprised," said Ovid, smiling now. "Poets have a reputation for thirsty minds. And throats."

They continued walking in silence for some time. Ast did not once hesitate, moving through the labyrinth with a familiarity that was slightly unsettling. Much like Ovid had in his large home back in Rome. Ovid followed nervously. Something was out of kilter here. Something wasn't quite right. His poet's intuition told him so and he had long ago learnt not to ignore it. He just wasn't sure what it was. With a growing sense of unease, he continued to follow the giant.

"And this is where Theseus slew the great beast?" Ovid asked eventually.

"Some say that," said Ast. Ovid couldn't be sure, but there was something in the big man's tone he didn't recognize. Something dangerous.

"That's what they *all* say," said Ovid. "Every single scholar and poet before me says that Theseus cut off the monster's head in this place."

"Don't always believe what you read," countered Ast.

"Oho," said Ovid, laughing gently. "Did you know I have written about this very subject before?" Ovid considered himself somewhat of an expert on the subject. He'd mentioned

Theseus and the Minotaur several times in his work.

Ast turned and faced him. He was completely motionless, as if made of the same stone that comprised the labyrinth. His eyes met those of Ovid's. It was a little frightening to be confronted by such a look. Ovid began to feel slightly intimidated.

"*The bones of my brother he crushed with his triple-knotted club and scattered o'er the ground; my sister he left at the mercy of wild beasts.*' I am aware of who you are and your work. Your *Heroides* is a work of pure fiction."

Ovid was taken aback. Ast had quoted directly from his work. In fact, from the speech written by Phaedra—the Minotaur's supposed sister—referring to the death of the monster at the hands of Theseus. "So you know more than scholars and poets now, do you?" asked Ovid, unable to control the amusement in his voice.

"Perhaps I do," said Ast finally.

"And how would you know that?" said Ovid, intrigued now.

"Because I was there," said Ast simply.

Ovid's mouth fell open in surprise. And then he began to laugh again. "You were there? Don't be ridiculous. We are talking over a thousand years ago." Clearly, the man was deranged. He didn't look any older than his third decade. Ovid began looking around as casually as he could, trying to remember the way out. He'd make his escape, return to port, and complain about Ast. He'd have him arrested and get those stupid legionaries at the garrison to give him a guide who wasn't mad.

"I can prove it," said Ast. "Long have I heard false tales of

Theseus and the Minotaur. You are a famous scholar and poet. In return for my tale, all I ask is that you record it faithfully. It is time the truth was finally heard. Come with me, and I will prove that I was there."

"Very well," said Ovid, thinking quickly. He probably wasn't going to be able to find his way out of here without Ast's help. If he fled, he wasn't sure if he'd be able to outrun him either. He'd have to wait, perhaps when Ast went to sleep, and then return to Iraklion. He'd encountered raving lunatics before and knew they had to be treated gently. Perhaps get him drunk? Ovid had plenty of wine strapped to the donkey. That was a good idea. Getting drunk was always a good idea. Perhaps he'd join him for one or two, just to keep up the appearances.

Ω

"Welcome to my home," said Ast. "It's not much but what hospitality I have is yours."

Ovid stepped warily through the doorway and into the stone cottage. It was a simple affair with an ancient wooden table dominating the center of the room. Four chairs were set around it. In the corner, there were kitchen implements and bowls atop another much smaller table. Shelves were cluttered with scrolls and sheaves of papyrus. An open doorway led into another room, presumably the bedchamber.

"Do you live here alone?" asked Ovid.

"Sometimes," said Ast. "I have visitors on rare occasions."

Ast put Ovid's bags and several wine skins in the corner. He placed Ovid's satchel under the table and set one of the wine skins on the worn table top. Grasping two goblets, he returned to the table and set them next to the wine. Ovid eyed the wine and goblets with something approaching hunger.

Usually, oblique answers like that only served to irritate Ovid. He let it pass this time due to the sensitivity of the situation.

"I have too many visitors," commented Ovid. "Those who want to discuss my works, some who just want to meet me. I wish they would leave me alone."

"I too, enjoy my solitude," said Ast.

"I live alone. By choice," said Ovid. "I was married. Three times, actually. All three ended in disaster. Thrice divorced by the time I was your age." Nervousness made Ovid prattle. He knew he was doing it but couldn't stop. "Do yourself a favor and don't get married."

Ast almost smiled. Ovid could see him trying to suppress the emotion. Perhaps, just perhaps, he wasn't mad at all.

"Shall we have a wine, then?" asked Ovid. He had an amazing tolerance toward alcohol, often able to drink larger men under the table. Even though Ast was far heavier than him, it was possible that the bigger man would collapse in a drunken stupor before him. Besides, it was hot outside and Ovid was thirsty.

"Yes," said Ast. "Why not?"

He filled both goblets with wine and offered one to Ovid, bidding the other man to sit. Ast eased himself slowly into the chair opposite.

"Your health," said Ovid and drained his goblet in one

gulp. Ast merely sipped at his before setting it down at the table.

"So, proof then," said Ovid. "What is it you wanted to show me?"

"What if I told you everything you know, have written about, or have read about the Minotaur is false?" said Ast. "What if I told you the Minotaur was not the beast of legend and Theseus was not quite the hero everyone believes?"

"I would say you have an interesting imagination," said Ovid. "Either that or you're completely mad." In hindsight, it was probably a poor choice of words, but the wine had made Ovid bold.

Ast took the remark without comment. His dull, blunt features displayed no emotion. "What if I told you the Minotaur was nothing but a man, a man with a slight deformity?"

"Then I'd say you have my attention," said Ovid. Thoughts of running off had diminished for the moment. Mad or not, Ast was beginning to interest him.

"I want you to look at something," said Ast. He leant forward on the table and swept his hair back to reveal two shining circular blots on his skull. "What do you see?"

Ovid bent forward and squinted sharply. Birthmarks perhaps? It was hard to tell. Closer inspection revealed that wasn't the case. The blots appeared to be made of bone. Or even horn. After a long moment, Ovid sat back.

"I don't know," he confessed. "They could be anything."

Ast sat down again, setting his hair back into place. "They are the stubs of my horns. The horns that gave me my name."

"And what name would that be?" asked Ovid, refilling his goblet.

"The name I was born with is Asterion. The name imposed upon me is something else entirely."

"Which is?" asked Ovid impatiently, taking another swig of his wine.

"Minotaur."

Ovid spluttered. A fine spray of wine filled the air between them. He began to laugh. Wine dribbled down his chin and onto his already stained toga.

Eventually, he recovered his composure. "You expect me to believe that you are the fabled half-man, half-bull of legend? For starters, you aren't nearly old enough."

"My father is Poseidon," said Asterion. "I am a demi-god. As such, I am immortal."

Ovid waved one hand dismissively. "Even if I accepted that, you died over a thousand years ago. Theseus killed you. Everyone knows that."

"Everyone is wrong," said Asterion impassively. "That is why you're here, is it not? You are a seeker of truth. A scholar and poet. I heard you were coming and offered to guide you around. That's why I was waiting at the port. I was waiting for you. I chose you. Do you not want to know the truth?"

Something strange was happening. Ovid, despite his misgivings, was hooked now. Even if he wanted to run, he knew he wouldn't. He wanted to hear. The ravings of a lunatic could still be thoroughly entertaining. Besides, he had a niggling doubt. He'd heard of these supposed demi-gods of course. Even heard rumors of their existence—that some of them still lived and breathed on Earth, a reminder of the golden age of gods long since passed.

Once, he'd possibly encountered one. A heroic figure who

dressed, acted, and spoke as if he came from a different time, convinced, like Asterion, he was over a thousand years old. Choosing to indulge the stranger at the time, Ovid had asked him about the path to demi-god status, why some were chosen and others not. Why weren't there more demi-gods running around?

The stranger had shrugged helplessly. "I don't know," he'd confessed. "I suspect it has something to do with self-belief and strength of character. Having the blood of the gods flowing through your veins is not always enough. Perhaps it is the gods themselves who decide?"

The conversation had amused Ovid at the time. Now all Ovid felt was confusion. The stranger spoke much like this Asterion did now. Why did the name Asterion suddenly sound familiar? He couldn't quite put his finger on it. Perhaps another goblet of wine?

"Here's what I'll do," said Ovid, filling his goblet again. Strange how it seemed to empty itself so quickly. "You start telling me your tale. I'll record everything you say. If, after a time, it starts sounding a little far-fetched, I am going to get up and leave. You will not stop me. Have we got a deal?"

"We have," said Asterion solemnly. "My words will have to convince you. Other than the stubs of my horns, I have little other proof."

"Let's pretend for a moment what you say is true, why reveal it now?" asked Ovid.

"Because of you. Your arrival on this island. Because history is written by those carrying the biggest swords," said Asterion. "At the time all these events took place, Crete was the most powerful state on Earth. Then, Athens became the most powerful. You have to remember that Theseus was Athenian. Even if the truth had emerged, those who wanted to preserve Theseus's memory would've ensured it never got out. I had to wait all this time for the power of Greece to diminish. Now is the time of Rome. Your time. Amongst your people, you have many scholars and your works are read and distributed to thousands. You are the perfect instrument of truth. I have been waiting for you, Ovid, here in my self-imposed exile."

Ovid nodded. He couldn't argue with Asterion's logic, even though he wanted to. "What makes you think anyone will believe your story now?"

"Because you'll be telling it. Your reputation has preceded you. It doesn't matter what you write now, others will want to read it. Surely some will see the truth in it."

Ovid watched Ast carefully. He knew the man was sincere. He certainly didn't appear mad or confused, just a little sad. Perhaps he really was the fabled Minotaur? Ovid had certainly seen some strange things in his time and birth defects much worse than horns.

Even if it was a complete fabrication, Ovid knew this was a story worth listening to.

CHAPTER 2

"Shall I begin then?" asked the man who thought himself the Minotaur.

Ovid held up one finger. "Momentarily." He rustled through his satchel, producing a quill and a thick sheaf of papyrus. He set them down on the table before him, squinting intently at both objects through bleary eyes as if trying to divine their origins. His eyes suddenly brightened. He bent down again, retrieving a small corked glass bottle filled with a dark liquid.

"Can't write without ink, now can I? This here is the best octopus ink you can buy. The merchant I purchased it from assured me it was from a giant squid fished from the deepest waters off Ostia."

Ast nodded disinterestedly. "Are you ready?" he asked in a tone that suggested he was losing patience.

"Yes," said Ovid. "No. Wait." He picked up the skin of

wine from the floor and took a mighty swig, smacking his lips in satisfaction before wiping his mouth with the back of his hand. He set the skin back on the table next to his writing implements. Ovid winked at Ast and smiled crookedly. "Writer's lubrication." He took a deep breath and blew it out, filling the air with alcohol fumes.

"All set," he declared finally.

"Where shall I start?" asked Ast.

Ovid made an expansive gesture with both hands. "Where else but the beginning of course."

Ast nodded his huge head. "Yes," he said. "Yes," his eyes already glazing over with the weight of thousand-year-old memories.

And then he began.

Ω

I was born only a few paces from here over a thousand years ago, in the once great palace of Knossos, certainly the greatest palace on Crete. My mother was Queen Pasiphae. I thought her the most beautiful woman in the world.

Much has been written about my conception and while certain facts have the smack of truth about them, others have been filtered, lost, and otherwise misinterpreted during the intervening centuries. What is true is that there was no love lost between my mother and Minos, the King of Crete. He was, not to put too fine a point on it, not a very nice man.

He treated my mother terribly. He used to beat her, and she

would hide the bruises that blotted her face in shame, unable to meet the eyes of others. I remember her walking around the palace with her eyes downcast. Her first son and my elder brother, Androgeus, brought her joy and the King an heir, so for a time she found favor with the King again. It didn't last. Minos rarely shared her bed after that, and I think my mother was relieved.

He, for his part, was happy to spread his seed amongst other willing, and sometimes unwilling, females in the palace and those unfortunate villagers who were pretty enough to warrant his attention.

King Minos was insecure in his rule. He prayed to Poseidon, the god of the sea, for a sign that he was the legitimate ruler of Crete, more to overawe the peasants than from any great interest in paying homage to the gods. Poseidon decided to test Minos's loyalty by sending a beautiful, giant white bull.

The bull was a glorious creature, the likes of which the world will never see again. It was taller than a large man at the shoulder and weighed more than three normal bulls. Its coat blazed pure white in the midday sun, forcing all who gazed upon it to shield their eyes.

King Minos, of course, was completely taken by it. He was present when it first appeared, lumbering magnificently out of the ocean, surrounded by spray. He knew what it was immediately—a sign of Poseidon's favor.

Minos had initially thought to sacrifice the mighty beast to the god but had second thoughts upon seeing it. Cows— bulls especially—were highly prized on this island, and the bull was too beautiful. Minos knew his prestige would rise by possessing such an animal. His pride and lust betrayed him.

He decided to substitute an inferior beast instead and had it sacrificed with due ceremony.

Did Minos think for a moment that Poseidon would not notice? Poseidon saw much of what transpired in the world those days. He did indeed witness Minos's betrayal and the displeasure of a god—especially one as mighty as the Sea God—is not something to be courted. Poseidon decided to punish Minos for his arrogance.

At that time, there lived a master craftsman. He went by the name Daedalus. The stories tell that my mother sought out Daedalus and asked him to craft her a device whereby she could conduct the act of love with the bull. I have heard that this device was made of wood and leather and would have enabled the bull to mount her. When I heard these rumors, I felt true rage. At that time, I conducted myself in a manner that probably added to my bestial reputation.

While it's true that Daedalus was a member of the King's court, Daedalus never crafted such a ludicrous device.

The gods have a certain bleak sense of humor. Poseidon wanted to remind Minos of his arrogance. When I was born, those present were horrified. One of the midwives screamed and fainted. Why? Because I was born with tiny horns on my head. My mother tells me that Minos's face blanched as white as the bull that was the cause of his shame and fled in a rage.

I suppose you might be wondering why Minos didn't have me killed immediately. Minos tried to do exactly that but was denied by Poseidon himself. The great god of the sea appeared just as Minos reached for me, presumably in the act of infanticide.

Poseidon commanded that I would never die at Minos's

hand. At first, I suspect Minos probably feared the wrath of Poseidon but this lessoned with the passage of time. Other emotions eventually overwhelmed this fear and his impulses were—unfortunately for me—finally acted upon. In all fairness, Minos did obey the letter—although not the spirit— of Poseidon's command. But I'm getting ahead of myself here.

Minos immediately hated me and his hatred of my mother knew no bounds. He refused to see either one of us again. This suited my mother, and for a while, she knew peace and happiness. She named me Asterion, the starry one, and loved me like all good mothers, despite my deformity.

Eventually, my father saw her again but only at night, fuelled by drunken lust, when there was no chance he could come face to face with me, his shame. She produced three more sons and a daughter with Minos: Catreus, Deucalion, Glaucus, and Ariadne. My half-brothers and half-sister. Minos had another illegitimate child with a village girl. Their daughter was called Phaedra. Even though she was a commoner, she was so beautiful and sweet natured that Minos brought her to court and treated her with almost as much favor as he did with my eldest half-brother, Androgeus.

My childhood was filled with mixed memories—some good, most bad. Androgeus was one of the good ones. He was four years older than me and was everything an older brother should be. Kind, patient, loving. Apart from my mother and Phaedra, he was my most formative influence. I remember him as a figure larger than life. He had almost a god-like presence to him. Everyone loved him but no one more than I.

I've been told I was extremely strong for my age and larger than a boy had a right to be, but clumsy with it. And of course, there were the horns. My robust size, however, made me a perfect playmate for my older brother. Most older brothers seek playmates their own age but for some reason, Androgeus and I bonded.

Androgeus was everything a father wanted in a son: tall, strong, agile, and handsome. While I might have been two of those things, only my mother considered me anything but clumsy and plain. My heavy blunt features hardly made the girls swoon.

Androgeus and I used to explore the myriad rooms, halls, and the vast grounds of the palace together. The palace was a source of wonderment. With over thirteen hundred rooms, there was always something new to discover. I was his constant shadow, and it was his presence that stopped others from treating me with the horror and distaste I became accustomed to later in life. I remember the looks servants would give as we played our games; their gazes would soften with love for Androgeus but harden as soon as they saw me. I was a freak. Not only that, but I had brought shame onto the house of Minos and the kingdom of Crete.

I must've been around five years of age when I asked my brother why they treated me like they did.

"Because you're different," he answered.

"Why am I different?"

Androgeus tousled my hair fondly. "Don't you know, little brother? What are these things here?" he asked, fingering the horns sprouting from my forehead.

"Horns?" I ventured.

He smiled at me. "Yes, they are! Do I have them? Does anyone else?"

I shook my head sadly, confused.

"Well, that makes you different then," he announced.

"Why do I have horns?"

"Ask our mother," he said and would say no more.

As he suggested, I took my concerns to our mother. She had her own suite of rooms in the palace, far removed from those of Minos. The palace was immense, large enough that Pasiphae and Minos only encountered each other by accident. Other than the times his desire overcame his disgust, when he'd creep around like a thief in the night, he and my mother only saw each other a few times each year.

When she saw me, Queen Pasiphae smiled sweetly and held out her arms. I rushed into her embrace, and she gathered me into her bosom. It was times like this when I felt truly safe, truly loved. I looked up at her.

"Why do people hate me?" I asked.

She looked slightly startled by the question. "What makes you think they hate you? And who are these people you talk about?"

"I don't know," I replied, gesturing vaguely. "People. Everyone. Well, everyone except you and Androgeus. No one looks at me. When they do, I see their faces change."

She rubbed my back. "Don't let it worry you, my sweet Prince. I love you, and your brother loves you, and that's all that matters."

"Why does my father never see me?" I asked. I had seen him around the palace, of course, but he always managed to make his excuses and depart as soon as I entered a room. I'd heard the rumors too, how the King wasn't my real father. Palace gossip reliably informed me that my father had been a monster.

Pasiphae looked down at me, wrinkles creasing her forehead. Even at that age, I suddenly realized that my mother was getting older. Having so many children was taking its toll as well.

"He's a busy man, your father. Being a king is a big responsibility."

"But he makes time for Androgeus," I complained.

"That's because your brother is older and will one day be the King himself. Your father is trying to teach him how to rule."

"Is my father really my father?" I asked, blurting the question out, not really wanting to hear the answer.

"Hush," said my mother. "Don't ask such silly questions."

And that was the end of the discussion.

It was a few years later that Androgeus began his real training to prepare him to be King. This meant (much to my disgust) that Androgeus was no longer available to explore and play. He was getting older and becoming a man while I was still but a boy.

As much as I resented the change, it did bring a new presence into my life. Phaedra. I was only around ten at the time, but other than my mother, she was the most beautiful thing I'd ever seen. She was about the same age as I but slim as a reed where I was thick and stout as a tree. She had long hair the color of gold and skin so tanned it shone with an almost otherworldly luster.

As one of Minos's favorites, she could do no wrong and her nature reflected this in some ways. She took risks where others wouldn't dare and possessed a restless, lively sense of humor I often couldn't compete with. I couldn't wrestle with her, but she could climb better than I could ever hope to. We spent days doing just that. She would climb to the very tip of the branches, causing my heart to quicken with fear. I stayed far below where the larger branches could support my ever-increasing weight.

There was a certain tree, a cypress, centuries old, grown huge and tall, far more massive than any other tree in the palace gardens. Our nurse, Alcippe, had told us to stay away from it as it was dangerous and full of rot. Large limbs had a tendency to fall with lethal effect on any who were unfortunate to be beneath them at the time.

Because of this, that part of the garden tended to be deserted. Perfect for young people to play their games. Phaedra, I, and the younger children would often use the tree as the center point for whatever other adventures the day brought.

My other siblings were away playing their own games. It was just Phaedra and I sitting quietly beneath the tree. Every moment we spent in its shadow made me more breathless as my fear threatened to overwhelm me. Phaedra appeared unconcerned. I could tell she was bored, fidgeting with the straps on her sandals.

"What shall we do?" I asked, more to break the silence than anything else.

Phaedra looked up at me, a calculating look in her eye. "What would you like to do?" she asked.

I shrugged. "Whatever you want." I was always keen to please her, and she often took the lead in any games we played.

"You could kiss me if you wanted," she said archly.

I didn't know what to say to that. What ten-year-old boy does? I blushed furiously. "But, I'm your brother," I stammered. "I can't kiss you." I knew I couldn't, but a large part of me really wanted to.

"Ah," said Phaedra, waggling one finger in front of my face knowingly, "But are you?"

"What?" I replied, too stunned to think of a more sensible response.

"Are you really my brother?" she asked again.

The question immediately placed doubts in my mind, doubts fuelled by the other palace rumors. "Yes," I said, sounding anything but confident.

"I heard a rumor the other day," she said. "A rumor that your father was a bull. That's why you have those horns."

I fingered the horns on my head self-consciously. Lately, they'd been getting longer and longer. It seemed that every year they grew, much to my embarrassment. Even growing my hair long couldn't conceal them. I snatched my hands away furiously and stood.

"My father is not a bull," I declared. "He's Minos. The King of Crete. The same father as yours except my mother is a Queen and not some village whore." That was a mistake. Unlike Phaedra, I was always a little clumsy with words. Sometimes they flew out of my mouth without me even realizing what I'd said. This time, however, I knew I'd said something unforgiveable and desperately wanted to suck the words back in. It was too late though. They were out there and had already reached Phaedra's ears.

Her mouth twitched in anger, and she sprang to her feet. The silence in the grove was broken by the sound of a slap, then another. I felt my cheek burn as blood rushed to my face.

"How dare you," she snarled through gritted teeth. "My

mother wasn't a whore. The King loved her. I loved her."

Her mother had died in childbirth a few years earlier, straining to push out another of the King's illegitimate children. To call her mother a whore was one thing, to dishonor her memory was another. Desperate to make amends, I looked around frantically.

"I'm sorry," I said. "I'll make it up to you."

With that, I began climbing the tree.

"Don't," said Phaedra. I felt a thrill as I heard the note of worry in her voice. She was concerned about me. She cared.

I ignored her, heaving myself up into the limbs of the trees. They creaked alarmingly under my weight.

"I know you didn't mean it, Asterion. I forgive you. Please come down. You'll hurt yourself." She knew I wasn't much of a climber.

I was beginning to have second thoughts. She was right—this was probably going to end badly. But I didn't care. I had hurt her, and now I'd make it up to her. Make her realize that I was sincere in my apologies.

I climbed higher. An ancient limb, thicker than my thigh, cracked, suddenly snapping under my weight. I saved myself by reflex, reaching out, desperately grasping another branch with one hand. Thankfully, it held, and I secured my hold with both hands. I breathed a sigh of relief, and it was only then that I heard it. Sobbing.

I looked down. The limb had crashed to the leaf littered ground below. Unfortunately, Phaedra was standing directly below. The limb had struck her and pinned her beneath its weight.

Heedless of my own safety, I plunged downward,

inadvertently dislodging smaller limbs, which rained down upon the ground. Fortunately, this time, none struck her.

I reached the bottom of the tree, breathless, and bent down next to Phaedra. Glistening droplets of sweat had broken out on her forehead and weak moans of agony escaped her lips. The branch was heavy but I didn't notice, tossing it aside easily. I examined Phaedra's leg. It appeared broken, the skin already discolored, the flesh surrounding it starting to swell.

"I'm so sorry, Phaedra," I moaned. It pained me to think I was the cause of her distress. Bravely, she tried to smile reassuringly, but it emerged as a grimace.

Unwilling to move her but frightened that more tree limbs might fall, I sheltered her with my body, making her as comfortable as possible. I called out, and eventually Catreus, Deucalion, Ariadne, and Glaucus returned.

The twins, Catreus and Deucalion, were the eldest of my younger brothers, and I sent them off to seek help. Ariadne and Glaucus stayed behind.

"You're in trouble now," smirked Ariadne. I flinched, knowing she was right. Ariadne, two years younger than I, hated me already. I didn't know what I'd done to deserve it, but she did. I suspected it was in order to curry favor with our father, but she was also mean-spirited and vain. She spent hours fussing over her long dark locks and was fastidious about staying tidy, regardless of how rough our games were.

"I'm going to tell father," said Glaucus. Temperament wise, Glaucus was very much in the same mold as Ariadne. He followed her around like a puppy, even though he was only a year younger than her. He seemed to lack a will of his own, content to follow Ariadne's lead. Neither one displayed any concern for Phaedra's predicament. It was merely an opportunity to get me into trouble—one they weren't going to miss.

I fussed about Phaedra, trying to ignore them. I felt like crying but wouldn't give them the satisfaction. Fear of my father and his displeasure started to override my concern for Phaedra. I almost wished that no one would come. But that would mean Phaedra's suffering would be prolonged, and that was unforgiveable.

We didn't have to wait long. Catreus and Deucalion returned with Alcippe and two guards.

"What happened?" demanded Alcippe. I explained, leaving out the details of why I climbed. Alcippe nodded curtly. "That's why I told you not to climb that tree. Children never listen." She was a good woman. Middle-aged and childless, she regarded all of us as her own—even me. I was not her favorite by any means, but she still treated me kindly, despite the circulated rumors, pettiness, and spitefulness indulged in by others in the palace.

She gestured to the two guards. "Pick her up. Gently. Take her back to the nursery." The guards complied. I held Phaedra's hand all the way back to the palace, trying to comfort her when the jostling caused her to cry out in pain.

A healer had already been sent for and waited in the nursery. Phaedra was set down on a pallet, and we children gathered around with a mix of curiosity, excitement, and, in my case, worry.

Unfortunately, Alcippe was having none of it. She ushered us out despite our protests. "Your time will come when you'll see all too much of this," she explained somewhat cryptically.

"And that time has not yet begun."

The waiting was terrible. The five of us camped out in the playroom—a vast open area attached to the nursery, the high ceiling supported by stone columns. Mosaics and paintings of children playing adorned the walls, and it had huge windows that were open all year long. Wooden toys of every description filled the room, some of which the other children began playing with. Not I. I sat on the ledge of one massive window, staring out gloomily over the palace grounds.

Catreus and Deucalion made an effort to comfort me, but I could tell they were more interested in sparring with wooden swords. I didn't blame them. They were good boys, almost identical and only a year younger than I, both fair to look on. Like Phaedra and Androgeus, they were palace favorites, their easygoing manners endearing them to most. Their ability to finish each other's sentences never failed to fascinate me.

"She'll be fine," said Catreus.

"Yes," said Deucalion. "Don't worry about her. It was ... "

" ... an accident, after all," finished Catreus.

I nodded but couldn't help but blame myself. I had done this to her. Because of my foolish words and actions.

Alcippe finally returned an hour later. It seemed like much longer. I hadn't moved, fidgeting nervously by the window. I rushed toward her, the others gathering around more slowly.

"Well?" I asked. "Will she be alright?"

Alcippe nodded. "Thanks to the healer. He has set her bones. They will heal straight and true. It was a very simple break, but she'll have to be treated gently for the next few weeks." She looked significantly at me.

"Lucky," sneered Ariadne.

"Can I see her?" I asked, completely ignoring my younger sister.

"Of course," said Alcippe.

Without bothering to see if the others followed, I scurried into the room next door. Phaedra was propped up on a pillow, smiling as she caught sight of me. I was enormously relieved to see she had apparently already forgiven me.

The healer was finishing wrapping her leg in white cloth, the splints already in place. He ignored me.

"How are you?" I asked. It was a stupid question, but I couldn't think of anything else to say.

"It hurts," she said, speaking around a mouthful of something. If the smell was anything to go by, it was probably the bark of a willow tree. Healers seemed to dispense it for any type of pain. My mother had chewed it through all her many labors.

"Of course," I replied. There was an uncomfortable silence as I furiously thought of something to say. "I'm sorry," I said eventually.

Phaedra touched my arm gently. "I know you are. It was an accident."

"That's not how Father is going to see it," said Ariadne behind me. I hadn't heard her approach. Behind her, the other children crowded forward.

I turned to see her smiling at me. A random urge to hit her flooded me, completely at odds with my gentle nature. That would only make my punishment greater still.

"Father probably already knows," said Ariadne, still smiling. I bet he did. She'd disappeared for a while when we were in the playroom, and I could hazard a pretty good guess as to where she went. The guards would've already informed Minos, but Ariadne was taking no chances. I kept expecting her to rub her hands together gleefully.

Punishment was inevitable. I thought it'd be meted out by some palace functionary later that night.

But I was wrong on both counts.

CHAPTER 3

I was summoned into a small audience chamber later that same afternoon. It is hard for me to explain the mix of emotions I felt that day. Fear, of course, was the most prominent. Underlying that was excitement and curiosity.

Up to this point, I had had nothing to do with my father. He avoided me. If I was to be disciplined, it was by someone else. He'd never spoken to me in my life. Never. Now, to be summoned before him, I was extremely nervous.

The audience chamber was like many rooms in the huge palace. Larger than most, supported by columns, walls covered with freshly painted murals, mostly depicting bulls in some aspect or another. At the base of the walls were several stone seats, all of them empty. I passed by the ceremonial pool but didn't pay much attention, my gaze being drawn toward the small ornate chair sitting on a raised dais at the far end of the chamber—and the figure sitting within it. The room had a slightly ominous and claustrophobic feel to it, more so because it was toward the center of the palace and blocked completely from all natural light. Oil lamps held within sconces on the walls provided illumination. My passage caused them to flicker, casting dancing shadows about the walls, giving the bulls the illusion of movement. The figure in the chair was, of course, my father, King Minos.

I approached on hesitant feet and stopped at the base of the dais at what I considered a respectful distance. Other than the guards lining the walls and the two flanking his chair, we were alone. I knelt but kept my eyes up in order to examine my father in more detail. I had never been so close to him. I had always considered him a young man and never had any reason to question that thought. If I'd thought about it, I would've worked out that he must've been getting on in years. I knew from palace talk that he hadn't married my mother until he was well into his fourth decade.

But my father, the King, was, like his daughter, Ariadne, extremely vain. Any signs of gray in his hair or beard were banished with dye. I suspected that the unnatural blush of youth on his cheeks was an extract from a plant applied in a judicious manner. He was, however, quite stout with the build of a warrior—albeit an aging one. In his heyday, he'd vied with and fought his brothers for control of Crete. Rumors, if they were to be believed, said he'd been a fearsome warrior in those days, and the evidence was still on show. His long black hair had been set with combs, and a small golden crown sat atop his head. His tunic was richly embroidered.

All in all, he didn't make an unfavorable impression. He

looked kingly. I was not disappointed. That's if you didn't look in his eyes. They were like blue chips of ice. I felt my heart freezing under his stare.

Complete silence filled the hall. Long moments stretched on and on until I felt almost compelled to open my mouth and say something, just to break the horrible silence. It would've been a terrible breach of etiquette to speak before my superior but I needed to do something. My father continued to stare at me. I noticed that his gaze was drawn to my horns, which, despite my best efforts to conceal, were well and truly on display.

Suddenly, my father stood. On long legs, he strode down the dais toward me, halting just before my kneeling form. Humbly, I averted my eyes, fixing them fearfully on the mosaic tiles beneath my knees.

I felt a finger slide under my chin, forcing my head up. I met the cold eyes of my father. He smiled at me and my heart leapt. Perhaps I had been forgiven? Perhaps this was the moment I had been waiting for? The moment I connected with my father for the first time. I felt elated, relieved, happy. I smiled back.

My father turned slightly. I saw a flash out of the corner of my eye and then something struck me with staggering force.

Even though I was still a boy, I had almost the same physique as a grown man. Solid muscle starting to layer into something even harder. Even so, the blow hurt, but it was the shock more than anything that dashed me into the tiles. My father was a powerful man and had obviously driven all his strength into the blow.

When I looked up, he was staring at his knuckles strangely.

The heavy rings that adorned every finger were covered in blood. He shook his hand gently, the expression on his face betraying that the blow had hurt him more than he'd obviously expected. At first, I thought the blood must be his and then I felt the trickles running down my face.

I reached up, touching my face, and held my fingers before my eyes. Red, covered in blood. My father's rings had cut me deeply.

To my shame, I started to cry. I felt lost, hurt, betrayed. To get my hopes up with a smile and do this? It was one of the worst moments of my life.

My father, in case you hadn't already guessed, was not a good man. But then again, he wasn't really my father, was he?

I crouched there, blood soiling my tunic and spilling onto the floor, weeping miserably. My father looked at me coldly and then turned and marched back to his chair atop the dais. He still hadn't said a single word.

Seeing that I wasn't going to receive any comfort from him or anyone else for that matter, I quickly sobered. It was the first time in my life that I worked out how to turn my emotions off. They were still there, lurking in the darkness, waiting for an opportunity to present themselves to the world but something happened to me that day. Cold stone entered my heart, and I vowed never to display such weakness again. Regardless of how I felt, I would not allow strangers to see how their words or actions could affect me. My father's humiliation taught me that.

My audience clearly at an end, I stood, wiping the mixture of blood and tears from my face with the edge of my tunic. I had entered the audience chamber as a boy. I would leave as a man. Without a backward glance at my father, I departed, walking as proudly as I could manage, hatred fuelling my steady stride. Hatred for my father.

As well as being a vain man, my father was appallingly stupid. Of course, he didn't know what I would become. If he had known, perhaps he would've conducted himself differently. Then again, perhaps not. He was convinced of his God's-given superiority. In my experience, such men never learn.

I should thank him, I suppose. He did teach me to grow up and to consider the consequences of my actions. Much earlier than I'd anticipated but in some ways, that was a good thing. It started to prepare me for the trials that were not too distant before me.

And I would need all my strength to survive.

Ω

"Are you trying to tell me that King Minos made you what you are?" interrupted Ovid, putting down his quill. He'd listened, fascinated, for what seemed like only a short amount of time. The reality was that a few hours had passed. Outside the tiny stone cottage, night was falling. Despite Ovid's initial reservations, the story was indeed compelling.

Ast shrugged his massive shoulders. "In a way, yes," he said. "We made each other. Perhaps he wouldn't have been bitter if Poseidon hadn't cuckolded him. If he had treated me better, my life would've been much different. I wouldn't be the man you see before you."

"That's if you are a man," said Ovid wryly.

"For the most part," replied Ast, without a trace of humor.

"So it was he who gave you those scars on your face?" asked Ovid. The marks seemed consistent with Ast's story. They even looked ancient. But a thousand years … ?

Ast nodded, reaching up and tracing the marks on his cheek for a moment, lost in thought. "They are a constant reminder of those times. They ensure I will not forget. You could say that Minos scarred me both on the inside and out."

"And King Minos was every bit as cruel as the legends say?" asked Ovid.

Ast stirred his great bulk and stood up. He stretched mightily. "He was. Probably more so. I bore the brunt of his cruelty." He paused and glanced around, becoming aware for the first time that it was almost night. "If we are to continue with my story, we will need light."

Ast bustled about the house for a while, fetching two oil lamps that he lit and set on the table. Ovid helped himself to more wine. His mouth had gone dry. So intent was he in writing down every one of Ast's words, he had forgotten to drink. Unthinkable! It was a testament to how involved in the story he had become. He still wasn't convinced that this man was the Minotaur of legend, but regardless, the story was compelling. His hand was cramping up but he still had an urge to continue.

"Do you wish to hear more tonight?" asked Ast, as if reading his mind.

Ovid nodded. "I do."

"Then I suggest we eat something first. My story is long and tales like this require stamina. You cannot write on wine alone." Ovid didn't agree but protested only mildly when Ast returned to the kitchen, preparing platters of food, which he set before them.

There was a bowl of olives, some dried strips of goat meat, beans still in their pods and some coarse brown bread. Ovid wasn't particularly hungry but ate mostly because he thought he ought to, picking lightly at a few things here and there. Ast himself ate enough for two men, which was appropriate given his size.

Finally, when the plates were almost empty, Ast cleared them away and returned to his seat at the table.

"Shall we continue?" he asked.

"Please do," said Ovid, settling himself into his chair. Despite his earlier protestations, the food had done him some good. He felt wide-awake, eager for the tale to resume. And he knew there was still much to hear.

Ω

That spring was a turning point in my life. Phaedra's leg healed cleanly and so well that her slight limp was almost unnoticeable. She began to explore the gardens again, and, more warily now, I accompanied her. I don't think I was terribly great company after the encounter with my father, but Phaedra still managed to elicit the odd smile and occasional laugh from me.

I was very conscious of not putting her in danger, unwilling to risk another bout of punishment from my father, but Phaedra was not easily contained. She was optimistic, as bright as the sun, the light of which I basked in. Her presence was a balm to my troubled soul.

She soothed some of the hurt away but it wasn't until we started lessons with a new tutor that I managed to dispel most of the disquiet that filled me.

Before the age of six, most of our education had come from our mother, her household staff, and some informal tutors. After six, we had real teachers, but none that I especially bonded with or felt inspired by.

That all changed when my father decided to make one of his resident scholars our new tutor. He was originally from Crete, but he had travelled widely, returning to the island of his birth after many years, bringing his son Icarus with him.

His name was Daedalus. You might have heard of him. He was a teacher, of course, but much, much more than that. His true skills lay in invention and design. He was both architect and mathematician—skills that, years later, would serve him well. For good or ill.

Ω

"Catreus, Deucalion, attend please." Daedalus rapped one of his knuckles down on the wooden desk directly in front of the twins. He held out his palm expectantly. "Hand it over."

Reluctantly, Catreus produced the offending article— a wooden horse that he and Deucalion had been playing with. Daedalus palmed it and then placed it in one of the many pockets adorning his tunic.

"Now then," he said, addressing the entire class. "Who has a solution to the problem?"

There was silence. Now there are two types of silences in a classroom. There is the silence when students are baffled into speechlessness, and then there is the silence where the answer wants to spring forth, but it is just too embarrassed or self-conscious. This was the second kind.

Apart from myself and the twins, almost all of my brothers and sisters were present. Icarus, Daedalus's son, was there too, although he contributed little or nothing to any discussion. He was a little older than I, about the same age as Androgeus, but where Androgeus was tall and strong with an athlete's build, Icarus was frail, with long spindly arms and legs. He didn't speak much either, content to bury his long nose in a bunch of papyrus.

I'm sure Daedalus was very proud of him in many ways—foremost being his interest in scholarly pursuits—but he wasn't the easiest person to talk to. I'd tried a few times, but he was even more awkward and nervous in the company of others than even I. In fact, I'd only seen him rarely before Daedalus was appointed our tutor, schooled by his father in their private chambers.

Androgeus had been present earlier before being called away for training with the shield, sword, and spear. He was sixteen now, four years older than I, and lately he'd been devoting himself more to the physical pursuits than anything else. I had been seeing less and less of him. The Panathenaic games were only two years away, and Androgeus was one of Crete's hopefuls. Held in Athens every four years, the games celebrated physical excellence. Androgeus hoped to enter both the wrestling and the marathon. Even though I was happy for him, I missed his presence.

I couldn't bear the silence any more. I felt some answers bubbling away within me. If I held onto them any longer, I'd burst.

"Lift," I said. Phaedra, sitting next to me, turned to me and raised her eyebrows. Even though I usually felt like I understood what Daedalus was saying, I often kept my mouth shut, unwilling to give Ariadne an opportunity to humiliate me. Despite being vain and nasty, Ariadne had a quick mind. Equipped with a sharp tongue, it was a fearsome combination.

"Explain yourself," said Daedalus. His top lip quirked ever so slightly, an indication that he'd just heard something amusing. I smiled back nervously. I liked Daedalus but he wasn't above chastising me in front of the others if I said something stupid.

"In order to fly, an object needs lift," I said. I cast a hurried glance in the direction of Ariadne. I couldn't help myself. To my relief, she wasn't smiling. Instead, her eyebrows were knitted together in concentration, staring at me intently. With a grunt of irritation, she began scribbling furiously on the papyrus in front of her. Even from a few paces away, I could tell much of it was nonsense. A horrendous waste of papyrus given that it was a rare and expensive commodity. But then again, we were the children of the King. Well, most of us anyway.

To demonstrate, I stood. "I just used lift to force myself off my chair."

"Yes, but you're hardly flying," sneered Ariadne.

"Ariadne," said Daedalus sharply. "Confine your observations to ones that are relevant."

Next to me, Phaedra chuckled as Ariadne blushed bright red.

"But that was relevant," protested Ariadne. "He's not flying. What has lift got to do with flying?"

"Asterion is right in some respects. In others, not so," said Daedalus, bursting my bubble of joy over Ariadne's discomfort. "Phaedra, have you got something to add?"

Phaedra nodded slowly. "I think I do," she said finally. She stood next to me and lifted one of the pieces of papyrus in front of her. She held it flat on her palm and then gave it a little push upwards. The papyrus fluttered upwards for a moment before slowly spiraling down to the floor. "See how the push I gave it caused the papyrus to float? I think Asterion was on to something. I believe lift is one of the things an object needs to fly—but there must be others."

Daedalus nodded. "Good, Phaedra. It's pleasing to see that at least someone has been listening all this time. Glaucus, you seem to be very quiet. Anything to add?"

Glaucus started, clearly not concentrating on anything rather than what was going on his head. Probably lunch, I thought. Lately, Glaucus had been putting on weight. Not surprising. He did little exercise and ate prodigious amounts of food. "I agree with Ariadne," he said automatically.

Phaedra and I unsuccessfully repressed laughter. It was what Glaucus always said.

Like Ariadne moments before, Glaucus blushed.

We spent several minutes discussing various ideas relating to the dilemma posed by Daedalus and then took a more hands-on approach, trying out our ideas using the papyrus in front of us. I enjoyed myself, as did most of the others in the class. Daedalus was an excellent teacher. Even Ariadne and

Glaucus were engaged. The twins, happy to have something more physical to do, were in their element.

Daedalus eventually declared it was lunchtime. As we shuffled out, I felt a light touch on my tunic. I turned to find Icarus standing next to me.

"You have some good ideas," he said very softly, almost like he didn't want the others to hear. Perhaps he didn't want to draw attention to himself. "I'd like to discuss those with you sometime," he said shyly. "If you'd like, we could talk about your horns, too. I have many questions."

I nodded. "That would be ... good," I finished lamely. I didn't actually relish the opportunity to spend more time with Icarus—I'd rather use what free time I had with Phaedra—but I could hardly say no. It must've been hard for him. He had no friends to speak of and was probably lonelier than I. At least I had Phaedra, Androgeus, and my mother.

It was an awkward moment, but fortunately for me, Phaedra saved me, grabbing my arm. "Come on," she said. "I'm starving."

"Do you want to join us?" I asked Icarus, blurting it out without thinking. It wasn't my place to ask him. He was, after all, the son of a servant. Daedalus, for all his standing, was still an employee of my father. Normally, Icarus and Daedalus ate with the other senior servants in the palace. Servants didn't eat with the sons and daughters of the King. I'd probably get in trouble but I didn't care. It felt like it was the right thing to say.

Icarus's lip quirked. It was only then, with that expression, that I could see the resemblance to his father. "No," he said hastily looking quickly in the direction of Daedalus. "Father wouldn't approve."

I nodded. It was probably for the best. I had overstepped my authority in any case.

Phaedra led me away. "That was nice," she said. "Not very clever, but nice."

"Not clever?" I asked, confused. "What do you mean?"

"I mean that you had no right to ask him to join us. Father would hear of it. Do you really want that?"

I shook my head slowly, raising my finger to trace the scars on my check. They had healed well, but I would always bear the mark of my father's displeasure. "I just thought he could do with some friends."

"There are plenty of children our age in the palace that aren't royalty. He can be friends with them. Besides, did you see the look he gave Daedalus? I'd imagine he'd get in trouble with his father if he joined us."

Phaedra was right. As usual. She was much wiser than I.

CHAPTER 4

Now that we were getting older, our daily lives were much more structured. We had routines. Failure to comply meant instant punishment. I, already having been on the receiving end of such punishment, did everything I could to obey both the letter if not the spirit—of the instructions given by our tutors.

Our day started at dawn with an hour's run. Glaucus struggled with this of course, and I often saw him sneaking away or taking short cuts. After that was five hours of unbroken tutelage at the hands of Daedalus. He taught us all manner of things, but his special interests lay in mathematics, physics, philosophy, and history, which suited me fine. Although I was not much of an orator, I excelled in these subjects. Daedalus was particularly interested in the practical applications of mathematics and physics. He had a large workshop in an outlying building not far from the palace, and I loved to watch him work. When I had the time, that is, which wasn't nearly as often as I would've liked.

After lunch, the boys and girls were separated. Much to Phaedra's disgust, she and Ariadne retired to my mother's quarters, learning how to manage and run a household and perfect other skills required to serve our father, and later, their husbands. Skills such as cooking, knitting, and weaving. My mother, Pasiphae, was also an accomplished healer, and she taught the girls much of what she knew. Phaedra, I knew, enjoyed this aspect of her education almost as much as Ariadne hated it. Both my mother and Phaedra even passed on some of their healing knowledge to me.

Although she enjoyed the healing arts, Phaedra would have much preferred to spend the afternoons training with me and my brothers, but my father had other plans. As much as he loved Phaedra and Ariadne (or as much as a man like him could love), his two daughters were valuable commodities to be sold or traded off to the highest bidder in Greece or to one of the rulers of the many islands scattered amongst the sparkling Aegean.

In this, Ariadne confused me. She made no protests at all regarding this type of education. Phaedra told me that Ariadne enjoyed all domestic tasks, approaching them with vigor and enthusiasm—traits Phaedra lacked. It seemed that Ariadne's great goal in life was to be married off to some powerful ruler's son and then manipulate him for her own ends and ultimate satisfaction.

As for us boys, the afternoons were a mixture of pain, excitement, triumph, and the occasional humiliation. For

Glaucus, it was mostly the latter. He approached our training sessions in the gymnasium with the same amount of enthusiasm he used for our early morning run. That is to say—precisely none. He was constantly derided and criticized by our tutors, and it made him even more bitter and petty than he was already. Icarus was excused from such activity, his life already being mapped out as a scholar.

For Androgeus, myself, Catreus, and Deucalion, our sessions in the gymnasium were mostly thrilling, times we'd look forward to with some anticipation. Make no mistake; it was not easy, but for me especially, it was easier than most.

Our tutors drilled us in wrestling, boxing, and the use of the shield, spear, and sword. Androgeus, who'd had a few years head start by the time our younger brothers and I entered the gymnasium, was already well accomplished in all these pursuits.

By the time I was twelve, I was almost man sized, with the strength to match. Because of this, Androgeus and I were often paired up—when he wasn't training with the men. I was as tall as him by now but much broader through the hip and chest, with arms and legs to match. Androgeus was slimmer, graceful, and much more agile.

The differences were clearly apparent in the heat of the midafternoon sun. We were naked to the waist, our torsos covered in sweat, our lower halves concealed by simple kilts.

Our weapons tutor was a man known as Paris. Not the same Paris that later abducted Helen of Troy starting the Trojan War, but a different Paris. This Paris was a grizzled man with a graying beard in his late middle age. He was still hale and hearty with muscles like corded oak, a veteran of hundreds of battles across mainland Greece and Northern Africa. He was a hard taskmaster but fair.

"Asterion. Stop gathering wool. Concentrate. You won't block anything that way." He marched up to me, clipped me smartly on the head with his bare hand, adjusted my shield grip, and then stepped back. Androgeus and I looked at him expectantly.

"Well!" he roared. "Don't just stand there. Fight for Zeus's sake!"

Androgeus and I went at it with a will. The shields were real enough but our swords were only wood. When Androgeus trained with the men, they trained with bronze weapons. Androgeus had the scars to show for it.

Although I enjoyed physical exercise, I never felt comfortable hurting anyone. I had a gentle disposition and rarely got angry. Paris despaired of ever turning me into a warrior. I lacked the ferociousness and passion of a truly great fighter.

I warded off a blow from Androgeus. It clattered harmlessly off my bronze embossed shield, sliding down. I took advantage of the fact that he was momentarily off balance and swung wildly at his head. I missed. In fact, I wasn't even close. Androgeus didn't bother to raise his shield; my blow was that clumsy. With agility that was quite mesmerizing, Androgeus blocked my shield with his and then slid under it, poking the wooden point of his sword right where my heart was.

"Asterion!" shouted Paris. "You son of a motherless goat. That was useless. Not only that, you're dead."

Androgeus grinned at me. "You almost had me then," he said encouragingly.

"Don't tell lies, Androgeus," growled Paris. "You'll only give him a false sense of confidence, which will kill him on the battlefield. And there's nothing worse than a man whose confidence outweighs his ability." He shook his head, grabbed my shield, and yanked it away from my numb fingers. "Put your sword down, we'll try something different."

I did what Paris ordered. "I don't think the sword and shield suit you," continued Paris. "You're big and strong, and you'll get more so with time. But slow with it. I think we'll give you a weapon to match." He thought for a moment and then marched over to the weapons rack, selecting a wooden club.

He threw it to me. I almost missed it, which would've been incredibly embarrassing. My reflexes were not like those of Androgeus. As it was, I just managed to grasp the handle of the club before it hit me in the head.

Like me, it was a clumsy thing, large and unwieldy, as long as my arm, and thick at one end, tapering down to a size that I could just grasp. It felt good in my hand though, almost like it belonged there. I'd heard rumors lately of a hero using a weapon like this. Heracles. On the mainland, he'd reportedly accomplished great and heroic deeds with such a weapon.

"Now try again," commanded Paris. "And this time, Asterion, try and show some spark."

Androgeus moved in instantly for the kill. He knew my abilities by now, only too aware that I was much slower than him. He did, however, sometimes forget about my strength, which seemed to grow daily. Not only that, but he appeared a little confused by the club. He was used to facing me shield to shield, sword to sword. Normally, he'd use his usual tactics, blocking my shield and using his superior speed to strike like a snake.

This time he had no shield to block.

He thrust his shield forward. I knew what it was. A decoy. He thought I would attempt to block his shield thrust with my club, and then he would strike with his sword while I was distracted. This, I realized, would once again end in defeat. Instinct kicked in then. I did what came naturally. Holding the club in both hands, I swung mightily at his shield. A bestial roar emerged from my throat. I wasn't angry—it just seemed like the right thing to do.

Nobody in the gymnasium that day expected to see what happened next.

By rights, the shield should've stopped my blow, at the very least deflect it. Instead, the club smashed into the shield with enough force to shatter it, blasting Androgeus off his feet. He lay before me stunned, looking up at me with what might have been fear. I felt confused. I wasn't even sure what had happened. I had just channeled all my strength—strength I'd never properly used—into that one blow. I knew I was strong; I just didn't know how strong.

I felt elated, invincible, powerful, but also I regretted that I'd possibly humiliated and angered Androgeus. Quickly, I dropped the club and extended a hand to my brother. He took it gratefully with a wry grin, and I let out a long breath of relief. He grasped my bicep with his other hand. It didn't even cover a third of it.

"My, we are getting strong, aren't we?" he said, clapping me on the back. All movement had ceased within the gymnasium. Glaucus, training with the son of a noble from a nearby city, Catreus, Deucalion, and some other sons of senior servants—

all had frozen.

I blushed, lowering my head to conceal the rosy glow. The movement almost caused Androgeus to lose an eye to one of my horns. He released his grip, hastily moving backward.

"Good," said Paris. It was the highest praise I'd ever heard spill from his mouth. "I think we've found you your weapon."

We continued to train throughout the rest of the afternoon. Androgeus left to continue his training with the men. I was paired with Glaucus, who eyed me nervously. He was no match for me physically. In fact, Glaucus was no match for anyone physically. Both Ariadne and Phaedra consistently beat him in impromptu wrestling matches held in the gardens of the palace, much to his embarrassment.

Paris got us all to lay down our weapons, and we boxed and wrestled for the rest of the day. It wasn't much of a workout, and it was quite unpleasant to lay hands on his flabby flesh. Even though I took it easy and wasn't trying to hurt him, I somehow managed to blacken one of Glaucus's eyes. I think I cracked one of his ribs too by throwing him gently to the ground. He protested hotly to Paris, who looked on unsympathetically.

"My father will hear of this," he declared, glaring at me.

"Don't you mean *our* father?" I asked.

"I meant what I said," he shouted. "Haven't you been listening to palace gossip? You're illegitimate. Our mother fornicated with a bull. You're no son of my father."

I took a menacing step forward and was pleased to see Glaucus cower before me. Like him, I'd heard the rumors. It didn't mean I liked them though. I'm not sure what I would've done then but for the intervention of Paris. Probably nothing pleasant.

"That's enough," said Paris, stepping between us. "Control your anger," he said to me. "A warrior who loses his temper, loses his head."

Behind him, I could see Glaucus smirking. Almost like he had eyes in the back of his head, Paris whirled on him. "Glaucus, close your stupid, fat mouth. If your father does hear of this, I'll tell him the truth. That you fought badly, put no effort in whatsoever, used poor tactics, and generally complained like a child. In short, you're a dog's behind."

That put Glaucus in his place. I tried not to grin, but catching the eye of Catreus and Deucalion, I couldn't help it.

Glaucus saw. "You'll regret this," he spat at me. My grin widened, but I suddenly felt a little uneasy. No doubt he and Ariadne would plot some petty revenge. I'd have to be on my guard.

He stalked off, regardless of the fact that we still had at least another hour of training time left.

Paris strolled over. "Looks like we'll have to find you another training partner," he said and then burst out laughing.

Ω

Before supper, we all had to spend some time practicing with the lyre and flute. It was all part of becoming a well-rounded member of the ruling class. A leader who could write, spell, complete mathematical sums, fight, orate, and play musical instruments. Although why exactly that last one was important was beyond me. It was the only part of the day I truly detested.

My large fingers, fingers that felt comfortable and deft on the grip of my club, were incredibly clumsy—more so than usual. The others would laugh at my inept attempts to coerce something resembling music from my instrument. The discordant sounds were reminiscent more of animals fighting or mating than actual music. I even caught Phaedra laughing on occasions, unable to stop herself. I didn't blame her. In her position, I probably would've reacted in the same way.

Ariadne and Phaedra were of course both quite excellent, the skill being more important for them apparently. They were forced to practice during their afternoon sessions in addition to learning how to be a dutiful housewife. Phaedra informed me that she would have to play for her husband's guests once she was married.

Catreus and Deucalion played with passable skill, while Androgeus played both instruments with his usual competence. Glaucus was a surprise. His chubby fingers were quite agile as they danced over the strings of the lyre. But, it was Icarus who was the true revelation. He played the flute like someone born to it. He began to surpass even the skills of his tutor and became largely self-taught. When he played for us, I watched him carefully. He would close his eyes, completely lost in the music. Only when he finished would he become aware of his audience, shaking his head like a dog clearing a vivid dream from his head. I discovered a newfound respect for him.

It was later that same evening, long after our evening meal, when I was summoned before my mother. Even though I sought out opportunities to see her, our daily routines were so busy that I didn't get to see her with the same frequency as I had when I was young. I missed her.

Every time I saw her, however, she seemed to age. It was almost like having her children around her kept her young. Now that they didn't need her as much, she seemed to shrink and collapse within herself. Not that she still wasn't beautiful and vibrant, but she had become less so, which saddened me.

"You wanted to see me, Mother," I said, lightly brushing my lips against her check, careful not to let one of my horns graze her face.

"Asterion, my beloved son," she said, holding me close. "I don't get to see you nearly enough these days."

"I know, Mother," I replied. "Our tutors keep us busy."

"Yes, I've heard. Take a seat." I pulled up a stool and perched next to her where she sat on a couch. From our vantage point, we could see the sea shining brightly under the glowing orb of a full moon. I found her looking at me sharply, but I could see the humor behind her eyes.

"I heard about you and Androgeus today. I also heard about you and Glaucus. It seems you're becoming a man."

I nodded, unwilling to meet her gaze. I didn't exactly feel good knowing I'd harmed or potentially harmed her other sons. My brothers.

"And a man has a right to know who his father is. His true father."

My heart skipped a beat. My breathing suddenly quickened, like I'd just been running. This was the knowledge promised me, the knowledge that Phaedra had hinted at. Knowledge that I wasn't sure I wanted. I desperately wanted to fit in with my other brothers and sisters. If a new revelation served to make me different, then I'd probably rather not know.

I had long ignored palace rumor and gossip as the work of

idle mouths. Yes, my horns were an oddity but no more so than someone born with an extra finger or toe. They were just more obvious. There was no way I could be the son of a bull. That was absolutely ridiculous.

"My father is the King," I said. "Minos."

Pasiphae pursed her lips. "Is that what you want to believe? That your father is that man? The same man who beat you because of an accident? The same man who shuns his wife in favor of harlots he finds in nearby villages?"

I didn't know what to say to that. My mother had always had a tongue much better suited to oration and debate than I.

Pasiphae saw the confusion clearly etched on my face. "If your concern is that your father is the white bull, then wipe that from your mind. Can you imagine me mating with a bull? Even with the assistance of Daedalus, the act would've been impossible."

I knew she was right. Oddly, the white bull had disappeared not long after my birth. One of my regrets is that I never got to see it for myself. I presumed my father had dealt with it to disperse persistent rumors.

"No, my son. Your father is a much greater man than Minos. In fact, much greater than any man. He's not even really a man. Your father is a god."

"What?" I exclaimed, jerking to my feet in shock.

"Your father is Poseidon, god of the sea."

I stood there, a mass of turbulent emotion, unable to speak, my mouth open like a dullard. My father a god? Was it true? Of course it was. I felt the truth of it. And why would my mother lie to me? She never had before.

"But how?" I exclaimed when I recovered my wits, sinking

slowly back onto my stool.

"Poseidon appeared to Minos as a white bull, a bull he was meant to sacrifice to him as a sign of his loyalty and respect. Your father, being who is he, decided not to. Poseidon punished him by seducing me. Not that there was much seduction going on. A god is hard to resist." My mother looked wistful for a moment, remembering the events of long ago.

"One moment he was a bull, the next, a beautiful man. I didn't even count it as a betrayal. I knew Minos was having affairs with other women, so why couldn't I? At least I didn't lower myself to sleep with common villagers."

A thought suddenly occurred to me. A happy thought. "That means that Phaedra isn't my sister," I said, feeling an overwhelming sense of relief flood through my body. I'd often thought my feelings for her were inappropriate. It was a joyous thought to discover that we weren't related.

"No," said my mother. "She is the product of your father's amorous affections on giggling, dim witted, large breasted village girls. Your other brothers and sisters are still related of course. They are merely your half siblings."

I felt relieved by that too. The thought that Androgeus was not my brother would've saddened me.

"But," said Pasiphae, "this knowledge comes with a warning. You are the son of a god, and you'll be a target for others as such. Not just mortals either. You will also have to be careful with your power. You will find that you are stronger than other men. This is not to say you are superior. Digest this knowledge humbly."

"What about my horns?" I asked.

Pasiphae smiled. "That was to remind Minos of his

arrogance. You will always be around to remind him. That is why he hates you so. One day soon, you must leave this place before his hatred manifests into something more. I know him. I know how the knowledge of my betrayal gnaws at his heart. Soon, it will be too much for him to bear, and he will have no choice but to remove that reminder."

"Leave this place?" I said, aghast. "But this is my home."

My mother placed a gentle hand on my arm. "It will always be your home but still you must leave. Not now, but soon. This will give you time for you to become acquainted with your heritage, to achieve mighty deeds. Then and only then, will you be free from the rage of Minos."

I nodded slowly, digesting the facts, knowing my mother was right. I still remembered the look on Minos's face after he'd struck me. I had never known someone so cold before.

"When shall I go?" I asked. "Where?"

"You will know the time," she said, smiling gently at me. "Perhaps the gods will send you a sign. Maybe even your father himself. As for where, that is for you to decide. Come," she said. "Give your mother another embrace."

I did so, hugging her more tightly than I'd ever hugged anyone. So tightly that I felt like I'd crush her. I didn't want to release her, now that I knew my time with her was limited.

Eventually, she pushed away and looked me full in the face. "Know one more thing, my son. No matter what happens, no matter what you do, no matter what anyone says, I will always love you. You are my son. My precious boy. You will always be my precious boy."

CHAPTER 5

I have always felt more comfortable alone than in the presence of others. Even though I welcomed the companionship offered by Phaedra and most of my brothers, I often preferred solitude. Perhaps it was because of my horns. They always made me feel different. I often felt self-conscious of them, and being with others made me only too aware of how different I was.

Sometimes, on rare occasions when I wasn't obliged to train or study, I would sit in an isolated spot under one of the trees in the palace gardens, completely alone with my thoughts. Occasionally, I would take some food—perhaps some bread or fruit—which I would munch on distractedly, often sharing it with the birds.

I must've been around fourteen when I encountered the first of my two animal friends.

It was a mangy dog, half-starved with a dirty dull brown coat. I don't know how he managed to get into the gardens without being chased away by one of the gardeners or guards, but there he was.

At first, I thought I had imagined him and started slightly as I suddenly became aware of his presence. He stood nervously less than a stone's throw away from where I sat. I could tell he was ready to bolt at any moment.

I have always felt an affinity toward animals, perhaps because of my supposed links to the bull. They, in turn, have sensed that about me, which has enabled me to get closer to wild animals than most people. This is probably the reason why I easily befriended this dog.

Careful not to make any sudden moves, I gently extended one hand containing a small chunk of bread and made soothing noises. The dog didn't approach for long moments, sniffing the air cautiously. Eventually, he must have realized that I was no threat and moved toward me warily, his eyes never leaving the bread held in my hand.

He stopped several arm lengths away from me but approached no further. Realizing that he wasn't going to take the offered food from my hand, I threw it gently at his feet.

Most dogs in his condition would have gobbled the food hastily. Not this one. He sniffed it before taking small, gentle bites. This immediately endeared him to me.

I named him Kyon, which means dog in Greek. I'm not sure why I gave him such an uninspiring name. It was a spur of the moment thing and once named, it stuck. I could've given him any number of heroic names and often thought about it but never did. Odysseus, for instance, named his dog Argos, meaning "fleet-footed." I guess Kyon was none of these things. He wasn't fast; he wasn't large or strong. He was just a dog.

He was also my friend.

After that day, I went as often as I could to the same spot in the hope that I would see Kyon again. I didn't see him for a few days and feared the worst. But my heart surged with relief when he suddenly appeared again. I saw him nearly every day after that.

I fed him. He still wouldn't take the food from my hand, but each day he got closer and closer. Eventually, on a day I still remember with great fondness, he took the food gently from my hand. That marked a new aspect in our relationship, and he began to tolerate my touch, even though he would often flinch and growl. After a while, he stopped doing that too. I suspected that he had been beaten, which had made him understandably wary around humans.

In the weeks that followed, I was able to stroke him, and he would nuzzle my hand affectionately. We played together, Kyon excitedly fetching sticks that I would throw into the gardens. I inspected his coat and found evidence of several scars, some still scabbed over. I did my best to clean them even though he growled.

I knew I would not be allowed to have him in the palace, so I didn't even try. I feared my father's displeasure. I have no idea where he slept, but he was often waiting for me in the gardens. If he wasn't there, I would whistle and he would soon appear.

He filled out substantially. His ribs disappeared under a layer of healthy fat and many of the scabs on his skin flaked off. I managed to bathe him once and discovered that his coat was not brown at all. It was a luxurious golden color. I don't know why I bothered because he just rolled in the dirt straight afterward. He learnt from the experience, however. Never again was I able to corner him to give him another one. He had a sixth sense in this regard.

Occasionally, Phaedra and I would make the two-hour journey to Nirou Khani that served as the official port of Knossos. Kyon would sometimes accompany us, but I could tell that he, like I, was not always comfortable in the presence of other humans. He was extremely protective of me and only tolerated Phaedra despite her best efforts to win him over with food. He didn't accept her at first, and often growled, but eventually he realized that she was no threat. She was never able to touch him, however.

Months later, that distrust of others brought disastrous consequences.

We were playing together, Kyon and me, in our usual spot in the palace gardens. It was a beautiful day, and I was enjoying the simple pleasure of our companionship.

That pleasure was brought to a sudden halt by an unwelcome presence.

"Dogs are not allowed in the gardens," snipped an acidic voice that I knew only too well.

I turned to see Ariadne and Glaucus standing nearby, watching. Kyon began to growl, a low menacing sound deep in his throat.

"That's true," chimed in Glaucus. "If Father finds out, say goodbye to your little friend."

I thought of several responses, but I really didn't want to antagonize either of them. "Please don't tell him," I said, trying not to sound too desperate. I could've threatened them, I suppose, but that would have resulted in an even worse punishment.

"Why not?" asked Ariadne with a sneer. "What will you do for us?" Ariadne must have been around twelve at the time, Glaucus one year her junior. Both of them had quickly learned how to manipulate people for their own benefit.

I thought desperately. I didn't really have any leverage over them. "I will let you play with him, too. You can throw sticks for him," I said hopefully.

"Why not?" agreed Ariadne. "It looks like fun. Glaucus, get me a stick." I thought nothing of it at the time, taking what she had said at face value. I thought perhaps Ariadne was making an effort to be nice for a change.

Glaucus, like the sniveling obsequious boy that he was, dutifully got his older sister a stick. She held it out for Kyon.

Kyon understood the game by now. He knew what was required of him. He edged closer, his nervousness around others forgotten for a moment by his desire to play. Ariadne made to throw the stick. But she didn't throw it. She hit Kyon with it instead.

He gave a yelp of pain that quickly turned into an angry growl. He lurched at Ariadne. Glaucus, displaying bravery I didn't know he possessed, kicked Kyon.

The result was predictable. Kyon bit him. Hard. Glaucus cried out in pain and tried to thrust Kyon off his leg, but Kyon was having none of it. Ariadne, I noticed, didn't try to help at all.

"Kyon!" I shouted. "That's enough." With one last jerk of his head, Kyon released his grip on Glaucus's leg and returned to my side, still growling. The boy fell to the ground and started crying.

"That's a vicious dog you have there," said Ariadne, smiling grimly. "It's not safe to have such a dog around the palace. Something will have to be done."

"Please," I pleaded. "Please don't say anything. Phaedra will look at the wound on Glaucus's leg. Nobody else has to know. It was an accident. Kyon wouldn't have bit anyone if you hadn't treated him like that."

"Are you saying this is all our fault now?" sneered Ariadne. "Plead all you want, it will make no difference."

"Kill it," sniveled Glaucus. "Kill the stupid dog."

"Now that," said Ariadne coldly, "is a good idea."

Ω

I knew I had no other choice. If Ariadne and Glaucus got their way, Kyon would be killed. I did the only thing I could do.

I ran away.

After Ariadne and Glaucus had slunk back to the palace, I told Kyon to wait and followed them. Entering my room, I loaded a few items of clothing into a satchel and tucked a purse with a few coins into my loincloth.

I risked one final detour. I went to the kitchens and threw in as much food as my satchel would hold. I tossed it over my shoulder and returned to the gardens as swiftly as I could.

I had feared the worst. I thought perhaps that Kyon would run off, never to be seen again. He'd already had many bad encounters with humans, this was one too many. I thought perhaps his trust in me was broken. I also worried that maybe Ariadne and Glaucus would call out the guards immediately and have him killed.

You can imagine my relief then when I saw Kyon waiting patiently for me under our tree. I could tell from his posture that he knew something was wrong, but dogs have limited ways of expressing themselves. His tail wagged nervously.

"Come on," I said.

I led him out of the palace gardens. The guards had seen him many times before by now, often in my company, so our presence went unremarked. I had no idea where we were going, only that Kyon and I had to leave. If we stayed, Kyon would surely die.

We headed for the coast. In my innocence, I thought perhaps I could get work in one of the villages. Maybe I could become a mercenary and take ship for some foreign parts? Of course, everyone knew me for who I was. My horns and size marked me as the King's son.

As night fell, a farmer and his wife took pity on me and allowed Kyon and I to sleep in one of their out buildings used for storing grain. Kyon and I cuddled together to keep warm, and eventually I slept, although it was a restless sleep filled with disturbing images of Kyon lying dead at my feet. Around midnight, a low rumble awoke me. It was a tremor, something most Cretans were accustomed to, and I thought little of it at the time. The granary shifted around me but thankfully didn't collapse, and I finally went back to sleep.

Kyon's barking woke me again at dawn. Before I could get to my feet, several guards burst into the granary and seized me.

Kyon did his best to fight them off but was clubbed ruthlessly into submission.

Both I and my dog were bound. Kyon was carried on a stout pole, much like a wild pig captured during a hunt. I was forced to march in front of him with guards at my back to ensure I didn't run off again.

To my surprise, we weren't taken back to the palace. Instead, we met another group of palace guards on horseback.

I was hoisted into a saddle and tied on. This was fortunate as I didn't know how to ride and would've fallen off otherwise. Two other guards carried Kyon suspended between them on their horses.

The journey took all day. Finally, as night fell, saddle sore and exhausted, we arrived at our destination. It was Monastiraki. I had heard of the place but had never had an opportunity to visit up to this point. I knew the place was home to a small village and a temple where sacrifices to the gods were often performed.

I felt a sudden surge of hope. Although it was hard to tell with his covering of dirt, Kyon had a golden coat and golden dogs were sacred to the goddess Diktynna. Many of them guarded her temples throughout Crete. I thought perhaps Kyon was going to be one of these dogs, living out his life in relative comfort. Even though I wouldn't get to see him often, I thought he would be safe here.

I was helped down from my saddle and guided to the temple. Two guards brought Kyon, still trussed and bound. The temple was filled with people. Most of them seemed to be simple villagers but three figures, sitting in a place of honor, caught my eye.

King Minos was flanked on either side by his son and daughter. Ariadne and Glaucus. If they were here, I knew something was very wrong. I was brought to the front of the temple, just before the altar, and made to kneel. The altar, I knew, was used to appease the gods in the form of sacrifices. Sacrifices that often took place after events like earthquakes.

At first, I thought Minos was planning to sacrifice me, and I was filled with sudden terror. Suddenly, I caught Ariadne's eye and knew that her revenge was altogether more subtle. Glaucus was smirking. I would've spat at him if the spittle had any chance of reaching him. As it was, he was well out of harm's way.

Kyon was carried up to the altar, growling and yelping piteously. My heart went out to him. If I could've switched places with him, I would've. I said nothing, my mouth dry. I knew it wouldn't make the slightest difference if I protested.

They released him from the pole but kept all four paws bound. Even so, he struggled mightily and tried to bite. I only wished he had succeeded. Two acolytes held him down.

I could do nothing, bound as I was with two guards standing over me. A cowled priest approached the altar and loomed above the squirming dog.

He went through the normal rituals and formalities. I tried to rise to my feet but was held down by the guards. The priest, having finished the preliminaries, produced a long knife. He held it high in the air and I, unable to watch, lowered my eyes.

Minos was having none of it. He barked a command, and the guards raised my head, forcing me to watch the horrible scene unfolding before me. The knife thrust down in a glittering arc. Kyon yelped once, a high-pitched bark of pain, and then there was silence. Just like that, my friend Kyon was dead.

Minos nodded once, stood, and left the temple accompanied by his children. Ariadne and Glaucus looked back once and were rewarded by seeing the tears streaming down my face.

Ω

"Why ... why that's monstrous!" exclaimed Ovid, slurring drunkenly. "Your brother and sister were monsters."

Ast nodded sadly. "Yes, I'm afraid they were much like their father. They had his same basic desires for petty revenge. Thankfully, not all of my mother's children were like him. Most inherited her kind nature."

It was well after midnight. Ovid knew he would have to stop soon. Even fuelled by constant alcohol, his energy reserves were waning. His writing hand shook, and his eyes stung, but it was hard to stop. He wanted—no, he needed—to hear more. If it was true, the things this poor misunderstood man—yes man, not beast—had gone through was more than anyone should have to bear. And Ovid suspected he had only heard the start of it.

"How do you feel about Kyon now? Do you still think about him?" asked Ovid.

"I haven't thought about him in a long, long time. The memories are ... painful," said Ast, his face betraying little emotion.

"What happened afterward?" asked Ovid.

"I was taken back to the palace. There were a few

cells beneath the palace. Minos had me thrown into one of them to reflect on my ways. I was guilty of having a pet he hadn't sanctioned as well as running off rather than face my punishment. I was kept in that cell for three days with no food and only a little water. It was a small taste of things to come."

"So you were put in the labyrinth then?"

"No," said Ast, slowly shaking his head. "Not until many years later. The labyrinth wasn't built yet. But I will answer all your questions tomorrow. I think you've heard enough for now."

"Perhaps a little longer?" asked Ovid hopefully.

"I am tired," said Ast. "My tale is more draining than I thought. I need to rest. We will continue tomorrow."

Ovid knew there was no point in arguing. Besides, he was dreadfully tired himself. He stifled a huge yawn and looked around. "Shall I sleep in here then?" he asked.

"Take my bed in the adjoining room. I will not need it tonight. I have … much to think on, and I wish to be alone."

Ast helped Ovid stagger to his feet and half carried him to his small cot. Almost as soon as the poet was horizontal, he was asleep. He started to snore. Loudly.

Ast watched him for a while, then, content that the other man was comfortable, left him to his dreams.

He ventured outside. It was a clear night. The skies were alive and bright with stars. Ast sat down. He reached into his tunic, and his questing fingers brought forth a small figurine in the shape of a dog. A figurine he had carved with his own hands to honor and remember the bond between him and Kyon.

And then he began to cry, remembering a friend who was over a thousand years dead.

CHAPTER 6

Life moved on. I gradually came to terms with the death of Kyon although I never forgave Ariadne and Glaucus. In fact, I only spoke to them when I had to, and even then, it was an effort to be civil. Apart from my father, I have never hated two people more.

We grew older, and apart from little mischiefs stirred up by Ariadne and Glaucus, I was happy. Not only that, but relieved too. Even though I wanted to believe that I was the same as my brothers and sisters, now I embraced the truth. To confess, there was a part of my mind, deep, deep below my conscious thoughts that always knew Minos couldn't be my father. That didn't want him to be my father. I guess I didn't want to discover that my father was some common fisherman from one of the nearby villages. Not that I had a problem with that as such, but it would've been another reason for my siblings and others at the palace to hate me. Besides, if Minos had discovered that my mother had cheated on him with a commoner, I would've been banished with her from the palace, never to see Phaedra again.

As it was, my father was a god. A god! And not just any god. Poseidon, one of the great three gods. Brother of Zeus and Hades. The sons of Cronos and Rhea, they divided the world up amongst themselves. Zeus, being the most powerful, took the sky, Poseidon the sea, and Hades the underworld.

It was odd thinking I was the son of Poseidon. I never had any affinity with the sea. Despite it being less than two hour's walk to the coast, I rarely made the effort. If anyone was a child of Poseidon, it should've been Phaedra. On hot summer's days, when our busy schedules permitted, she would make the journey, often by herself, with only a servant for company. When I was able and inclined, I occasionally accompanied her. I confess I had an ulterior motive. The water clung to her long dress, emphasizing her curves that were no longer a girl's.

Ariadne and Phaedra both flowered into extraordinarily beautiful woman. Both were fourteen now, two years younger than I and ripe to be married off to some King or Prince somewhere. I often lay awake at night, my heart filled with longing and despair. We could never be together, despite the fact that we were no longer related. Even if Minos had viewed me with favor, I was not a suitable husband for his daughter, having no kingdom, advantageous political alliance, or dowry to offer.

Age had not mellowed Ariadne at all. If anything, she had gotten worse. Her tongue spat acid, and she used any opportunity to deride me. I avoided her as much as I could.

The warning of my mother was never far from my thoughts. There would come a time when I needed to leave the island and seek out my destiny, but I delayed mostly because I dreaded the separation from Phaedra. But the time was coming.

I was sixteen now, a man. And not just any man. I was taller than anyone, including Androgeus, by a head and massive with it. I weighed as much as two smaller men. My vigorous training regime ensured that most of it was thick muscle. I stood out amongst my smaller fellows like a sapling amidst grass and drew attention wherever I went. Even my father couldn't ignore me. Catching glimpses of him around the palace, I noted that he would stop to consider me, looking me up and down, assessing with cold eyes.

It wasn't just my body that had grown. Unfortunately, the horns atop my head kept pace with the growth going on in other areas. They were a source of embarrassment. I drew enough attention with my size alone; the horns were an unwelcome addition. Not only that, but I was painfully aware of my looks.

Compared to Phaedra, Ariadne, and Androgeus, I was almost ugly with thick, homely features. Not exactly looks which made the girls flock around me like they did with Androgeus.

When time permitted, I had been spending a few hours with Daedalus and Icarus in their workshop. I loved to watch them work, and Daedalus would often get me to help out. Icarus and I began to bond. He was extremely bright, with long dexterous fingers. I also discovered that he was willful, often arguing with his father over small matters. Although we seldom talked casually, we would often discuss projects until late in the night. It was he who came up with a solution to at least two of my problems.

More than once, I caught him looking at my horns.

"Do they bother you?" he asked one evening.

"What?" I replied, knowing exactly what he was talking about but choosing to be deliberately uncooperative. My horns were a bit of a sensitive issue.

"Your horns."

"What do you think?" I said, unable to keep the sarcasm from my voice. Luckily, Icarus seemed to be almost immune to sarcasm.

"I think they probably do," he replied eventually, giving the matter some thought. "Not only do they draw attention to you, but I'd imagine it makes physical activity difficult."

I blushed heavily. I knew he was probably referring to my sessions in the gymnasium, but I couldn't help but think about the kisses and caresses I'd shared with Phaedra. I'd told Phaedra about my conversation with my mother and my heritage. She'd never had any doubts, always knowing in her heart that I wasn't her brother. Of course, the knowledge, now out in the open between us, freed us to pursue ... other matters.

He was right though. The horns did make life difficult. They were as large and impressive as a fully-grown bull by now, curving first outward and then in to point directly in front of my forehead. I had to be extraordinarily careful when kissing Phaedra for fear of damaging her. Likewise in the gymnasium. I'd inadvertently gored a few of my opponents several times. Androgeus bore several scars even though I'd taken to blunting the ends with a file. He, of course, never said a thing to his father. My brother was a great man, more so due to recent events, having won the marathon at the previous

Panathenaic games, despite being only sixteen at the time.

"What do you suggest?" I asked. I'd thought about it before, but the only solution that came to mind was cutting them off. I tried that. Once. The pain was just too intense. I tried to saw through one, only to black out after the first few cuts, regaining consciousness face down on the cold marble floor.

"You've tried cutting them off?" he asked, almost like he was reading my mind. When I nodded, he ruminated further.

"If removing the problem isn't the answer, how about concealing it?"

"Concealment?" I spluttered. "How am I supposed to conceal these things? Cover them with flowers? Paint them to match the colors of the sky?"

"No," said Icarus finally. "I have something else in mind." He explained and the simplicity of it astounded me. Why hadn't I thought of that?

We worked together on the project with what free time we had. Icarus was a skilled craftsman, having learnt from his father. I in turn, learnt from him although I lacked his gift and the dexterous fingers needed for such fine work.

Daedalus helped, but even so, it took us two weeks of hard labor. But it was worth it.

Icarus helped put it on my head and then moved a mirror of polished bronze into a position where I could see my reflection.

"Well?" he asked finally.

We'd constructed a helmet. Not just any helmet either. Most helmets during this time were made from slivers of boar tusks, sewn onto a leather base. Mine was different in several ways. Holes had been bored into the front plates, cleverly enabling my horns to slide through. So skillfully had Icarus wrought that only a close inspection would reveal that the horns weren't actually an extension of the helmet itself. To a stranger, the horns would appear as a fearsome adornment of a battle helm. It wasn't unknown to wear such things although most helms had boar tusks instead of those of a bull. The helmet was also strengthened with strips of layered bronze making it extremely strong. Not only that, but Icarus had constructed a hinged plate that could slide down over my face.

I fixed the faceplate into position and regarded myself in the mirror.

"Do you like it?" asked Icarus hopefully. I could tell he was excited. I never would've believed it, but it seemed like Icarus had a sense of humor after all.

The face of a bull stared back at me from the mirrored surface.

Ω

My new helmet, despite its clever design, was not much use in day-to-day living. I could hardly walk around the palace of Knossos wearing it, could I? It was designed for battle, its practical use to disguise myself in front of those who didn't know me. Unfortunately, everyone on Crete knew who I was by this point.

Icarus must've somehow guessed my ultimate intention to leave the island. Perhaps I'd let something slip during our conversations. Regardless, I knew the helmet would have its uses in the future. In the meantime, my life was unaltered by the new addition to my wardrobe.

My relationship with Phaedra blossomed. I spent more time with her than any other, including Icarus. She was clever and kind and had a sense of humor I enjoyed, although could rarely compete with. She also possessed a beauty that made my heart ache. I had no idea what she saw in me.

I was large and clumsy. I was not poetic or gifted with the same ease around women Androgeus had. I was not even handsome. That's not to say I was ugly, but my features were rough clay compared to the sculptured brilliance of my brother's dazzling looks. I sometimes wondered how we were brothers. My mother was a beauty, and Minos, despite his meanness of spirit, did not lack in that department either. I could understand why their children turned out so well formed. Even Glaucus, fat and slovenly, was better looking than I. It did occur to me that it was part of Poseidon's revenge against Minos. Why else would I look the way I did when by rights, I should have inherited some of my mother's features?

And of course, there was the matter of my horns. The horns that marked me as someone abnormal and peculiar. A freak of nature. A monster.

I guess that was part of the reason I didn't particularly enjoy walking to the coast with Phaedra. On the few times I had gone there with her, I had found it a little overwhelming. The bustling port was filled with people, Cretans and Greeks from the mainland and more exotic types from places like Egypt, Syria and places I'd never even heard about. Phaedra loved to go, to sample strange foods, perfumes, and spices, to caress new types of fabrics.

The only thing I liked about our trips were the weapons.

Minos imported a great deal of bronze and tin. Most of it was used for weapon production to equip his growing army. With his great wealth, he was also able to buy already forged weapons and armor. It was these that attracted my attention. Massive bronze shields and glinting spears, greaves and breastplate armor, clubs, knives and tridents. A huge array of equipment with only one purpose—to intimidate and subdue other rival states.

I would often pause to look or touch these instruments of death, fascinated by them in spite of my gentle nature. As I did this, I could not help but attract attention. Both Cretans and foreigners alike would stare at me and point. Some would laugh. The only reason I wasn't taunted further or physically abused was because of my status. My clothing marked me as a member of the royal family and most people were probably intimidated by my size. Not only that, but I was also in the presence of Phaedra. She was a favorite of King Minos and many were too scared to risk offending her. With one obvious exception, Minos took a dim view to any who offended his children. On some occasions, he actually put a few unfortunates to death for apparently insulting Ariadne. I doubt whether they'd actually insulted her—it was just Ariadne playing her games with the lives of those she considered irrelevant.

The end result of all this was that I preferred to walk with Phaedra in the countryside, outside the vastness of the palace grounds. We stayed off the major roads, and there we could be largely alone, only rarely meeting the occasional farmer.

Besides, I had another motive for getting Phaedra alone. Despite what I knew about my parentage, I was still considered a son of Minos by the general population of Crete. Therefore,

Phaedra was my half-sister, and any physical relationship was deemed inappropriate. In order to pursue our love, we had to conduct our affairs in private. We were very careful not to demonstrate overt affection in the company of others. We knew our other siblings probably suspected, but without proof, they could do nothing about it. I'm talking, of course, about Ariadne and Glaucus. In hindsight, we should have probably been more careful, but I believe that at the time, we were being as cautious as youth allowed.

When I say love, we were young, and it was largely innocent—kissing, caressing, and the like. Still heady stuff for a young man, so of course I tried to lure Phaedra away from the palace at any opportunity.

Sometimes, we would lie sheltered from the sun amongst the cypress and oak trees, talking, kissing, and doing what other young couples in love did. They were probably the best times of my life.

On one such occasion, Phaedra and I had taken some food and a little wine I'd stolen from the kitchen and wrapped up in cloth. We set it down in a clearing amongst the trees and ate and drank our fill. I confess I'd probably drunk more wine than was good for me and was feeling more than a little bold.

We kissed. Reluctantly, I broke the embrace to ask a question that had been plaguing me.

"Why do you love me?" I asked.

Phaedra looked at me askance, her head tilting slightly to show the perfection of her jawline. I desperately wanted to kiss her again.

"Do you really need to ask such questions?" she replied, her face serious.

"Of course I do. Look at me. Look at you. Don't you think we are an odd match?"

"Asterion, you of all people should know I don't judge based on appearances. To me, you are the most handsome man in the world because of who you are. You are gentle and have a kind soul. That's more important to me than looks. Besides," she said, with a twinkle in her eye, "you have big muscles. Every girl likes big muscles."

"Is that all I am to you? A slab of meat?" I tried to joke, but my tone was all wrong. I knew I half meant what I said. I was only too conscious of my massive size and, like my horns, knew it marked me as an oddity or a strange freak of nature.

Phaedra slapped me playfully. "Most of the time. Sometimes you're able to string a sentence together that is almost intelligent."

We both laughed, breaking the tension. Laughter led to more kissing. Through trial, experimentation, and experience, Phaedra and I had worked out how to kiss properly without me goring her to death with my horns. I won't go into the details here but suffice it to say it took some adroit twisting and dexterity I didn't know I possessed. I put my experience to good use and soon we were locked in an embrace that even a blind person would interpret as anything but brotherly.

Unfortunately, that was exactly the same time we heard the thud of horses' hooves. If we hadn't been so thoroughly intent and otherwise occupied in our pursuit of pleasure, I probably would've heard them earlier. As it was, the riders had ample opportunity to witness our love.

If it had been a farmer or woodcutter passing through, we might have gotten away with it. Minos did not like hearing bad news, often punishing the messenger in addition to those who crossed him. Because of this, news of Phaedra and I never found his ears through common people. Although we had always taken pains to be careful, we had been discovered once or twice before, but nothing, as far as I knew, had been said. But these weren't common people. They were soldiers. Minos's soldiers with loyalty bought by gold.

I looked up at the sound and discovered with some alarm that four riders had entered the clearing and were watching us with interest. I should've immediately known who and what they were. Only soldiers and the ruling class generally rode horses, common people were forced to walk or make use of donkeys. If that wasn't enough of a clue, their emblazoned kilts and weapons clearly marked them for what they were.

They whispered amongst themselves. A couple of them laughed, nasty sounding chuckles.

Phaedra sat up angrily. "What are you doing here?" she demanded.

"We are just passing through, Princess," said one of them, leering at her. I felt myself bristle but, with an effort, remained calm. If we had hoped to remain unrecognized, we were out of luck. Even if Phaedra had been with someone else—someone normal—I doubt we would have gotten away with it.

"Well pass then!" she said.

The soldiers laughed but offered no further comment and soon departed.

The mood broken, Phaedra and I decided to return to the palace, our hearts heavy. We spoke little on the walk back, dwelling on our own dismal thoughts. It was a forlorn hope to think the guards would remain silent. Minos, although happy to punish any of his people for idle gossip or rumormongering, took a more pragmatic approach to his soldiers. He needed their loyalty. They were his strength, his power. Without them, he was nothing. If he punished them for telling the truth, for essentially doing their jobs, he would lose them. The soldiers knew it and were motivated by winning Minos's favor. Everyone in the palace—no, everyone on Crete—knew Minos hated me and welcomed any opportunity to punish or humiliate me.

They must have galloped straight back to the palace because, by the time we had arrived, guards were waiting to escort us to the throne room.

Minos was waiting there, sitting on his throne, his face grim. We knelt before him, lowering our heads but not our eyes. I could tell that Phaedra was scared. Her chest was heaving, and her eyes were wide. I felt the same way, but after my other encounters with Minos, I was not about to give him the pleasure of witnessing any weakness.

He looked from one of us to the other, his eyes completely devoid of warmth. Finally, his gaze settled on Phaedra.

"You will not see this … creature again," he snarled. "From now on, you will be kept apart. If I hear or see you together, I will have him killed. Do you understand?"

Phaedra, bolder and more courageous than I, did not take this well. She was also a favorite of Minos and tried to use this to her advantage.

"We were doing nothing wrong!" she cried. "Asterion is not even my brother. You know that as well as I. Everyone knows that."

She dared too much. Minos's eyes went wide with rage. He gestured to a guard. "Get her out of here. She is not to leave her chambers for one cycle of the moon." Guards took her away. Only Minos, a few guards, and I remained.

"Remove this *thing* from my presence," he snarled, not bothering to look at me. "Have him beaten and thrown outside the palace. He is not to return for the same period. If he does, kill him. If you see him with my daughter, kill him."

I was beaten half to death with wooden staves. The soldiers, eager to win Minos's approval, were possibly a little over enthusiastic. My body was blackened with bruises for many days after. I hobbled away from the palace and into the nearby forest to lick my wounds.

Of course, I contemplated leaving then but had nowhere to go. I had no money, no weapons. The kilt I wore and the sandals upon my feet were my only possessions.

When I was able to, motivated by hunger and thirst, I sought to satisfy these basic needs. I soon discovered that Minos had issued a decree that if anyone aided me, they would be punished by death. I was forced to steal food and always felt guilty about it. I stole from those who could least afford it— the common people who worked the land outside the palace grounds. I had no choice. If I didn't, I would've died.

Occasionally, when it was dark, I crept into a grain store and slept. More often than not, I made my uncomfortable bed in the forest, usually tucked into the base of a tree. I didn't know it at the time, but this experience in survival would serve me well in the future.

Eventually, a month passed and I returned to the palace. My bruises had all but healed. The only evidence of my beating were fading blotches of yellow discolored skin scattered over my body.

Under the watchful eyes of the guards, I made my way to my bedchamber, threw myself down on my pallet, and slept for two days.

After that, I rarely saw Phaedra. I was forced to take my lessons privately with Daedalus. I ate alone. Phaedra and I were constantly watched. It was one of the unhappiest times of my youth.

Ω

A few miserable months passed. A time for a festival approached however, one that I was looking forward to. The knowledge raised my spirits considerably. Although many Cretans worshipped the Greek gods of mainland Greece, the bull was still venerated as a holy animal. I still consider it odd that so many reviled me, I who bore the horns of an animal held in such high regard. I put this down to the King's influence. A wiser and kinder king would've perhaps used me to emphasize his divine favor. Unfortunately, Minos was neither of those things.

In the annual festival, games were held to celebrate and honor the bull. One of the highlights of the festival was the famous bull leap. For the last ten years of my life, I had watched those competing in this event with something approaching awe. It was incredibly dangerous and as you can probably imagine, many died from gore wounds. Enraged bulls trampled some. Those who succeeded were heaped with accolades and rewards. The rewards, it seemed, outweighed the risks as many entered.

You had to be sixteen to participate. Androgeus, four years older than I, a superb athlete in his prime, was the resident champion. He had successfully somersaulted each year to rapturous applause and praise. I was hoping to emulate him, not to win favor from Minos but to perhaps gain acceptance from the people. Not only that, but I wanted to impress Phaedra with my physical prowess. I was, after all, just a sixteen-year-old boy.

The bull arena was situated outside the palace grounds, not far from the sea. People from all over the island attended, in numbers so great that they spilled out of the stands like an overfilled bucket. It was the last day of the festival, the climax and culmination of all the other celebrations. The air was filled with happy, excited laughter. The mood was infectious.

The hopeful bull leapers gathered together outside under the shadows of one stand, clad only in simple loincloths. Androgeus and I stood together. I fidgeted nervously. Androgeus stood easily, a relaxed smile adorning his handsome features.

We'd practiced together using smaller bulls, and Androgeus had made it look easy. He used the bull's back instead of its horns to aid with the somersault but that took immense courage and few risked it. I had seen several try it but only a handful could successfully pull it off. Only those possessed with amazing physical grace and ability could leap high enough to avoid being gored.

I, however, was not equipped with his speed and agility. Not only that, but I was far heavier than my brother. Unless I timed it perfectly, my great weight would often force the bulls head down rather than up, which would lead to a wrestling match rather than an exercise in grace and speed, much to Androgeus delight.

"You're not trying to seduce it," he had said during one failed attempt, laughing as I struggled to pull the bull to the ground. "Leap over it, not through it." At first, I thought Androgeus was referencing my supposed conception. But I knew he would never dishonor our mother with such words. He was not that type of person. I had told him about my true origins, and he had accepted it without question.

"Makes sense," he'd said. "The horns, your great strength, and size. Who else could be your father but a god?" And that was the end of it. It didn't change our relationship in the slightest. I worshipped him, and he in turn treated me with kindness, respect, and understanding.

Out of ten attempts, I had succeeded only twice. Androgeus told me not to worry. The bulls in the arena were much larger and had the necessary strength to throw me. I hoped he was right.

As sons of the King, Androgeus and I had the honor of going last. Actually, Androgeus would go last. I would compete just before him. We watched the other competitors try. Some failed, some succeeded. Two died. There was only one more athlete in front of me. The competitor—a young man not much older than myself—cautiously approached the bull from the front. Suddenly, he sprinted toward it and leapt, grasping the cloth wrapped horns and flipping himself over it to land on his feet behind the animal. Fortunately, the bull's instinctive response aided the athlete. Once it felt the young man's hands on its horns, it tossed its head upwards and back, helpfully providing the momentum for the somersault. It was beautifully done and the crowd went wild, showering the happy young man with flowers.

Then it was my turn. My fear had almost unmanned me. I was shaking uncontrollably. Androgeus attempted to reassure me. "You'll do fine, brother. Remember, it's all about timing. Get that right and you've got nothing to worry about. Besides, if you fail, the bull will probably turn tail and run. I would if I was a bull." He smiled happily and patted me on the back. The words caused most of my fears to evaporate. I couldn't have loved my brother any more than I did at that moment.

I strode out into the arena, expecting to be greeted by cheers. Instead, I heard only silence. Minos, my mother, and my other siblings sat on a raised dais at the far end of the arena, protected, like the other spectators, by tall wooden walls. My father stared down at me, his expression unreadable. I felt like fleeing in shame. All the other competitors had been met with raucous applause. Did the people of Crete really hate me this much?

Suddenly, ragged cheering broke the silence. Behind the King, Phaedra, Catreus, and Deucalion were attempting to break the mood of the crowd. No doubt, they would suffer the King's displeasure later on. The crowd took their cue and some began to join in. Others followed, and soon the arena was filled with the sounds of support and encouragement. It wasn't as great as it had been for the other athletes, but it was more than enough for me.

The bull was ushered into the far side of the arena. It was a massive beast, much larger than any other I'd seen that day. Not only that, but it was white. Minos, in his none too subtle way, was sending me a message.

The bull was already in a lather. Someone had been working it up into a killing frenzy. It caught sight of me and immediately charged, giving me no time to plan my assault. As it got nearer, I finally noticed something else different. Its horns, more massive than my own, were uncovered. They glinted wickedly in the sun. This was not how it was supposed to be. I sensed the hand of Minos guiding events once again and knew his intention. He didn't want me to leave the arena alive. He could get rid of his hated son without fear of reprisals from his family, the people of Crete, or Poseidon himself. Not that many would have likely cared if I died but even a king couldn't kill his son without consequence.

Poseidon had decreed that I could not die at the hand of Minos but he said nothing about a bull. Minos' hatred knew no bounds and he was prepared to risk it. Perhaps he thought that if I died in a supposed accident, Poseidon would not avenge my death. Minos was never the wisest of men. The gods may be many things but they are neither blind nor stupid.

The knowledge was sobering, but it also filled me with determination. Determination I'd never felt before. I would succeed here. I would show Minos and the people of Crete that there was more to me than just a lumbering, deformed giant. I would survive despite the intentions of my father.

I sprinted directly at the charging bull. When I say sprint, it was more of a lumbering plod but you get the idea. It had lowered its head, intent on goring me. Unlike most of my practice sessions, this time I got my timing right. Well, almost.

I grasped the bull's horns, but not before I felt a slight nick as one sharpened point grazed my palm. And then I was soaring through the air. As Androgeus had predicted, this bull was strong enough to provide the lift necessary to propel me upward and over. I flipped in mid-air, hoping to land on my feet behind the bull.

My timing was almost perfect but not quite. The bull, as I mentioned earlier, was huge. The push I received was not enough. Not only that, but I hadn't had time to accelerate to full speed. As a result, I landed almost head first on the back of the bull. I felt the sickening impact as my own horns penetrated deeply into the beasts flesh. It roared in mortal anguish. My momentum carried us both to the ground, with me still pinned to its back.

The bull was clearly in its death throes. It thrashed about, leaking copious amounts of blood over me, pooling on the soil beneath us. It gave one last bellow of pain and then succumbed to its grievous injury.

I got to my feet and pried myself away from the dead bull. More blood spurted from the parallel wounds as I yanked my horns out. It was only then that I noticed the absence of noise in the arena. All was deathly quiet.

I looked up, catching the eye of my father. His mouth was twisted in hatred. Before I could move, he was already on his feet, furiously marching out of the Monarch's box.

There was a grumble of discordant noise from the crowd. A few cheers cried out but they soon quieted down. Most in the crowd realized what this meant. This was a sign from the gods and not a good one either. I had killed a sacred animal. Not only that, but I had killed a sacred animal with horns that were universally regarded as a sign of divine disfavor. This was not good.

I felt an arm tug at mine. I looked down in a daze and saw Androgeus there.

"Come, Asterion. Time to leave."

Numbly, I let him lead me out of the arena. Phaedra was waiting for me. She was taking a huge risk seeing me like this but concern for my safety had overridden common sense.

She and Androgeus guided me back to the palace. The festival was over. Despite my grogginess, I felt a little guilty. Because of me, Androgeus would not be able to compete this year.

"I'm ... I'm sorry," I slurred, gripping Androgeus's shoulder. "You didn't get your go."

He patted me on the back and smiled reassuringly. "Don't worry about it, little brother. How could I possibly have competed with your performance anyway? Hard act to follow."

The journey was a blur. I don't remember arriving back, only that suddenly I was sitting down with Phaedra. She was dressing the wound on my palm. We were in her bedchamber. Androgeus stood at the window, gazing out at the ocean, his face blank. It was dusk. I felt weak, nauseous. My stomach was churning.

"Are you all right?" asked Phaedra. I could tell she was worried. "You've turned white."

I wasn't feeling well at all. Something was wrong. My palm was throbbing. Through the pain, a thought occurred. Had Minos poisoned me? Would he do such a thing? I knew with sudden certainty that he would. It wasn't enough to uncover the bull's horns. He had to make certain that I died.

"I don't feel so good."

Phaedra and Androgeus helped me lie down on a couch.

"I think he's been poisoned," said Phaedra. She knew me. Knew how strong I was. Something was very wrong when a slight scratch could have this effect on me.

Androgeus looked frightened for a moment and then nodded his head ever so slightly. "We have to send for a healer."

"No," said Phaedra. "The healers will do our father's bidding. They will probably let Asterion die or even poison him again. Now that Father has tried once, he's got nothing to lose by finishing the job he started."

"Well, what then?" asked Androgeus impatiently.

"We'll send for Daedalus. He'll know what to do."

Androgeus ran off to summon the master craftsman while Phaedra stayed at my side. Catreus and Deucalion arrived, crouching next to me, offering whatever support they could. Of Ariadne and Glaucus, there was no sign. For that at least, I was grateful. The last thing I wanted was for them to laugh at me.

Daedalus bustled into the room, already briefed by Androgeus. He examined me closely, even going so far as to unravel the bandage Phaedra had wrapped around my palm, sniffing the injury. He opened the wound and placed a gentle finger inside, tasting what he found there.

"I don't know," he confessed. "I think it could be nerium, but I'm not sure. I've seen similar effects before. There's not much I can do. Keep the arm down so that the poison doesn't travel to his heart."

Phaedra did what he asked and Daedalus applied a compression bandage to my lower arm. "That's all I can do for him. We'll just have to hope his natural strength can overcome it."

"You have our thanks, Daedalus," said Androgeus. "When I am King, you will be richly rewarded. This will not be forgotten."

"Certainly not by the current King," replied Daedalus drily. "If he finds out I've helped, that is."

"He will not find out through us," said Phaedra, trying to reassure him. "But make sure you are not found here. Go. Now!"

"In a moment," said Daedalus. "I may be of more assistance to you yet."

"Asterion can't stay here," said Androgeus. "Our father will find him, and if he does ... ."

"I know where we can take him," said Daedalus.

And indeed he did. A place where even Minos couldn't find me. A place I didn't know existed.

CHAPTER 7

It took me two full days to recover, covered in sweat, passing in and out of consciousness. Not that I was aware of the passage of time. Androgeus told me later that Phaedra stayed at my side for much of that time. It seemed that my part-god constitution was a match for the poison employed by Minos.

Under the cover of darkness, Daedalus had me taken to his workshop outside the palace, carried by my brothers and Phaedra. Unknown to any of us, Daedalus had constructed a series of rooms underneath the workshop itself, accessed through a small, cleverly concealed trapdoor. The rooms were devoted to secret projects, projects he felt the world was not yet ready to see. Icarus knew of them, but his father had sworn him to secrecy. The rooms, I guess, were a forerunner to the labyrinth.

There were all manner of devices contained within. Some I

vaguely recognized, but the purpose of most escaped me. Most intriguing of all was a set of wings, which I assumed were for Daedalus's next stage in his exploration of flight.

In the world above us, Minos was conducting a frantic search. Androgeus and my other brothers had to leave. Their absence would have caused too many questions. It was bad enough that I had disappeared, let alone Phaedra, but most of the King's children? Too much of a coincidence.

Even she had to leave eventually. The King had been asking about her. Once she saw I was going to recover, her fear lessoned and she left me under the care of Icarus. Daedalus continued to work in his workshop above us to allay suspicion. Guards had already searched the place, leaving disappointed.

On the second day, I began to feel stronger. Icarus fed me broth and made me drink prodigious amounts of water, thinking the water would help flush the poison from my body. Who was I to argue?

Later, I was strong enough to rise and dress. That done, I started to consider my options. They were depressingly few.

"What are you going to do?" asked Icarus.

"I don't know," I confessed. "My mother told me I would have to leave the island sooner or later." I shrugged helplessly. "I suppose I hoped it would be later." I had delayed my departure too long, and now I was paying the price for my indecision.

"You have no choice but to flee," said Icarus. "Even if this place is never discovered, Minos will find you eventually. You can't stay here forever."

Icarus was right. I knew he was right, but I still dragged my heels.

We discussed options. Eventually, our conversation moved on to the wings nestled in the corner of the underground workshop. They intrigued me.

"Did your father make these?" I asked, standing and moving across the room to examine them more closely. There were two separate wings, feathers fixed on brackets of wood. On closer inspection, the feathers had been attached using wax. There were straps where presumably the wings were attached to the body of whoever was brave enough to try them.

"No," said Icarus quietly. "I did." I could tell from his tone that he was proud of his achievement. He was never boastful. This was about as close as he got to anything resembling arrogance.

"Have you tried them?" I asked, full of wonder.

"Not yet," said Icarus. "Father doesn't want me to risk them yet. He wants to help me make some changes. I know they will work though. I'm certain of it."

I knew the answer before I asked the question. I would've seen or heard something if he had. It did surprise me though. Icarus, although quiet and thoughtful, was also willful and sometimes rash, often doing the opposite of what his father told him. There must have been another reason why he hadn't tried them out. Then I knew. He was afraid. I didn't blame him. Just looking at them made me afraid. But then again, lots of things scared me, foremost among them heights.

Icarus looked me up and down, calculating. "I never designed them for someone of your weight, but it might just work."

"What!" I exclaimed. "You can't be serious. Even if I did get into the air, do you really think they will get me to the mainland?"

"Maybe," said Icarus. "With the right wind behind you. What other choice have you got?"

"I could get a fisherman to take me?" I asked hopefully.

Icarus shook his head. "What fisherman around here would defy the King? Would they really risk it for you—someone who clearly hasn't got the favor of the gods? Even if they did decide to take you, they'd probably huddle in fear the whole voyage, waiting for a lightning bolt hurled from the gods."

"I could steal a boat?" I suggested.

"Can you sail then?" asked Icarus, raising one eyebrow at me. He knew just as well as I that I didn't know the first thing about boats.

It was hopeless. We spent the next few hours suggesting and then abandoning various ideas.

It must have been after midnight when Phaedra and Androgeus returned. Unfortunately with bad news. Androgeus had a large sack slung over his shoulder.

"Our father knows you're here, somewhere," exclaimed Phaedra, breathless.

"How?" I asked but it was unnecessary. I knew.

"It must have been Ariadne and Glaucus," said Androgeus. "They know you spend your free time here. They probably saw us carry you. We were careful, but Ariadne is not stupid. Now that our father is getting desperate, she has finally played her hand in order to reap the greatest reward."

Already, I could hear the tramp of heavy feet above us. The King's guards had arrived. They would tear the place apart, eventually finding the secret trapdoor. I didn't have long and all I could do was wait. They wouldn't get me without a fight though. I started looking around for a useful weapon, hastily pulling items away from the wall, frantically searching.

"No need for that," said Icarus. "My father planned well. There's another way out."

And indeed there was. A hidden access way in one of the walls opened to reveal a rock passageway.

"You go on," said Icarus. "I'll catch up."

I was about to protest but Androgeus took my arm, forcing me into the narrow rock passage. He passed me a burning torch liberated from one of the sconces to light the way. It was a tight fit for someone of my size. Claustrophobic. I still wasn't fully recovered from the poison, and my body poured sweat, which leaked into my eyes, obscuring my vision.

I could hear Androgeus and Phaedra shuffling behind me. They weren't breathing nearly as hard as I.

It seemed like we were in the passage for hours, but it must have been less than one. Eventually, the passageway sloped upward. The flickering light from the torch revealed a dead end above me. It was stone. I immediately started to despair but then logic—logic painstakingly drilled into me by Daedalus—kicked in. He wouldn't have built an escape tunnel without a way out. Experimentally, I gave the stone a push. It rose easily, revealing a dark, cloudless sky punctuated by stars.

I squeezed myself out and reached down to help Androgeus and Phaedra. Not that they needed my help. If anyone needed help, it was probably me. Phaedra closed the stone hatch. It really was a piece of clever engineering. Designed to look like any other stone, it would go unnoticed. The field around us was littered with similar rocks. On closer inspection, I discovered that Daedalus had attached a lever that made lifting and closing easy enough for a child to manage.

We stood together, saying nothing. I quickly got my bearings. We were facing toward the north. The passage had somehow taken us to the cliff tops outside the palace grounds. The Cretan sea spread out below us, a vast never-ending expanse of water that glittered in the starlight. I would've thought it was beautiful had it not been for our predicament.

"Now what?" I asked eventually.

Androgeus set his sack down and leant over the cliff face. "I see a path," he declared. "Not much of one. Probably used by goats but we should be able to get down to the beach."

"And then what?" I asked. "Am I meant to swim?"

"No," said Phaedra, a grim smile on her face. "I've seen you swim. It's not a pretty sight."

"After that?" I asked, my voice rising. Conscious of being heard, I asked again, this time in a whisper.

"I organized a boat," said Phaedra. "I gave a fisherman that I know some of my jewelry. He won't take us himself, but I know enough to manage. He should be here." She joined Androgeus at the cliff face, her face contorting into a worried frown.

"What's this about 'we?'" I asked. "You're not coming with me. It's too dangerous."

"Don't be ridiculous," she said. "You don't know the first thing about boats. You'll drown before you even lose sight of this island." I felt relieved and slightly selfish. She was right—I couldn't handle a boat by myself. But equally, I didn't want Phaedra to give up her life for me. She had it good here. The King loved her in his own strange way. She'd be married off soon and have a life where she wanted for nothing. But, as usual, Phaedra had her own ideas.

"Well," I asked, wisely choosing not to argue further. "Where's this boat then?" It still hadn't appeared. The sea below us was devoid of anything floating.

"It's not coming," said a voice behind us.

We turned as one to see Icarus forcing himself through the concealed entrance. He knelt down behind him and began dragging something out. Anything else I was about to say dried up immediately when I saw what it was.

Ω

"All set?" asked Androgeus. He tried to smile reassuringly at me, but I could tell it was forced. He was as worried as I was.

He and Icarus had helped me don the wings. There was a lot of adjustment necessary, given that they had been originally designed for Icarus himself, but eventually we got there. I flapped them experimentally. They felt light and flimsy. I was having some serious misgivings about this whole thing, tempted to tear them off and give up.

"This is ridiculous," said Phaedra. She sat on the ground nearby, refusing to help with such a misguided venture. "I'll find us another boat."

"I doubt that," said Androgeus. Icarus had already told them that any fishing boats, or in fact anything floating, were now guarded by the King's men. He'd overheard the guards talking as he made his escape through the tunnel.

"I still think he's going to wind up dead," said Phaedra. She rose to her feet and faced me. She was so close I could smell the sweet scent of her perfume. I desperately wanted to gather her into my arms, but that was now almost impossible. Not to mention awkward.

"Don't do it," she pleaded. "We'll think of something else. We can hide together, you and I. We'll find a way off the island."

"There's no other option," I said. "I have to do this."

Androgeus was staring back toward the palace. "Someone's coming," he declared.

I turned to look. I could see the light of several torches in the distance. They looked to be heading in our direction.

"It's the King's guard," said Icarus. "They probably found the tunnel but I collapsed it behind me. Only a fool wouldn't be able to be able to guess where it came out though."

"It's now or never," said Androgeus. He moved Phaedra aside and embraced me. "Good luck, brother. I'll see you again. I know it."

I nodded mutely, clumsily trying to return the embrace, hampered by my wings. He tucked the sack into my belt. I already knew what it contained, and it was much lighter now than it was before. Icarus had insisted that the less weight, the better. Food was the first thing to be removed, followed by some items of clothing, a short stabbing sword, and some other sundry items deemed to be unnecessary.

Only a small purse of money, a flask of water, and a fishing line remained. Androgeus had had the foresight to bring my helm. It was too cumbersome to put in the sack, so he set it on my head instead, strapping it into place but leaving the faceplate undone.

Icarus approached and grasped my hand in a clumsy

warriors grip. It was an awkward gesture given that he was no warrior, but he tried and that was enough.

"Thank you," I managed. "For everything."

"Just remember you have to tell me all about it," said Icarus. "Don't forget to tilt the wings for more lift."

"How am I meant to steer?" I asked belatedly. It was a bit late for that, but the thought had only just occurred to me.

"Use your legs," he replied mysteriously.

I didn't have a chance to question him further. Phaedra was in my arms, weeping softly. "Don't go," she said one more time. "I want us to be together."

I enfolded her in my winged arms. "I have to. You know I do. I will return one day. I'll come for you. Will you and the others be all right without me? Minos … "

"Don't worry about us," she said. "Our father won't dare punish Androgeus. He'll be King one day. I'll bat my eyes prettily at him and say it was all my idea. That'll get Icarus off the hook. You just worry about yourself."

"If you don't go now, you won't be going anywhere," said Androgeus, a note of worry in his voice. "They're almost here."

He was right. I could see the bronze glint beneath the torches. The King's guard was almost upon us.

I kissed Phaedra softly, and then gently pushed her away and moved to stand on the edge of the cliff. I looked back at the three of them, trying to burn their images in my mind. It might be the last time I saw them. My gaze lingered on Phaedra. She looked so beautiful and so sad. With an effort, I tore my eyes from her and took stock of the task at hand.

"Look for me in Athens," said the voice of my brother.

"I'll be at the games in three months. Poseidon be with you and watch over you."

I certainly hoped so. I needed every bit of help I could get. I sucked in a huge breath, flexed my thick legs, and jumped. It really was one of the stupidest things I have ever done. In hindsight, I should've listened to Phaedra.

Ω

"You flew then!" asked Ovid, his eyes wide.

"You will have to wait and see," said Ast patiently. "I think this is a good time to have a break. You certainly look like you could use one."

It was true. Ovid was suffering. When he'd awoken, simply raising his head off the pillow had been an effort. His head had swam, and he'd felt a little nauseous. He'd put his head back on the pillow and tried to go back to sleep, but it was hopeless. Outside the tiny uncovered window, the sun had already risen. The bright light had done nothing for Ovid's hangover or his already irritable temperament.

Accustomed to overindulgence, Ovid knew he had a remarkable capacity for wine. Many had commented over it. Indeed, few men could match his ability to consume it. Like any true alcoholic, Ovid rarely suffered from debilitating hangovers. He got them, sure, but only mild versions. They were never like this. This was something special.

He really had overdone it the previous night. So engrossed had he been by the story, he'd hardly noticed that he'd emptied two full skins of wine.

"Perhaps a little fresh air would clear my head," he admitted grumpily. Ast accompanied him as he stumbled outside.

When he had first awoken, he had been a little disorientated. After finally levering himself out of bed, the enormity of where he was and who he was with threatened to overwhelm him. Sitting down on the bed again, he had slowly become aware of his surroundings.

The windowsill had a delicate little pot sitting on it. Inside were white flowers. Ovid, a poet and scholar in the truest sense of the word, always interested in the details that would give a sense of reality to his writing, knew they were sea daffodils.

Strange, he'd thought. In his experience, men who lived alone rarely adorned their homes with such, well, feminine things. Now a confirmed bachelor with three broken marriages behind him, he could say he was almost an expert. When he'd lived with his wives, often the home they shared would be decorated with flowers and the like. Since then, he couldn't remember a time that flowers had ever graced his windowsill.

"Are you sure you live alone?" he asked, breathing deeply.

Ast eyed him strangely. "Yes. Why do you ask?"

Ovid shrugged. "The flowers in your bedroom. Don't see that very often in a man's home. Almost suspected you were hiding someone from me for a moment there."

Ast allowed the remark to pass without comment.

Ovid sucked in a few more deep breaths. There was a large ceramic pot outside the door filled with fresh water. He dunked his head in until he could hold his breath no longer and then surfaced, spraying water in every direction. Drying himself with a cloth provided by Ast and feeling a little better for his efforts, he declared himself almost human and fit to continue.

They resumed their seats at the table.

"A few questions," said Ovid. "How did Daedalus know what poison it was?"

"He didn't," said Ast. "He guessed. Daedalus wasn't just a master craftsman. His knowledge was extremely broad. I have never met anyone more knowledgeable. He travelled widely and, as I mentioned, had seen similar effects before. It didn't really matter what poison was used though. The effect was important. I was very lucky I didn't die."

"Did you see Phaedra again?"

Ast nodded. "I did, but I will come to that part of my story in due course."

"Not really helping me a whole lot here," grumbled Ovid. "What about the helmet? It does, I confess, intrigue me. Why didn't you use it more often? Do you still have it? Can I see it?"

"I will answer all your questions eventually, but you will have to be patient," rumbled Ast.

Ovid could see that his large companion was losing patience, but Ovid's curiosity was getting the better of him. Despite his initial misgivings, he was really starting to see Ast as the fabled Minotaur of legend. Could it be true? It was an unbelievable story but somehow it had the ring of truth to it. Not only that, but Ast oozed sincerity. He was a hard man not to believe.

Being a little drunk seemed to help swallow such an unlikely tale. Maybe more wine? Hair of the dog that bit you and all that. He was confident that a few goblets of wine would get rid of his lingering hangover and his doubts.

He poured himself one as Ast resumed his story.

Chapter 8

In hindsight, I was just a boy, ignorant, naïve, stupid. Boys have a tendency to act before thinking. Consequences are rarely considered. Stupid boys do stupid things. Despite my fear, I thought it would work. It didn't really occur to me that it wouldn't. Like Icarus, I had thought of flight. His design seemed sound to me. He was far smarter than I, and so I had the greatest confidence in him.

Unfortunately, the wings had never been tested. Certainly not on someone of my weight and size. Icarus got many things wrong, things he corrected later on in life to his ultimate loss. His later success cost him his life, as you probably know.

I wouldn't have survived but for the favor of my father, Poseidon. As soon as I flung myself from the cliff face, I became airborne above the sea, Poseidon's domain. In or above the sea, Poseidon could defy the laws of nature, the laws of physics. I know this now because he later told me. At the time, of course, I didn't credit him, putting my survival down to Icarus's clever construct.

At first, I thought I was going to die. I plunged headfirst toward the waiting sea. The speed was immense. To my shame, I screamed, the noise emerging as a roar of fear. Just before I plunged to my death, a mighty wind suddenly sprung up, blasting into my wings and catapulting me into the night sky.

I soared then. A feeling of power overcame me, freedom. Joy. My one regret was that I had not had the chance to look back. I wondered for a fleeting moment what was happening to Phaedra, Androgeus, and Icarus. I hoped they wouldn't be punished too severely. The thought was pushed aside by my elation. I had never imagined that flight could be like this.

High across the wine dark Cretan sea I flew, kept aloft by a divine wind pushing me northward. Daedalus had given us enough geography lessons for me to have some understanding of the journey I faced. The immensity of it. If I continued in this direction, eventually I would reach the islands of the Aegean. Thirty leagues would take me to the first inhabited island, Thera. After that, I had no idea how I would get to the mainland. As I said, I was just a boy. There were many islands scattered throughout the Aegean. I had a vague idea that I would simply fly from one to the next, stopping only to eat and drink before continuing my journey to the mainland.

Reality and perhaps fate unfortunately interceded. After several hours of thoroughly enjoyable flight, my arms started to ache and my great strength to ebb. I didn't know how much longer I would be able to hold them out. Not only that, but my endurance was already seriously taxed by the poison that

I had only just overcome. On top of that, I was exhausted. My eyelids began to flutter tiredly.

At that moment, Poseidon once again took an interest in me.

The wind dropped so suddenly that before I was even aware of it, I was plummeting toward the waiting sea. I flapped my arms desperately, but they were too weak. I plunged into the water with a mighty splash. The water wasn't cold, but it was sufficient to revive me. I surfaced, spluttering, flailing wildly with my arms. The impact had torn the wings from me. I paddled over to them and made a raft of sorts. This was fortunate. As I have already mentioned, I had no affinity with the sea. Unlike Phaedra, I couldn't swim.

The wings gave me buoyancy. I collapsed onto them, resting my face on my arms, my legs dangling in the water. I don't know how long I slept for but I did, lulled by the gentle lapping of the waves. I didn't stop to think about how lucky I had been. Normally, the Cretan sea was churned up into ship destroying waves by storms at this time of year. My true father had once again smiled upon me.

I was woken by something brushing against my naked feet. I was dreaming about Phaedra at the time. As first, I thought it was part of my dream and smiled lazily. Then, I felt a second impact. I awoke with a start. Something was in the sea beneath me.

Just then, a fin emerged, slicing through the water. A shark! I panicked, my frantic motions causing me to lose my grip on my wings. I sank beneath the water, my helmet and heavy body dragging me down. I tried to thrash to the surface, but I was weak. I considered discarding my helmet but was reluctant to do so. It was that or drown, though. Frantically, I began to fumble with the straps.

Suddenly, a massive dark shape appeared at my side, sliding under my arm and lifting me up to the surface. I was too exhausted to protest, waiting for the shark to finish me off. It was just toying with me. My head brushed against its smooth flanks. Wait! Smooth flanks. Even with my limited experience, I knew sharks didn't have smooth bodies. I had felt them at the fish markets. I'd even eaten a shark. I knew their skin was rough with thousands of tiny teeth. A brush like that would've taken the skin off my face.

I lifted my head, examining the creature underneath me. It was, of course, a dolphin. I might've been lucky. I might've been in the right place at the right time. But it did occur to me that perhaps, just perhaps, my father was taking an active hand in my fate. Regardless, I was alive for the moment. It was more than I had hoped for.

Ω

I must've fallen asleep again. I awoke, confused, to find my arm draped over the back of the dolphin, my cheek pressed into its sleek skin. The sun had risen. A wave slopped into my face, waking me fully. I took stock of my situation. In the distance, I could see land. Dark cliff tops rose out of the sea, breaking the monotony of the water with their cold bulk. I relaxed. The dolphin was bringing me to land.

Distances are misleading at sea. Tired as I was, I thought

perhaps land was close enough to paddle to. It was fortunate that I didn't try. I would've surely drowned. It wasn't until another hour had passed that my feet brushed against something harder than mere flesh. I had finally reached the beach. I staggered to my feet, somewhat unsteadily. The dolphin raised its head and eyed me with what I was sure was recognition. I patted it on the side and muttered words of thanks.

With a quick flick of its tail, it turned for deeper water and disappeared. I was alone.

I waded to the shore and flung myself down on the beach. I lay there for long moments, grasping the sand like a lover. I had never been so happy to see land before. Finally, I sat up and looked around. At first, I thought the beach was deserted, and then I noticed a tiny upright speck in the distance. It was moving. I lurched to my feet and set off in that direction.

As I got closer, I realized that the speck was a man. A simple fisherman casting his net out into the waves. He was old and bronzed and so slim he looked almost emaciated. Thin wisps of gray hair failed to hide his almost complete baldness. He saw me, and his eyes widened with surprise or perhaps fright. I must have cast a strange image. Clad only in a loincloth and my bull's helm, he might have first surmised that I was some god emerged from the sea. Perhaps Poseidon himself. He approached me nervously, fearfully.

"How can I help?" he asked timidly. I'm sure if I had appeared without the helm, the encounter would've been altogether different. From my limited experience with fishermen on my own island, I had found them to be on the whole a distrustful, superstitious bunch. They survived because of the whim of the sea and the winds. Elements controlled by Poseidon. Clearly, he wasn't taking any chances. If I was a god, he wasn't about to offend me and risk being cursed by an empty net or a rotting hull. Or worse.

"Greetings," I said. "Can you help me? I need food and water. I have money." I reached down to the sack at my waist to find that it was gone. The waves must have washed it away. Gone were my money, my water, and my precious fishing line.

He watched me curiously as I fumbled at my waist, desperately hoping to find the sack somehow snagged within my loincloth. It wasn't.

"Actually, it turns out that I don't have any money after all," I said, feeling a little embarrassed. "But I will work for whatever you can spare. I also seek passage to the mainland."

If he wondered why a god needed food, money, or passage, he never asked, unwilling to cause offense. I was, you have to remember, an extraordinarily large person. Regardless of whether I was a god or not, he was probably motivated by fear more than anything else.

He nodded and gathered his net without a word and indicated that I should follow him. In the days that followed, he spoke very little. To this day, I still do not know his name.

I spent a week in his simple cottage, in the cliffs above the beach. He lived alone. Food was simple, mostly stews made from fish, tomatoes, and olives plucked from his garden. I slept on a pallet made from straw. It was a far cry from the luxuries I had grown up with in the palace of King Minos. Surprisingly, I didn't mind it at all. I had recently adjusted to living rough during my banishment from the palace and my current situation didn't seem terrible by comparison.

The fisherman had a small boat, but it was propped up

on logs some distance away from the beach. As part of my lodging, he had me work on the boat under his guidance, repairing several holes and damage from long disuse. My tutelage under Daedalus once again came in useful.

Eventually, he declared the boat ready to face the challenges of the sea.

We set off. The old man had supplied me with kilt. It was in serious disrepair, but it was better than the loincloth I had been wearing. I helped where I could on board the small boat and learnt a thing or two about navigation, knots, and sails. Not enough to make me a sailor by any stretch of the imagination, but it was better than nothing.

We were at sea for two days and a night. I had hoped that he would take me directly to the mainland, but we only got as far as the next major island.

And that was how I passed the next few weeks. I kept out of major population centers for fear of being recognized. By now, Minos must have realized that I'd left the island. I wasn't sure how far he would take his revenge, but I wasn't about to chance it. He had possibly sent out ships to search nearby islands. My helm was easily recognizable, but I could hardly take it off either.

Smaller fishing villages had everything I needed. Most residents looked upon me with fear, but once they saw how useful I was, they put me to work. I paid for my passage with odd jobs, mostly involving the use of my great strength. Many asked why I never took off my helm, and I answered that it was part of a vow. Oddly, it seemed to satisfy most of them. I have learnt over time that it's best to keep lies simple.

I island hopped. I didn't know why I was so focused on

reaching the mainland. Perhaps because of the stories I'd heard about Heracles. I wanted to win fame and fortune for myself, make myself untouchable to Minos. And also, of course, to be worthy of marrying Phaedra. Not that she cared about such things, but I did. My hopes were pinned to mainland Greece. I didn't know exactly what I would do once I was there, but I was confident I'd figure something out. I had a vague notion that I would kill monsters. Be a hero. Something like that.

I finally reached the mainland three weeks later. The small fishing boat dropped me at the port of Troezen, the capital of the small territory of Troezenia on the Peloponnese peninsula. I had hoped to be taken directly to Athens, the largest city in mainland Greece in those days, but it was well out of the fisherman's way. I counted myself lucky that I had made it as far as I had. I thanked the fisherman and considered my options.

Troezen was about twenty leagues southwest of Athens as the crow flew, on the opposite side of the Saronic Gulf. On foot, it was at least three times that distance. I could possibly manage ten leagues at day, so I was looking at a journey of around a week.

I was hungry and thirsty. The only thing I'd had to eat in the last day was a bit of raw fish and some figs given to me by the fisherman on the last leg of my journey. I wandered about the city, marveling at the sights and sounds. Even though I had been brought up in a palace, my experience with cities was rather limited. Most villages on Crete were tiny by comparison.

Troezen was a proper city, with stone walls and cobblestoned paths. It was filled with small groves of trees, providing shelter and places to sit. The people were dressed differently from what I was accustomed to. Men preferred tunics rather than kilts or loincloths. The style of dress for women was more conservative as well. On Crete, women's dresses were such that one breast was often exposed. Not so in Troezen.

I attracted curious stares wherever I went. Some stared openly at me. I suppose I couldn't blame them. My kilt for one, cut as it was in the Cretan style, marked me as a stranger. Even without the helm, a man of my stature was a rare sight.

I found a fountain and drank deeply, satisfying my thirst. My belly still rumbled with hunger. For lack of other options, I followed the main path through the city. It led me uphill toward the acropolis. Eventually I reached a temple. I entered without challenge and found myself in a colonnaded court surrounded by rooms. The court led to a hall with several stone benches. I gathered from the people waiting that the temple was dedicated to Asklipion, the god of healing. Many of those milling inside bore signs of illness.

I took a seat for lack of anything better to do. It was pleasant just to sit out of the sun for a while and rest my weary legs.

Eventually, a priest approached.

"How can I help you?" he asked, not unkindly. He looked me up and down, searching for obvious signs of illness or disease. "You do not appear unwell. Actually, you look healthier and stronger than most."

I stood and the priest took a nervous step backward as I towered above him.

"I'm sorry," I said. "I was just resting. I am hungry though, but I have no money."

The priest looked from one side to the other before beckoning me close. "I normally don't do this," he said in a conspiratorial whisper, "but stay here and I'll bring you something. A big young warrior like yourself shouldn't go hungry."

I returned to my seat. Soon enough, the priest returned. He shoved half a loaf of bread at me. "Here, take this with my blessing."

I thanked him profusely, promising that I would make a donation to the temple when I could. He smiled. "You look the sort who will accomplish great deeds. Do so, and that will be compensation enough."

I thanked him again and departed, shoveling great chunks of bread into my mouth. So far, my impressions of Greece had been good. The sun was shining, my belly was full, and there was adventure before me. What more did a young man need?

I continued to amble around the acropolis. I came to a practice yard. It was empty save for one youth exercising on the packed earth.

I sat down and watched. The youth—I guessed to be about the same age as I—appeared to be a little over average height with a slim athletic build and grace that matched that of Androgeus. His long black hair was oiled and tied behind his neck by a simple leather thong. He was stripped to the waist, and his lean muscles gleamed in the early morning sun.

He must've noticed my stare because he suddenly stood before me.

"Would you like to train with me?" he asked. I stood and he gave no indication of being intimidated by my size or my horned helm. The expression on his face seemed to indicate approval. I looked him in the eye. He was an extremely good-looking man. Almost beautiful, with fine features and clear,

116

smooth skin. I felt suddenly conscious of my own plain looks. Unlike me, he must've made the girls swoon.

He held out his hand. "My name is Theseus. Yours?"

"Asterion," I said, grasping his wrist in the traditional warriors greeting.

"You aren't from around here, are you?"

"No," I said. If he was hoping for more information, he was destined to be disappointed.

"Ah. A man of few words. I like that. Shall we wrestle?"

I nodded. Now that my hunger had been satisfied, I felt the need for some physical exercise. Other than manual labor, I hadn't had a chance to train for weeks.

He eyed my helm with interest. "Are you going to take that off first?"

"No," I said again. "I have vowed not to."

Theseus made a wry face but shrugged in acceptance. "Fair enough. Try not to gore me with those things."

We wrestled. It soon became apparent that I was stronger than Theseus. I had yet to learn that no mortal could match my strength. But then again, Theseus wasn't exactly mortal either.

He was, however, much more nimble than I. His movements once again reminded me of Androgeus. Where I used brute strength, his much lighter weight forced him to rely on fancy footwork, trick holds, and using his opponent's momentum against him.

We were almost evenly matched. Eventually, more by good luck than anything else, I got a lock on him that was impossible to break. He yielded with poor grace and seemed rather angry about it.

We lay in the dirt, panting from the exertion.

"By Zeus's balls, you are strong," he grudgingly admitted at last, regaining his breath. "I have never encountered anyone as strong as you. Nor as large."

I nodded. "You almost had me there."

Theseus shook his head, his anger fading as soon as it had appeared. "I don't think so. I think you were toying with me. I'd love to match swords with you, though. Then we'd see who has the advantage."

I shook my head. "Perhaps another time. I have to go."

"Where to?" he inquired.

"Athens." I saw no point in lying to him. He seemed an honest enough man.

Theseus smiled broadly. "It seems as if the gods have brought us together. Our goals are the same. I was about to set off to that city myself. Perhaps we can share the road together?"

I hesitated for a moment. I hadn't planned on company. What harm would it do though? It would be nice to share my journey with a fellow warrior. Conversation would be welcome too. Not that I have anything against fishermen but I was weary of listening to lectures on fish, the weather, and knots.

"I accept," I said finally.

"Well, it's agreed then," he said smiling and jumping to his feet. He extended a hand, helping me rise. "One moment."

He darted to the side of the practice yard and came back moments later armed with a sword, spear, and shield. A satchel was slung over his shoulder.

"Do you need time to collect your things?" he asked.

"I have everything I need," I said. It wasn't true of course. The truth was that other than my helm and the kilt I wore, I had no other possessions in the world. I'd even lost my sandals during my long immersion in the ocean. But I didn't want to appear weak and needy in front of Theseus. I had my pride.

We set off, taking the road north out of the city. In those days, the roads were not like they are now under Roman rule. They were mostly dirt, sometimes overgrown, often impassable due to erosion or occasional flooding. Not only that, they were dangerous. Certainly, there were wild animals to contend with and even the occasional monster, but it was our fellow humans we had to be wary of.

Outlaws and brigands were commonplace in the wild lands outside cities, preying on unwary travelers. Despite our fearsome and well-equipped (well, in Theseus's case at any rate) appearance, there were still only two of us. An easy target for villains and thieves.

As we walked, I asked Theseus about his past and the reason for his journey to Athens.

"I'm the grandson of the King of Troezen," he replied. "I was raised by him and my mother, Princess Aethra. My mother told me I have two fathers. Poseidon is my immortal father but my mortal father is Aegeus, the King of Athens. He sent my mother and me away when I was a child, setting me a task to complete before I was ready to take my place at his side."

So, it appeared that Theseus and I had several things in common. We were the sons of royalty and both believed our father to be Poseidon. The story wasn't uncommon. Several heroes had divine as well as mortal parents. The knowledge comforted me. Theseus was perhaps my half-brother. I sensed the hand of the gods. It was not mere chance that we met. I voiced none of this, however, content to keep my origins a mystery for the moment. Even though Theseus appeared trustworthy enough, I wasn't about to reveal the fact that I was a hunted man. I doubted whether Theseus would have wanted to share the road with such a notorious figure.

"What was your task?" I asked.

"King Aegeus left me certain items that would identify me as his heir when I was ready. He placed them under a huge boulder in a forest clearing not far from here. A few days ago, I finally managed to lift the boulder. Admittedly, I don't have your great strength so I had to use cunning instead. Eventually, using a pulley and lever, I managed to pry the great stone loose."

"What did you find?" I asked, intrigued.

"These sandals and the sword I bear," he answered proudly. "They were my father's and will mark me as his son."

"So, it's that easy then? You'll just march into his palace at Athens and say 'here I am. I'm your long lost son.'" It was beneath me to criticize, but I couldn't help it. It did seem a little far-fetched. But then again, it wasn't like my own plans were any less ambitious or ridiculous. It seemed like Theseus had put about as much thought and planning into his journey as I had. In all fairness, at least he was better equipped than I.

Theseus's eyes narrowed. "Of course," he said sharply.

I raised my eyebrows but said nothing. Clearly I had angered him. I was to learn that Theseus was many things and like all men, he had his flaws, the greatest amongst them pride. He was also quick to anger and stubborn as an ox, though he forgave readily. He was not the sharpest spear on the rack either when it came to scholarly pursuits. Despite having access to the same sort of education as I, he never took to it and was extremely sensitive about it. I learnt later that he could hardly read.

"What about you?" said Theseus, his anger gone as swiftly as it had arrived. "What brought you here?"

"A boat," I replied.

Theseus laughed at that. Even I chuckled along.

"Well, you're from one of the islands then. If I had to guess from your clothing, I'd say you hailed from the Cretan sea."

It was a good guess. Theseus may not have been the most intelligent or well-schooled person I'd ever met, but he wasn't stupid either.

"I'm from Thera," I said, thinking quickly. "My father was a fisherman."

Theseus raised his eyebrows. "Fishermen from Thera get to wrestle and train regularly then? Seems things are done differently where you are from. Do all fishermen from Thera wear great helms like the one you sport? I've heard fishing can be dangerous, but I didn't think it was *that* dangerous." He laughed again.

He knew I was lying, but I couldn't tell him the truth. Not yet at any rate. "My father found it in his net," I lied. "As for wrestling, my brother was the village champion. He taught me everything I know." Which wasn't far from the truth. Androgeus had shown me a thing or two about wrestling.

Something compelled me to reveal more than was perhaps wise. I guess it was the feeling of camaraderie that made me open up.

"Like you, I have two fathers," I said. "Poseidon is also my father." I didn't see the harm in telling him that. I certainly didn't tell him I was from Crete. Besides, in those days, the gods were rather promiscuous when it came to socializing with mortals.

Theseus accepted that. It must have soothed his ego a little to know that he had been bested by an equal. To his credit, Theseus pried no further about my past, only my future.

"Why Athens?" he asked.

"Like you, I seek my destiny there. There are heroic deeds to accomplish. I hope to win fame and then return in honor to ask for the hand of the woman who has stolen my heart."

"Ah," said Theseus. "That I understand. Women are capable of making us do all sorts of things in the name of love. Believe me, I know."

I didn't doubt it for a second. With his looks, his experience with women was no doubt much greater than mine.

We journeyed on, finally making camp when it became too dark to see the road clearly. We moved into the trees next to the road and found a clearing. I collected some dry wood while Theseus used tinder and flint to strike a spark. Soon, we had a blazing fire and sat warming our hands in companionable silence. He shared what food he had from his satchel. He produced goat's cheese, some bread, dried figs, and a little watered wine from a skin. I was grateful given that Theseus probably had little enough food for himself, let alone me. The thought had obviously occurred to him too.

"We'll have to hunt," he said. "The food I have will not last until we reach Athens."

I nodded agreement. "Can you hunt?" I asked. I couldn't. Even if I had a bow, I was a poor shot.

Luckily, Theseus said he could. He'd brought a sling with him and assured me that he was proficient with it. Except for his ability to hunt, Theseus, like me, had lived a rather sheltered life. His experience was mostly limited to palace life. Other than my recent journey and brief banishment from the palace, I had rarely spent extended periods of time in the wilderness. We weren't exactly seasoned travelers. We were also a little foolish. More wary and wise adventurers would probably not have risked a fire. Not in the wild. Not in those days.

We may as well have put up a sign saying "easy pickings."

CHAPTER 9

A sharp crack of a breaking twig alerted me to the fact that we were not alone. I roused myself and sat up. I have never been a deep sleeper, and I struggled to get comfortable on the hard ground when I was used to soft palace beds. Even my recent exposure to sleeping rough at the bottom of boats or on straw pallets had not changed that fact.

The fire had burnt down to glowing coals. It was very dark under the trees. I could only just make out the dark huddled shape of Theseus still asleep on the other side of the fire. I heard another crack, and my head twisted in that direction. We were definitely not alone. Something told me that it wasn't an animal lurking amongst the trees.

I stood and looked around desperately for a weapon. Theseus's sword was the obvious choice. I took a step in that direction, but I was too slow.

My suspicions were confirmed when four men suddenly stepped out of the shadows of the trees. Before I could shout a warning, two immediately jumped atop Theseus, pinning him to the ground. He thrashed around but groggy with sleep, was no match for his assailants.

The other two approached me warily, stepping closer to the fire. One, a large, powerfully built man dressed in clothing that had once been fine, carried a great club wrapped in bronze. The other one, smaller and clad in rags, was armed with a short bronze sword. Despite their superior numbers, they were hesitant. My great size was often intimidating. One tried to circle around behind me rather than face me, even though I was unarmed.

Their intention was clear and I was not about to be slaughtered like a goat. I darted forward and kicked hot coals into the face of the outlaw in front of me, scorching my bare foot. He frantically dodged aside, but that was merely a ruse. My goal was one of the stout branches stacked near the fire. I grabbed it. It was a large limb, not too dissimilar from the clubs I was familiar with in the gymnasium.

"What have you got there then, young fellow?" asked the large outlaw in front of me. Given that he was slightly better dressed than his fellows, I guessed him to be the leader.

"Come closer and find out," I growled, sounding more confident than I felt. I had never been in a real fight before.

"There's no need for words like that," he said, smiling. Three of his teeth were missing. He slung his great club over his shoulder. "We saw your fire and thought you would welcome some company. Perhaps share some of your food as a sign of good faith."

"Let go of my friend then, and we can discuss it," I said.

"And have him do something hasty?" he asked. "Hasty actions cost lives, and no one here wants to lose their lives now, do they? Put down your weapon, such as it is, and let us talk."

"Don't do it!" said Theseus. "It's a trick. Don't trust these sacks of wine." One of the two men sitting on him struck him a blow to the side of head, silencing him.

I hardly needed him to tell me. Even someone as ignorant as I could see that.

"There, look what you've made us do," said the man facing me. "All is not lost though. Despite your mistrust, we can still resolve this with words. My name is Periphetes." He held out his arm. "And yours?"

I hesitated. It would be rude not to take a hand extended in friendship. Perhaps this was all just a big misunderstanding? As always, I liked to avoid conflict as often as possible. As I hesitated, distracted, the man behind me took the opportunity to launch his attack, just as Periphetes had intended.

Lucky for me, the outlaw was not exactly well versed in battle. His bronze sword, poorly kept, was blunt. He aimed for my head, intending to cut me down before I had a chance to do anything else. He was only partially successful. The bronze sword clattered against my helm. Daedalus and Icarus had made that helm, probably the world's best craftsmen at the time. Against an inferior sword, there was only one possible outcome. To the outlaw's surprise, his sword shattered.

The impact was still enough to shake me. My training, however, ensured that I didn't freeze. To freeze in combat was to die. Paris had told me that on many occasions. Instinctively,

I swung in the direction where the blow had come from, feeling a satisfying thud judder through my arm as my makeshift club contacted flesh. My attacker gave a yelp of pain and toppled to the ground.

"Now that wasn't very nice," hissed Periphetes. His eyes narrowed with angry concentration. He approached menacingly and swung mightily with his club.

I brought my own club up to block, but to my dismay, it snapped under the impact. The momentum of Periphetes's blow carried his club on. It struck my helm. This time the outcome was altogether different. Periphetes's club was not a common one. It was constructed of seasoned wood and covered in bronze. A heroic weapon completely mismatched with its wielder.

The blow knocked me from my feet. I sprawled on the ground, stunned as Periphetes moved to stand over me triumphantly.

"And thus do the young learn," said Periphetes, grinning. He brought his club down in a vicious arc to finish the job.

Unbelievably, I caught the club before it struck me, stopping it dead. I still remember the look on his face. One moment it was a mask of evil triumph, the next one of comical dismay.

Frantically, Periphetes tried to yank it from my grip. He may as well have tried to move a mountain. I jerked my arm, pulling him off his feet, causing him to lose his grip on his club. He fell over me and crashed onto the ground. I staggered to my feet. Blood was leaking into my eyes from where his blow had caught me. Despite my protection, I hadn't emerged unscathed.

I reversed the grip on the club and hefted it experimentally. It felt good. I looked down at Periphetes dispassionately. Although gentle by nature, sudden hatred filled me. I don't know what it was—perhaps the blood rage of battle that Paris had talked about so often, perhaps I just believed that this horrible human being didn't deserve to live.

"Can we talk about this?" he pleaded.

"I think the time for talk is over," I said. He screamed as his own club descended.

"And thus do evil doers pay," I said grimly.

Ω

"Thank you," said Theseus. "You saved my life. I owe you a debt." I knew how much the words cost him. He seemed a little sullen, as if resenting the fact that I had rescued him, unable to forget that he had been taken without a fight. His pride had been injured.

"Forget it," I said, waving his words away. I lowered myself wearily next to the fire that was now almost completely out.

"I won't forget," insisted Theseus.

"I told you to forget it," I said, angry now. I wasn't really angry with him. More with myself. Up to that point, I hadn't really considered myself able to kill someone, to take another's life. Paris had told me there were two types of warrior. The first type had doubts during battle. They were the ones whose self-doubt often resulted in their own deaths. Then there were the second type—the ones who were able to cast aside such doubts, doubts that would only come back to haunt them long after the battle had ended. These warriors triumphed. Paris had told me it was only natural to think about death after the fact. He often saw the faces of those he'd killed in his dreams. But he was able to turn that off during battle, to live in the moment, to do what had to be done. Remorse came later.

It seemed like I was numbered amongst this second group.

After I had killed Periphetes, his two remaining thugs had fled in terror, taking their injured friend with them. As for Periphetes's body, Theseus had kindly dragged it into the trees, away from sight. He was away for some time and carried several items that he tucked into his satchel when he returned.

He tossed something at me. They were sandals. "Here," he said. "Periphetes's sandals. He won't be needing them anymore. He's food for the maggots now."

I stared at the footwear of a dead man without touching. I couldn't do it. Not just yet at any rate. They probably wouldn't fit anyway.

Theseus himself was uninjured, the blow he had been struck a minor one. My injury was a little more serious. The blow had broken the skin on my forehead, despite my helm's protection. The wound was still leaking as I slumped next to the fire. I wiped at the blood, thinking of the body of Periphetes lying lifeless and cold amongst the trees.

"How is your head?" asked Theseus.

"Fine," I said gruffly.

"You'll need to clean it," he said. He tore a strip from what had presumably been Periphetes's tunic and soaked it in water. He crouched down before me and began wiping the blood from my forehead.

I let him work without protest. I didn't really care, but Paris had told me how important it was to clean wounds. Paris had seen too many soldiers die over wounds more minor than mine.

"It's not deep," said Theseus. "Luckily."

I said nothing. "We won't have to worry about food for a few more days now," he continued. "Periphetes had a pouch of food and a water skin. I also found a purse tucked up against his skin."

I knew what Theseus was trying to do. Distract me and perhaps make me realize that some good had come from Periphetes's death. It seemed like a high price to pay. Some food, water, and a few coins in exchange for a life. Instead of making me feel better, I felt worse.

"Have you ever killed a man?" I asked.

Theseus paused. I could tell he was wrestling with his pride again, unwilling to admit his inexperience and lose face in front of me. He pursed his lips but finally told the truth.

"No," he admitted. "But I will soon. That's what heroes do."

"Be careful what you wish for," I said.

He thrust himself to his feet angrily, throwing away the bloodstained rag. "You need to be stronger than this," he said. "We are bound to meet more outlaws or worse on the road. This will not be your last killing. I need you to be strong at my side."

"Easy for you to say," I said. I knew it would make him angrier, but I was too busy wallowing in my own misery and regret to care.

"Yes, it is," he said, his voice rising. "Periphetes deserved what he got. Do you think he would be dwelling on your death if your positions were reversed? I don't think so. Think of the lives you have saved by killing him. He would've preyed on other travelers and taken their lives without remorse. One life for many. It was the right thing to do."

"I could've let him live," I said glumly. "I could have made him swear on his honor to change his ways. To promise to give up the life of an outlaw."

"Do you really think he would've listened to you?" Theseus sneered. "Promises extracted from someone like him would never last. But I'll tell you this now; when I have to kill someone, especially scum like him, I will not hesitate and I will have no regrets. Whatever harm they seek to inflict on me or others, I will rain down upon them a thousand fold."

Theseus threw himself down by the fire and said no more.

$$\Omega$$

"You're telling me that you and Theseus were friends?" said Ovid with open disbelief. "At the very least, companions?"

"That's what I said, wasn't it," replied Ast mildly.

"But you are never mentioned in the stories" said Ovid.

Ast sighed impatiently. "That's because the myths were retold and passed down by the Athenians. I have told you this already. His stature would've been lessened by my presence."

"I have to confess," said Ovid, "that this is quite difficult to believe. Surely there should have been some mention of you?"

"No," said Ast. "The deeds Theseus and I accomplished together have been altered to suit." He thought for a moment. "I can see that you doubt me now. That you doubt my honesty. Is there something I can do that will prove what I say is true? That I am who I say I am?"

"I doubt that very much," said Ovid with a note of scorn in his voice. "What evidence could possibly remain after all this time?"

Ast said nothing. He rose to his feet and disappeared into the adjacent room. When he returned, he was carrying a cloth wrapped bundle. He set it down on the table between them.

"Open it," he said.

Ovid didn't move for a moment. He had no idea what lay concealed amongst the cloth wrappings. Suddenly, he felt a little afraid. With nervous fingers, he picked up the bundle and cautiously opened it.

His mouth fell open when he saw what was revealed.

"Do you believe now?" asked Ast.

Ovid steadied himself with a gulp of wine. For once, words had abandoned him. He nodded slowly.

"Now can I continue please?"

Ovid nodded again but he found it hard to concentrate on the papyrus before him, his eyes constantly drawn to the object sitting on the table.

It was an ancient helmet, smeared with the grime of accumulated centuries. A mask was bound to it, hanging off to one side. The face of a bull stared out at him. But it wasn't just that. Two holes were bored through the helmet, holes where horns had once been. The holes were exactly the same size as the marks that Ovid had seen on Ast's head.

Ω

Our path became more difficult, often overgrown with shrubs and weeds. Slowly, we followed a steep dirt trail that wove up into the hills, forcing us to revise our schedule. It was going to take much longer than I'd thought to reach Athens.

Food was scarce. Even with our supplies bolstered by Periphetes, we were still on the verge of starvation. Theseus wasn't as good with the sling as he'd boasted, only managing to bring down one small rabbit, which we roasted over the fire and devoured eagerly. I started to daydream about food.

We had to have our wits about us though. The uneven terrain, heavily wooded with thick pine trees, had a tendency to conceal sudden drop offs that would plunge a careless traveler to their deaths.

Theseus tried to lighten the mood and pass the time by telling me stories of his childhood adventures. He was, in all fairness, quite the entertaining storyteller. Most of his tales seemed a little farfetched but I never suggested they were anything other than the truth for fear of offending him.

I said little, still dwelling on the death I'd caused. I knew that Theseus was right—that killing Periphetes was the right thing to do—but it was a hard thing to let go of. Having a death on your hands is not an easy thing to bear. It doesn't get easier either.

It was hot. Not a cloud in the sky. The sun blazed down, evaporating the sweat from our skin almost before it had time to cool us. We were running short of water too, having last filled our water skins at a stream over a day earlier. They were now all but empty save for a few precious drops.

As well as my new club, I carried the satchel of food and water. Theseus had his sword, shield, and spear. I was impressed by his stamina and started to appreciate how hard it must be for soldiers to bear forced marches, day after day, loaded down with weapons and armor. By contrast, Theseus and I were travelling light.

I was glad Theseus forced me to wear Periphetes's sandals. At first, I had resisted, but after picking several thorns out of my heels, I decided to relent. Periphetes had been a large man but his sandals were still too small for me. My toes stuck out, and I stubbed them several times, but the sandals were better than bare feet.

We stopped for a rest, sinking wearily onto a warm bed of needles beneath a cluster of pines.

"How far do you think we've come?" I asked. Even though I had covered the geography of Greece with Daedalus and my knowledge was fairly-broad, it was not enough to give me any idea of where we were. Theseus had much more detailed local knowledge.

He thought for a moment. "I think we've probably walked ten leagues."

I was surprised. I thought we'd travelled further than that, but I was rather inexperienced in such matters. It didn't seem like much.

"How long until we reach the next city?"

"We've been walking for three days. I'd guess another two to reach Ismthmia. We could travel a bit further north and get to Corinth but that's a little out of our way. Ismthmia will have everything we need."

Two more days. I hoped our water would hold out. Even though our energy reserves were low, we were unlikely to starve before we reached the nearest city. Water was the real problem.

Too exhausted and hot to talk further, we lapsed into silence. I began to think about food again. No doubt Theseus had similar thoughts.

Suddenly, the silence was broken by the quick slap of sandals on earth. People were heading in our direction, and they were in a hurry. We jumped to our feet.

Down the path came several figures: an ancient man, two older children running on foot, and three women, the eldest carrying a small child. Their eyes widened in fright when they caught sight of us. They made as if to turn around and retreat the way they had come.

"Peace," said Theseus. "We mean you no harm." I think his handsome smiling face went some way to reassure them, especially when two of the women were not much older than us. They smiled tentatively back at him. Theseus often made a good impression with members of the opposite sex. Unlike me.

The group of travelers eyed me nervously, but the presence of Theseus calmed them. Although still obviously alarmed, they made no move to get past us.

"What troubles you?" asked Theseus. "Why the haste?"

"It's my husband, eldest daughter, and my two older sons," said the mother. She began to sob. "We were set upon by bandits. My husband told us to flee while he and my sons fought them. They grabbed my daughter. We heard screams behind us. I fear the worst."

"We will deal with these brigands," said Theseus, sounding overconfident to my ears. "We will find your husband, daughter, and sons and return them to you safely."

"Thank you," sniffed the woman, wiping away her tears with the sleeve of her dress. "Please be careful. I think they were many, and there are only two of you."

"Yes, but we are two heroes," said Theseus, puffing out his chest. He hefted his shield and sword with a swagger. The two younger women looked him up and down with bright eyes.

The woman gave us directions and we were about to head off when she stopped us.

"What is your name?" she asked. "So I might tell tales of your bravery."

"Theseus," he said, "and this is my companion, Asterion." She seemed satisfied by that.

"Theseus," she said. "I will remember. May the gods be with you."

Theseus strode off with me travelling in his wake. With only a moment's hesitation, I fixed my faceplate into place with the leather thong. In a fight, it might terrify an opponent long enough to give me an advantage.

Theseus turned to make sure I was keeping up. His face betrayed his fear for a moment before being replaced with a grim smile. He nodded. "Excellent. You scared me for a moment though. I would not like to face the likes of you in battle."

We reached the spot described by the woman. Even though Theseus and I were hardly skilled in tracking and woodcraft, we could still tell that a scuffle had taken place. The shrubs were beaten down and several footprints led off the path, deeper into the trees.

Cautiously, we followed them. Shortly, we came across a clearing. Even from this distance, we could hear weeping and cries of pain. We crept closer, hugging the ground, trying not to make a sound.

I have never been able to move quietly. My sheer size makes it all but impossible. Theseus, on the other hand, moved like a ghost, his passage hardly disturbing the undergrowth or needles beneath his feet. Thankfully, there was enough noise coming from the clearing to mask our approach.

A quick glance into the clearing confirmed that we were well and truly outnumbered. There appeared to be six bandits. Those we could see at any rate. Three figures, presumably the daughter and sons of the woman we spoke to, lay on the ground not far from the remains of a campfire. They seemed to be bound, hand and foot. One of them wasn't moving. Three men stood guard over them.

The bandits had built a lean-to, using the hide of a deer as a makeshift doorway. Next to it, two smaller pine trees had been bent almost to the ground, held in position by ropes and stakes. The trees were facing each other with just enough room between them to put a man.

A man was being forced to his knees by a huge bandit while two other bandits were binding his wrists to the bent pine trees. I didn't like the look of what they were doing.

Before we could act, the bandits finished their bonds and took positions on either side of the pines. The bandit in the middle stepped back and nodded to his fellows. Ignoring the pleading and screams of their prisoner, they drew blades, simultaneously cutting the ropes securing the pines to the ground.

The result was horrifying, sickening. The trees, no longer bound, sprung back into their normal upright position. The man trapped between them was torn apart. I felt bile rise in my throat, and it was only through great force of will that I didn't throw up.

The huge bandit laughed. Moving toward the three younger prisoners on the ground, he yanked the girl to her feet and began dragging her into the lean-to by her hair. His intentions were clear.

"Enjoy yourself, Sinis!" laughed one of the other bandits.

"I will," said the huge bandit. "Fresh meat. Young too, just the way I like them."

"Save some for us," said another bandit. "That's if she still lives."

I felt a rage growing within my breast. I didn't completely agree with Theseus, but these bandits deserved to die.

"What's our plan?" I whispered, the sound muffled by my faceplate.

"Simple," said Theseus. "We kill the bandits and free their prisoners."

"Not much of a plan," I grumbled.

"Whilst we debate, more innocents will die." He was right. Even as we whispered together, the bandits were leading a young man toward the blood-splattered trees. The trees had already been bent back into position once more. "What do you suggest?" hissed Theseus impatiently, struggling not to raise his voice.

"Some tactics," I offered. "Maybe one of us creates a distraction while the other frees the prisoners? That's if they're still alive."

Theseus narrowed his eyes. "Agreed," he said. "You do the freeing, I'll create the distraction."

Quickly, he crawled further around the campsite, making no discernible sound. I had a sudden thought, scattering the pine needles and pawing at the earth around beneath me. I unearthed a couple of large stones that I had felt under my body and hefted them in my free hand.

Suddenly Theseus sprung up from cover, clashing his spear against his shield. "Oi! You loincloth sniffers!" he yelled. "Let's see how you go against a real man."

The sound and his sudden appearance caused the bandits to flinch. Their surprise lasted for only a moment. Yelling, three of them immediately charged toward him, brandishing a variety of weapons.

Theseus, fleet of foot, darted into the trees and disappeared. The three bandits set off in pursuit.

I made my move. Approaching as quickly and as stealthily as I could, I reached the edge of the clearing. I needn't have bothered. The bandits were already on high alert and didn't look surprised by my sudden appearance. I suspect a charging bull would've made less noise. Three bandits remained—the huge man known as Sinis and two others.

Sinis released his grip on the woman's hair and pulled out a sword, striding toward me. His companions weren't so keen. I'm certain my huge size, massive club slung over one shoulder, and my bull's helm unnerved them somewhat. They approached more uncertainly.

It didn't matter. I was still outnumbered, but this time, I kept a tree to my back to offer some protection from an attack in that direction. I dropped one of the stones to the ground and squeezed the other firmly. Taking aim, I hurled the first rock at the nearest assailant—Sinis. He ducked, and the rock sailed harmlessly over his head.

Cursing silently, I quickly picked up the other. I chose one of the other bandits instead and threw my last remaining rock with all the strength I could muster. Fortune finally smiled on me. The rock hit him squarely on the forehead, dropping him to the ground like a sack of wheat.

I brought my huge club down off my shoulder and readied myself. Dismayed, the other smaller bandit backed off.

"Get him!" roared Sinis. As fearsome as I was, I suspected the smaller bandit was more scared of Sinis. Instead of fleeing, which he clearly wanted to do, he approached me tentatively, his sword outstretched.

I didn't need another invitation. The sword was too easy a target. I swept my club down and shattered his sword. Sharp fragments sliced through the air, one whistling past my neck. One of the fragments struck the bandit in the eye. With a howl of pain, he tumbled to his knees.

One on one then. Much better odds. I squared up against Sinis. He was almost as massive as I, with a bull's neck and shoulders large enough to lift boulders. He eyed me evilly and charged. Not wanting to kill, I didn't see how I could avoid it this time. I couldn't risk disarming my opponent. He was clearly too powerful for that. Besides, I was probably too clumsy. I had gotten lucky with the other two bandits—there was no way I could pull it off a third time.

Sinis roared and stabbed with his sword. Despite his size, he was remarkably quick. I attempted to parry with my club, but I was much too slow. Not only that, but I was tired and hungry. I had very little energy left—certainly insufficient to move fast enough to block.

I felt a burning pain in my side. Sinis withdrew his sword. It had my blood on its point. He grinned at me, sensing victory. He had my measure by now. He knew that I was slow with the club. Sure, on a good day, I would have bested him, but this was not one of those days. Now that I was injured, it was only a matter of time before he wore me down.

Confident, Sinis went in for the kill, darting in close and aiming for my neck. It was a foolish move, arrogant even. The blow was so obvious even a child could see it coming. It was, however, a move designed to nullify my club. By moving in so close, I simply didn't have room to swing it. Sinis knew it; I knew it. I couldn't bring my club up in time.

So I didn't. I dropped my club instead and crouched down under the sword stroke. It sliced the air above my head, narrowly missing my horns. I lowered my head and with an ear splitting roar, I charged. Sinis was too close. He had no room to dodge. Frantically, he tried anyway. Tried and failed. My horns speared him in the stomach, driving in deep.

A lesser man probably would have died, but Sinis was certainly not a lesser man. His strength and endurance were almost equal to my own. I suspected that he had divine or even titan blood running through his veins.

At first, he tried to hammer his sword hilt against my helm. When that didn't work, he dropped his sword, got a solid wrestlers grip around my neck, and began to squeeze.

I, in turn, wrapped my arms around him, forcing my horns in deeper. So deep in fact that his body was pressed up hard against my helm. It didn't seem to matter. Sinis's strength seemed to have no limits.

Roaring with rage, I lifted him from his feet. He twisted, forcing my neck sideways. Off balance, we both toppled to the ground. He landed on top of me, driving the wind from my lungs and freeing himself from my horns.

He used my momentary breathlessness to press his advantage, tightening his grip. I began to see bright sparks before my eyes as lack of air began to affect my vision. I suspected that Sinis had me.

Just before I began to black out, however, I felt him starting to weaken. Blood loss was beginning to take its toll. Not that I was in any better shape. The wound in my side hurt badly, and I could hardly breathe. But I was still alive, and where there is life, there is hope.

Rallying, I unclasped my hands from around his waist, breaking his grip around my neck. I grabbed him by the throat and began to squeeze. He flailed against my hands, hitting my armored face, anything he could to dislodge my grip. But it was useless.

He was almost unconscious when his eyes went suddenly wide. He looked down, terror etched over his face as he saw a spear point protruding from his chest. He stared at me for a moment, confused, and then collapsed to the ground. Gurgling sounds came from his throat. Somehow, he still lived.

Wearily, I lurched to my knees and looked up. Theseus was standing above me, his spear point dripping blood. His eyes were wild, and there was a splattering of blood on his face.

Dropping his spear and picking up Sinis's sword, he grabbed the huge man by the hair and dragged him toward the pine trees.

Suddenly I realized what he intended. I still tell myself that I was too injured and exhausted to stop him, but perhaps the truth is that I really didn't want to stop him. In my heart, I knew that Sinis was getting what he deserved. It didn't mean that it was right though. No man should have to die that way.

Theseus dragged Sinis in between the trees. The bandit leader was too far gone to protest. Almost dead. Almost, but not quite. Swiftly, Theseus bound each of Sinis's wrists to the pines. Then, drawing his own sword with his right hand and with Sinis's sword in his left, he swept both blades down simultaneously.

The effect was just as gruesome as it had been the first time we witnessed it. Sinis would never again trouble innocent travelers.

CHAPTER 10

Directly after this event, I didn't know what to say to Theseus. I didn't thank him, probably because I had nothing to thank him for. Although he didn't know it, I had already defeated Sinis before the spear had entered his chest.

Theseus did what he believed to be right. He was a stubborn and pride filled man. He believed he had saved me. We were even. Without doubt, the fact that I never thanked him rankled. I suppose he was left a little hurt and confused, but we never got to discuss it until much later.

Theseus went around and finished off the two injured bandits dispassionately. I don't think I could've stopped him if I tried. He seemed a little bit possessed, and I doubted whether I had the strength to resist him.

We had much to do after Sinis was disposed of. I untied the prisoners and made them as comfortable as I could. Other than the father, one of the men was already dead. I left them to mourn their brother and father while I bound my wound with strips torn from dead men's clothes.

Theseus retraced our steps, intending to find the women, children, and old man we had met on the path. By the time he returned, I had gotten rid of the dead bodies and cleaned up the campsite as best I could. I was thoroughly exhausted, but my strength was returning quickly thanks to the ample supply of food and water I found in the camp. I shared it with the survivors—the daughter, who was in her early twenties, and her surviving brother, who was probably only a few years younger. Both continued to weep for their dead.

Although clearly distraught by her loss, the mother thanked us profusely, promising to sing the praises of Theseus. She made no mention of my contribution. We loaded them up with as much food and water as they could carry, as well as a purse of coins we found on the body of one of the bandits.

After they left, Theseus and I sat in silence, both lost in our own thoughts.

He'd been injured. He had a few sword cuts to his legs but they were relatively minor. Once again, I had fared worse than him. My injury wasn't life threatening, but it would take time to heal. Theseus washed and cleaned his wounds and then bound them with strips torn from the clothes of the bandits. He washed the worst of the blood off his face. It seemed it wasn't his.

"What happened out there?" I asked at last. I didn't need to explain. Theseus knew exactly what I was asking.

"I killed them," he said. The crazed look in his eyes had been replaced with something colder.

"What, all three of them?" I said, shocked.

Theseus nodded. "Yes. All three of them. They chased me around the trees. I separated them and took them one at a time."

"And … and how do you feel about that?" I ventured.

"Satisfied," he said, looking me square in the eye, challenging me. "They were fatherless sons of whores."

Theseus was always made of sterner stuff than me. The death of Periphetes, the first man I'd ever killed, still haunted me. Theseus appeared unconcerned that he had killed all six bandits.

"Remember, they deserved it," said Theseus. "Think what they did to that woman's husband. Given the chance, they would've done the same to us, and raped and killed the woman. Don't you think the world is better off without them?"

I nodded slowly, knowing the truth when I heard it. "What about Sinis? Did he deserve to die the way he did? You could've just put him to the sword."

If Theseus was confused by me naming the bandit leader, he didn't show it. "I could've, but I chose not to. I think it was fitting that he died the same way as those he killed. Don't you?"

I frowned, not knowing what to say. Theseus didn't press me for an answer.

"We are even now," he said. "A life for a life. I saved your life just as you saved mine. But we are brothers now too, bonded by the blood we have spilt together."

We spent the next hour preparing for the next leg of our journey. We were well supplied now thanks to the bandits. Not only that, but we had several coin purses that would come in handy when we reached Ismthmia.

We distributed our supplies evenly. Although I found it distasteful, I tried on several pairs of sandals. I left Sinis's for last, reluctant to go near the scattered remains of his corpse. As I suspected, his sandals fit me perfectly.

Thus prepared, we set off. The next two days passed uneventfully. We took our time, now that water wasn't an issue. Theseus and I spoke little at first but he attempted to break the mood with more stories. It worked to some degree, and by the time we reached Ismthmia, we had regained a certain level of camaraderie.

Now, after the passage of many years, I remember those days we spent together fondly. At first, we weren't exactly the best of friends, but we were comrades, united in our goal to reach Athens. The events that occurred in that place ensured that we would forever be tied together by fate. Over time, our bond grew and he became my friend. Perhaps my only true friend. A bloodthirsty one at that, but I wasn't exactly in a position to be picky. It's not like I had a queue of friends waiting to take his place. We were never enemies like other poets and scholars would have you believe.

My relationship with Theseus was, for lack of a better word, complicated.

Ω

Ismthmia was a city no larger than Troezen and in some respects, inferior. Its gardens were overgrown in parts, largely untended. Some of the buildings were in a state of disrepair.

Like Troezen, it had a stone wall to protect itself from bandits and other rival city states. Its market was a rich, vibrant place filled with the cries of vendors trying to sell all manner of goods including fruit and vegetables, wine, freshly baked bread, clothes, and weapons. With the money we had obtained from the bandits, we succumbed and stocked up on supplies.

With my share, I purchased a new tunic and sandals. My kilt marked me as a foreigner, which brought me even more unwelcome attention than my size or bull's helm. Wearing dead man's sandals had always sat badly with me. I was relieved to see the last of them. I threw them in the ocean and watched them float away on the lazy swells.

Theseus also bought some new clothing: a richly emblazoned tunic and a belt sewn with gold thread. He planned to arrive in Athens in triumph and wanted to make a good impression with his father, the King.

Word of our exploits, or more specifically, Theseus's exploits, had somehow already reached Ismthmia. Presumably, some of the survivors of Periphetes's band had spread word about us, as had the woman whose family we had saved. I'm not sure how the news got to Ismthmia so quickly. Perhaps by ship or passed onto those travelling faster than us on horseback or donkey.

I was unmistakable of course. Theseus for his part was marked by his confident bearing and godlike handsomeness. Some vendors even offered to give us free produce for ridding the land around Ismthmia of bandits. We could've easily stayed in the city for a week or longer. We had several invitations to stay in wealthy citizen's homes, the implication being that our food and lodging would be free, paid for by tales of our exploits. I suspect some of the attraction was to keep heroes in the city to deter attacks, but I think that many just wanted to be in Theseus's presence, to bask in his handsomeness. Theseus could also be incredibly charming when he wanted to be.

We ended up staying for two days, attending dinner parties where Theseus related our adventures to universal applause, praise, and admiration. I said little, uncomfortable with the attention.

I know Theseus's exploits have been sung about and retold many times over the years. Some of those stories are about his adventures before he reached Athens. None of those stories in the decades and centuries that followed mention me. Theseus, to his credit, did relate our adventures with a certain level of truth, although he was prone to exaggeration and embellishment. I guess other storytellers and poets believed that the stories sounded better with just Theseus in them. For many years, I featured in them, but over time, as Athens became the most powerful city in Greece, my contribution was conveniently forgotten. I was not, after all, Athenian. I wasn't even Greek.

I didn't resent it at the time because I—or my appearance at least—was part of the tales. I think I would've felt a little aggrieved if I hadn't been mentioned at all. Although I was not vainglorious like Theseus, I was in Greece to increase my status. That and to avoid the wrath of Minos.

Theseus turned down several more invitations. He was eager and impatient to reach Athens and to claim his title as Prince of that great city. I, on the other hand, wasn't in such a rush. Ismthmia, I realized, was a place where I could build my reputation and wealth, enough that I would be able to claim Phaedra as my bride.

Theseus insisted we move on however. I had promised to accompany him to Athens, and I wasn't about to break my word. I have broken many things in my time but never my word.

It was another fifteen leagues to Athens from Ismthmia. Perhaps another five or six days. Theseus and I had been rather ignorant when we set off, thinking we could get from Troezen to Athens in the same amount of time it had taken us to travel to Ismthmia.

We were slowly becoming more proficient travelers though and more realistic in our expectations. We set off again, our heads held high, ready to embrace our destiny.

Ω

The road to Athens was much busier with traffic than the earlier part of our journey. Many travelers were headed to that place, largely comprised of traders seeking to make their fortunes. We encountered several families on the road, but there were others like us too—adventurers, heroes. We swapped stories with many we met, ensuring that our fame spread. We passed through the cities of Megara and Eleusis only long enough to replenish our supplies.

There seemed to be fewer bandits on the road, primarily because travelers were not so isolated. As a result, we didn't encounter trouble until we were only a few leagues from Athens.

The path branched at that point. The main route headed further inland. It was a safer, wider route used by most travelers. Theseus, however, had a strong desire to see the ocean. He'd often been told stories of this coast from his mother and wanted to see it for himself. So we took the smaller route that led to the coast.

By this point, we were dusty, tired, and footsore. Our tunics were soaked through with sweat. After walking for an hour, we came to a cliff top with a majestic view of the Saronic Gulf. The island of Salamis loomed massively nearby. Further in the distance was another island—Aegina. I knew that many leagues past that was Theseus's home city of Troezen, almost directly across the gulf.

We stood side-by-side, gazing out at the white-topped waves whipped up by the strong wind threatening to blow us off the cliff. The wind was not unpleasant, drying the sweat from our bodies.

After standing there for several minutes in silence, I thought of where we'd come from. A thought occurred to me.

"Wouldn't it have been easier to take a ship?" I asked. "I mean from Troezen to somewhere along this coast. It would've been a lot quicker too."

Theseus smiled. "That's exactly what my mother said. She warned me the road was too dangerous, but I wouldn't listen. I knew I had to take the road. To make a name for myself so my father will be forced to recognize me. My mother didn't understand."

"I see," I said. And I did. Knowing Theseus as I did by now, I knew how his mind worked. It would not have done for him to arrive in Athens as an unknown boy. He wanted to make an entrance. I confess, so did I—I just wasn't as driven as he.

"Not everyone thinks as heroes do, Asterion. You and I are the same. We are both heroes. And heroes find their own path in life. We do not always do what others tell us to do."

"We do when it means our exploits will be sung about," I said wryly.

Theseus missed the tone in my voice. "And isn't that what it's all about?" he said happily, clapping me on the back. I almost toppled off the cliff and hurriedly steadied myself.

"Come," he said at last. "Athens awaits."

As we walked along the cliff, we encountered a strange sight. A large bronze tub sat on the edge of the cliff. It was curious to see such a thing in a location like this. Wary, but with our interest piqued, Theseus and I decided to investigate.

As we got closer, we realized we weren't alone. A man sat beneath a nearby cypress tree, peeling an apple with a knife. He set them down and stood, smiling at us invitingly. A few paces from him was a fire with a large pot bubbling merrily away.

"Greetings, friends! You must be wary from your travels. Please, feel free to use my tub to wash the dust of the road from your bodies. The water is fresh and warm."

We exchanged names. His was Sciron. Despite my initial mistrust, he seemed like a decent sort of man. I liked him immediately.

"Why do you offer this service?" asked Theseus warily. "What is the price?"

Sciron inclined his head and spread his arms warmly. "No charge. I do this as a service to my fellow man. I was once a trader and accumulated great wealth. Now, I attempt to give something back."

Theseus considered this. I could tell he didn't trust Sciron like I did, but it would've been rude to refuse such hospitality. Besides, after a tiring few days on the road, a soothing bath was a welcome invitation. It was hard to resist.

"I'll go first," I offered eagerly.

Sciron smiled at me warmly. "Please, young warrior. In the interests of privacy, go behind the cloth, disrobe, and then you will be free to use my bath." He indicated a large blanket that was hanging between the branches of two trees. I stepped behind it and stripped, keeping my helmet on for obvious reasons. It was doubtful whether Sciron would be keen to offer the same hospitality once he saw my horns. I emerged moments later and stepped gratefully in the tub. It was as Sciron promised: warm and fresh.

I relaxed in it for as long as I could while Sciron chatted idly to us both. Sciron disappeared a couple of times, excusing himself by saying he had to fetch fresh essences for the water. He was gone for quite a while, but his absence went unremarked.

I got out, and Sciron handed me a towel while Theseus went to disrobe. Sciron retrieved the pot from the fire, using it to fill the tub with fresh hot water.

Theseus returned and plunged into the bath while I retreated behind the makeshift barrier to get changed. I had an unpleasant surprise. My clothes and all my equipment, including my club, were gone. I thought that perhaps Sciron had been exceptionally kind and had decided to wash my clothes, but why hadn't he asked? I suspected something wasn't right.

My suspicions were confirmed by a scream. I pushed aside the barrier, prepared for a fight even though I was naked and unarmed.

I was initially confused by what I saw. Theseus stood on the cliff face, naked as I, his back toward me, looking at something below. There was no sign of the bronze tub. Or

Sciron for that matter.

"What happened?" I asked, darting my eyes about hurriedly, searching for danger. "Where's Sciron?"

Theseus turned to face me. "I knew this was too good to be true. As soon as I hopped into the tub, Sciron attempted to tip me over the cliff."

"What did you do?" I forced the words out of a suddenly dry mouth, already knowing the answer.

"I did to him what he planned to do to me," he said, watching me carefully for my reaction. "I sent him to Tartarus."

A surge of anger washed over me. At that point, I was heartily sick of Theseus. Sick of him killing people seemingly on an idle whim. I seized him by the throat and lifted him off the ground.

"You didn't have to do that, Theseus," I raged. "You don't always have to kill."

Theseus grabbed my hands but made no other effort to free himself. "Stop, Asterion," he gurgled. "Look over the cliff. See the truth."

I frowned and shook my head, thinking I hadn't heard properly. Still clutching Theseus by the neck, I approached the edge of the cliff and looked down.

There was a huge creature far below us with a mottled green shell. It appeared to be a giant turtle, a monster from an earlier age, more massive than any beast I had ever seen, its enormous bulk crouching atop a cluster of rocks above the reach of the thrashing waves. It was surrounded by clusters of white, which looked like branches of trees whitewashed by the sea. It was also feeding on something. I realized it was Sciron.

With hands suddenly gone numb with shock, I released

Theseus. He dropped to his knees, grasping his throat and breathing hoarsely. Eventually, he recovered his composure and stood to face me.

"I've said it before, but it seems you are hard of hearing," Theseus replied coldly. His eyes blazed. "Those who seek to harm me will get what they deserve. Sciron tried to kill me. I just turned the tables on him."

I closed my eyes and clenched my fists for fear that I would hurt him again. With an effort, I restrained myself.

"Before you judge me, brother, look more closely at what lies below."

Despite my anger and frustration, I did what he asked. On closer inspection, the pile of white objects that I initially took for tree branches were actually bones. Human bones.

My rage started to leak out of me.

"It would seem that Sciron has been at his game for some time," said Theseus. "That son of a goat lured weary travelers here, threw them to the turtle below and kept their belongings."

It was true. Undeniably true. I still couldn't help but feel angry at Theseus. Once again, he'd solved a problem with violence, without remorse, almost like he relished it.

I took a deep breath, letting the anger pass.

Theseus looked me up and down and smiled. "Now, I think we'd better find our clothes before another traveler comes this way."

Ω

I was forced to concede that killing off the bandits that inhabited Greece at that time was making us rich. Sciron had accumulated quite a pile of treasure that he'd taken from unsuspecting travelers. As well as a sack of coins, there were bracelets and necklaces set with precious gems, weapons, armor, and a pile of clothing large enough to fill a decent sized room. It was quite sobering and a little disturbing to think that these items had once belonged to those whose bones decorated the rock island inhabited by the giant turtle. We filled our pouches and sacks with as much as we could easily carry—enough to make us both extremely wealthy—and buried the rest.

We found Sciron's treasure—including my own equipment—after a thorough search of the area. Hidden further back in the forest behind the cliff was a large stone house disguised by tree branches stacked against it. If we hadn't suspected that Sciron had a stockpile somewhere, we would've never found it.

I later discovered that Sciron was quite an infamous brigand, wanted in Athens and other cities for his crimes. He'd been operating his scheme for years but had never been found, moving every few months to avoid detection, presumably leaving his treasure unguarded or perhaps under the protection of the giant turtle that dwelt at the bottom of the cliffs. Maybe the turtle followed Sciron about given that he was a source of constant fresh meat?

Theseus smiled smugly at me when he heard that Sciron was a wanted criminal. Eventually, word also spread that Theseus had done the bandit in, thus further enhancing his reputation.

I had originally thought that it would take me at least a

couple of years to gather the wealth and prestige I needed to return to Crete. I had a vague idea that I would use the money to buy a small ship, approach Crete by night, and rescue Phaedra. I would then set myself and her up on an island far away from Minos.

Sciron's wealth filled me with hope. I would be able to return far sooner than expected. Theseus and I would arrive in Athens rich men indeed.

I also began to reconsider my feelings toward Theseus. He was what he was. He wasn't an evil man; he just had a slightly warped sense of justice. He hated bandits, outlaws, and brigands with a vengeance and was determined to punish them using their own instruments of death. He thought it rather fitting. I considered it a little barbaric.

I longed to reach Athens by now. I'd had my fill of adventures for the moment and wanted nothing more than to spend a few uneventful weeks in that city without being surrounded by death.

We set off again. Night was beginning to fall when we came across a house built of rough-cut blocks standing by the side of the road. We were tired, having made good progress that day. We guessed, correctly, that we would reach Athens after another day's travel.

It was a little cold that night. Both Theseus and I didn't relish another night out in the open, especially when we were so close to Athens. We were about to knock on the door of the house, willing to spend some of our wealth on a bed and hot food for the night, when the door opened, seemingly of its own accord.

A man stood there, small, wizened. He had a gray wispy

beard with hair that matched. He squinted heavily at us.

"Hello," he croaked, his voice dry as a sun dried leaf. "Do you seek a bed for the night?"

Theseus and I looked at each other. I knew what Theseus was thinking. This old, shriveled man couldn't possibly offer us any threat.

"We do indeed," said Theseus. "A bed, a hot meal, maybe a goblet of watered wine by the fire. We'll be on our way come sunrise and can pay with good honest coin."

"Enter and be welcome," he said, standing to one side to let us pass. He smiled a toothless smile. We found ourselves in a square room, furnished simply with an old wooden table and four chairs. Another couple of chairs were being warmed by the fire, which blazed invitingly. I wanted nothing more than to go and rest my weary legs beside that warmth.

"Take a seat, gentleman," said the old man, indicating the chairs by the fire. "Supper is not far away. I hope you like soup. It's the only thing that I eat these days without my teeth. Fortunately, I always make more than I need. Old habits."

Theseus and I made ourselves comfortable. My chair creaked alarmingly as it took my weight. Fortunately, it didn't break.

"Your name, sir?" asked Theseus. He took off his sandals and wiggled his toes closer to the fire.

"Procrustes," said the old fellow, bustling around his tiny kitchen adjacent to where we sat.

"I am Theseus. This is Asterion."

"And where do you venture?" he asked, shuffling over with two wooden bowls that he set in our laps. He handed each of us a wooden ladle.

"Athens is our goal," said Theseus. I had begun to notice that Theseus always took the lead in conversations, relegating myself to the background where I said little or nothing. Not that I minded, but I found it interesting that Theseus had begun speaking for me. His pride ensured that he would always take the role of leader. It made sense. Most people addressed Theseus instead of me. I guessed it was partially due to my fearsome appearance. Then again, Theseus was much fairer to look upon and much more charming. I have noticed over the years that it is often the most handsome or beautiful individuals that get all the attention, even if they are as dull as a mud stained rock. I understand that. It is human nature.

"Athens, yes. Lovely place that," said Procrustes. "I once lived there."

As we ate, Procrustes told us about the life he once lived. He had moved out to the countryside once his wife died and his children had left home, preferring the quiet and isolation to the bustle and noise of city life. I joined in the conversation where I could.

Procrustes asked us many questions. He was particularly interested in my horned helmet and asked where I'd gotten it. I told him the same story I'd told Theseus.

The soup was unremarkable, but he served it with rough bread, which we used to mop up the juices puddling the bottom of our bowls. After dinner, he brought us a large goblet of watered wine each.

"A toast," declared Procrustes. "To adventures and long life." We touched goblets and drank.

It was an enjoyable evening. Procrustes was a fine host, eagerly replenishing our goblets as soon as they were empty.

Theseus and I thought nothing of it given that Procrustes was clearly not a threat.

I assumed it was the wine making me tired. I felt groggy and a little dizzy. Looking over at Theseus, I could see he was also suffering. His eyes were bleary and he swayed slightly in his seat.

Procrustes looked at us both and smiled, his gums gleaming in the firelight. "I believe it is time for you young heroes to take to your beds."

Theseus and I were in no position to disagree. Wordlessly, we followed him to an adjoining room. Inside were two beds.

"You are fortunate, young warriors. I had these beds specially made for my sons."

"What … what's so special about them?" Theseus slurred, supporting himself against the doorframe.

"Why, it has the amazing property that its length exactly matches whosoever lies upon it," said Procrustes. They didn't look so special to me, but then again it was hard to tell through my blurred vision.

Eagerly, we both lay down. My great size ensured that my feet hung over the end of the bed. Procrustes had been exaggerating, but I was so tired I didn't care. As soon as my head hit the pillow, I was asleep.

Ω

I awoke from a restless sleep filled with faces of the dead. My eyes opened slowly, resentfully. It was still dark, but the gray light of dawn was just starting to peak in through the single window. Time to start the last leg of our journey.

I tried to sit up and failed. It was only then that I realized something was wrong. I found that my hands and feet were securely bound to the posts of the bed. I looked over at Theseus. He was still asleep but was tied in the same way.

"Theseus," I hissed. "Theseus, wake up!"

Theseus slowly roused, gradually becoming aware of our predicament. His eyes widened in horrified realization. We were trapped. Procrustes must have drugged our wine. Our confidence in our superiority had been our downfall.

Before we could begin to struggle free, Procrustes shuffled into the room.

"Ah, young warriors. I see you're awake."

"What is the meaning of this?" demanded Theseus. "Free us immediately!"

Procrustes shook his head and smiled sadly. "I'm afraid I can't do that. I have promised my beds new victims and new victims they must have."

He was clearly mad. Not that I'm an expert but anyone who wants to sacrifice you to a bed can't be completely sane.

"You are probably wondering about the magical properties of these beds," he said, insanity sparkling in his eyes. "Their length does indeed exactly match those who lie upon them. Of course, that's only with some adjustment."

He looked from me to Theseus. His eyes narrowed thoughtfully when he saw that my feet dangled over the end of the bed. "I think we'll start with you," he said, eyeing up Theseus. "Your large friend here presents more of a challenge. Not to mention a mess."

He retrieved a bronze bar from a darkened recess of the room and inserted it under Theseus's bed. He then began to wind, singing softly to himself. Procrustes may have been mad but he meant what he said. The bonds on Theseus wrists and ankles began to tighten, trying to stretch Theseus so that he fitted the bed.

Theseus thrashed about wildly, struggling against the inexorable pull of his bonds. It was useless. Procrustes had tied both of us securely. I suspected this wasn't the first time he'd had visitors. Theseus began to scream as the rack took up the slack. It was muscle, sinew, and flesh against metal. The result was inevitable.

Procrustes was paying me no attention whatsoever. He was grunting and singing with his back to me as he slowly wound.

Desperately, I assessed my situation. I had to save Theseus. Not only that, but I had to save myself. Once Procrustes was finished with Theseus, he would turn his attention on me. I suspected that his solution to my size would be rather simple, hence his reference to mess. In order to make me fit the bed, he would chop off my feet.

During our drugged sleep, Procrustes must have taken off my helm, obviously thinking that my horns would provide me with a weapon during my struggles. I can imagine his surprise when he found that the horns weren't part of my helmet. But, there was nothing he could do about it. And that gave me an advantage.

While his attention was elsewhere, I twisted my neck. If I could only move my horns into a position where they could saw through the bonds securing my wrists. It was incredibly difficult. The angle was all wrong, but desperation drove me.

At last, I moved into a position where my horns could begin to saw through the rope on one of my wrists.

It was desperate, painful work, and I moved with as much haste as I could muster. Sweat began to trickle from my forehead, running into my eyes and ruining my vision. My neck began to seize up. I dared not look at Procrustes for fear of losing contact with the rope. I prayed silently to Poseidon for aid, hoping Procrustes would not glance in my direction.

Perhaps my father heard me. With a last flick of my horns, the rope parted. One of my hands was free! Quickly, I tore the rope from my other hand and sat up. The noise of my struggles had gone unnoticed by Procrustes, who was still busy winding. The screams of Theseus were drowning out all other noise in the room.

I freed my legs. Procrustes must have seen something in Theseus's eyes as he looked in my direction. The old man turned just in time to see me lurching to my feet. Before he could react, I wrapped my arms around him in a wrestler's embrace. Surprisingly, he was stronger than his appearance implied and struggled furiously. I had no choice but to tie him up. I could hardly release him while I freed Theseus.

The obvious choice was the bed. Despite his wild struggles, I tied him securely by wrist and ankle. Only then did I turn my attention to Theseus.

"Help me," said Theseus weakly, his voice hoarse from his screams.

I nodded and swiftly undid his bonds, helping him to stand. I had to steady him but he recovered his strength quickly. He was, after all, a son of a god. Luckily, despite Procrustes best efforts, his limbs had not been pulled out of their sockets.

Eventually, he gently pushed me away, standing without support. He looked down at Procrustes with a blank expression on his face.

Procrustes stopped his struggles to free himself, sensing impending doom. He met Theseus's stare and flinched with what he saw there.

"You might want to leave," said Theseus. Even though he wasn't looking in my direction, I knew he was talking to me.

I also knew what Theseus planned. I had no illusions as to what sort of man Theseus was by now. Although I didn't agree with his methods, I understood them. There was no sense arguing with him. I suppose I could've stopped him, but it was like the incident with Sinis and the pine tree repeating itself. A part of me knew that Procrustes was getting what he deserved. But, then again, he was just an old man. For a moment, I thought about forcing Theseus out of the room, leaving Procrustes tied to the bed, but what then? The next traveler who passed would free him, enabling him to try his evil madness on the next poor unsuspecting adventurer. I also was aware that once Procrustes had finished with Theseus, I would've suffered the same fate. Or worse.

I knew that there was no other option. I also knew that I wanted no part in it. Without a backward glance, I left Theseus to his revenge.

CHAPTER 11

I was sitting down under a tree, far from the stone house of Procrustes but still in view of it, when Theseus finally emerged. At first, I had removed myself just from the house itself, sinking wearily to the stone steps below the door but that wasn't enough. I could hear Procrustes's screams like he was next to me.

I was forced to walk several dozen paces before the wind carried the noise of his suffering away from my ears. And there I waited. It seemed like hours, but surely it wasn't. I doubt even Theseus could've been so cruel to extend the suffering of Procrustes that much.

I had our equipment and supplies stacked neatly next to me. I'd found them easily enough. Procrustes had simply placed them on the table in the main room. He probably thought there was no need to hide them. As far as he was concerned, we weren't going to be in a position to use them again.

Thankfully, my helmet was amongst the pile. After lowering it onto my head, I felt comforted. It's funny how you can get used to something so unusual. The helmet had become an extension of myself. I felt almost naked without it.

Theseus cast around, looking this way and that before locating me. He strode in my direction. As he got nearer, I saw his eyes. There was death in them.

"Is it done?" I asked. To this day, I don't know why I asked the question. Perhaps a part of me hoped that maybe Theseus had spared him even though I knew in my heart he hadn't.

Theseus nodded curtly and began loading himself with weapons and supplies. I noticed that he had another sack, presumably loot taken from Procrustes. More wealth covered with the blood of our victims.

I knew better than to remonstrate with Theseus by now. He did what he thought necessary. For his part, he probably scorned me as a weakling, squeamish, someone unable to do what must be done. Theseus always considered himself a leader of men, a risk taker, a decision maker. Leaders had to make difficult decisions. I guess that's why I was never cut out to be one.

It took us the whole day to reach Athens.

We said little to each other as we strode on, side by side. Finally, Theseus broke the silence.

"You have horns on your head," he said, not looking at me. "They're not part of your helmet as I supposed."

I nodded, not knowing quite what to say.

"I have heard of such a man. They say he is the son of King Minos of Crete. Others say he is the son of a bull."

"Theseus," I said, touching him lightly by the arm, forcing

him to stop. "I wanted to tell you, but I foolishly delayed. The King wants me dead. I thought it would be safer for you not to know."

"They say you are a beast," said Theseus, looking me in the eye. "That your horns mark you as such."

"Theseus, I can explain," I said.

"There is no need," said Theseus, taking me into his arms. "I recognized my brother straight away. You, like me, are the son of Poseidon. You saved my life. Again. You are not a beast. I name you for what you are. My friend."

And with that, Theseus and I dealt with the awkward subject of my horns. It was that easy. Despite everything, Theseus was extremely loyal and forgiving. He never forgot a debt and judged a man on his deeds rather than his appearance. In many ways, Theseus was a good man—a slightly mad one at times, but then again, who am I to judge?

Ω

Night was falling by the time we passed through the city gates, but not before guards challenged us.

"Who are you and what is your business in Athens?" asked their Captain.

"My name is Theseus, Prince of Troezen. I, along with my companion and brother, Asterion, a hero and son of Poseidon, have rid the countryside of bandits and outlaws."

The Captain and his men seemed surprised and perhaps a little intimidated by this statement. A man with lesser bearing than Theseus may not have been taken at his word. I suspected that if I had spoken instead, we may have been thrown out of the city. As it was, despite his youthful appearance, Theseus was believed, aided by the growing rumors of his deeds that had slowly trickled into the city.

"I have heard of you," said the Captain. I almost expected him to bow. "Have you some place to stay tonight?"

"No," said Theseus haughtily. "But we have ample funds. We will find an inn somewhere in the city."

"No need for that," said the Captain hastily, eager to please. "You would honor us if you stayed with the city guard tonight. We have good food, soft beds, wine, and a warm fire."

Theseus nodded. "We accept with pleasure," he said.

The Captain escorted us personally to the barracks of the city guard. True to his word, everything was as he said. Theseus stayed up late into the night, regaling a large group of guards with our adventures. They hung on his every word. I crept away as soon as I could and retired gratefully to my bed.

As I drifted off to sleep, I wondered why Theseus hadn't yet revealed his true identity. Perhaps he wanted his deeds to speak for themselves so the King would deem him worthy? I hadn't had a chance to ask him.

We arose late. Theseus seemed a little worse for wear from overindulgence. We breakfasted with the Captain and several of his men and then decided to look around the city. Theseus and I had never seen Athens before and were eager to explore.

Even in those days, Athens was a city to rival any other in the world in terms of size, grandeur, and beauty. It was the greatest city in Greece.

It was filled with grand buildings, statues, plazas, gardens, and markets positively teeming with people. I could see why Athens had a greater reputation than even Sparta or Corinth. Neither of us had seen so many people in one place before. I was a little overwhelmed, but Theseus took it in his stride.

News of our arrival must have spread. Everywhere we went, people stopped to stare and whisper, marveling at our appearance. We were a striking, unmistakable pair. People thanked us for our deeds, concentrating most of their attention on Theseus.

Purchasing our lunch from one of the many markets, we sat down in a public garden to eat.

"Why didn't you tell the guards who you really were?" I asked Theseus.

"It's a little complicated," he replied. "My mother told me everything before I left Troezen. My father has a new wife, Queen Medea. But before she became his wife, she was something altogether different. She was a witch and in all likelihood, is still one today."

A witch? I had heard rumors of women with magical powers. On Crete, there were several women known to be able to perform miracles, but I had never witnessed them myself.

"So why the secrecy?" I asked

"My father, so it is told, despaired of ever having an heir. He enlisted the help of Medea and her powers to aid him. He picked my mother, Princess Aethra, and seduced her, leaving his sandals and his sword for me when the time was right. I believe that Medea kept word of my existence from him. My mother sent several messages to Athens informing the King of my birth but never received a response. I believe he is still ignorant that I live."

"So why not just tell him?

"Because Medea now has her own son fathered by Aegeas. Without me, their baby son is the heir. I doubt whether Medea will be very pleased to see me. From what I've heard, Jason abandoned her during his quest for the Golden Fleece. She will not risk being abandoned again. If she knew I was in the city, I suspect she would make my life difficult and all but impossible to see the King. I'll have to find an opportunity to reveal my identity, proving it with the sandals and the sword."

I nodded slowly. If I had hoped for a few days of peace, I was mistaken. But how to get access to the King?

Fortunately for us, the King gave us such an opportunity. Even he was interested in heroes who could accomplish such feats as we had.

When we returned to the barracks sometime in the afternoon, a messenger from the palace was waiting for us.

"It would please King Aegeus and Queen Medea if the hero Theseus and his companion would join them for a banquet tonight." The messenger waited patiently for a response.

"Companion" indeed. I bristled a little but remained silent.

"Tell King Aegeus and Queen Medea that Theseus and Asterion accept gratefully." The messenger departed.

We prepared carefully. When I say we, I really mean Theseus. I was just his

"companion." He groomed himself so thoroughly his hair and skin seemed to glow from within. He wore his new tunic and tucked his father's sword into his belt so it was displayed prominently. On his feet were his father's sandals.

I did what I could to look impressive, also wearing my new tunic that wasn't nearly as grand as Theseus's. I wore my helm of course and completed my preparations by hefting my bronze encased club over my shoulder.

Dusk fell. Thus prepared, we set off to the palace, escorted by the Captain and several of his men. Theseus seemed confident all would go to plan and smiled easily, chatting as we walked.

We arrived at the palace and with due pomp and ceremony were ushered into the presence of the King and Queen, who were already seated in the feasting hall.

King Aegeus was a large, handsome man in his late years with a square cut, well-trimmed beard, mostly gray but speckled here and there with black. He welcomed us with a shining smile that was so similar to Theseus's I had no doubt that he was indeed his father. Medea was an altogether different story. Younger than Aegeus by a decade and with a cold, hard beauty like that of a diamond, her smile was so forced that I had to look away for fear of breaking into laughter.

Luckily, she spared me only a glance, her attention riveted by Theseus. Her calculating assessment made me realize that without a doubt, she already knew who he was.

I saw her whisper something in the King's ear. His expression darkened. I learnt later from Theseus that she was indeed aware that Theseus was the King's rightful heir and had attempted to poison the King against him. Playing on the King's insecurity, she warned that Theseus was already popular amongst the people due to his heroic deeds. With such popularity, Theseus could easily seize the throne for himself.

"Come, noble heroes," said the King. "Sit. Eat, drink, and tell us tales of your adventures." We were seated in a place of honor, only a few places down from the King and Queen themselves. Theseus started regaling the King and Queen of our exploits. He had a captive audience. Nearby, other guests leaned in to better hear of our deeds. As I've mentioned before, Theseus was a good storyteller. If my memory serves correctly, I believe Theseus was regaling them about Sinis and his bandits at the time.

"And once I had finished off Sinis's crotch sniffing followers, I made my way back toward the clearing," said Theseus, his eyes shining, grin so broad his perfect white teeth threatened to blind his audience. All eyes and ears were upon him now, eager to hear more bloodthirsty exploits.

"Yes … ?" asked King Aegeus, leaning forward no less eagerly than any of the other listeners.

For my part, I was hardly paying attention to Theseus. I'd heard the story before. Instead, I was watching Queen Medea. Something about her posture was wrong. Unlike everyone else in the room, she wasn't watching Theseus, her intense gaze locked instead on the object resting near Theseus's elbow. It was a wine goblet.

"And then," said Theseus, springing to his feet, "I saw the bandit leader Sinis atop my dear friend Asterion, clearly strangling the life out of him." A few of the listeners moved their eyes toward me for a moment and then, finding nothing of interest, returned their attention back to Theseus.

"With spear in hand I crept toward the huge and dreadful bandit leader. Asterion was all but dead by then. I knew I couldn't delay. I took my spear and thrust it through Sinis's heart." As Theseus said these words, he drew his sword for dramatic effect and stabbed it toward his enraptured audience. Almost unnoticed, the action of his arm knocked the nearby wine goblet from the table.

Still watching her closely, I couldn't fail to notice the look of horrified disappointment on the face of Queen Medea as the goblet tumbled to the floor, splashing its crimson contents all over the tiles, almost as if Theseus's sword thrust had actually drawn real blood.

It was all very contrived, of course. Theseus had always planned to draw his sword in order for his true father to get a good look at it.

Aegeus registered surprise and shock, immediately recognizing the pattern on the sword hilt. Medea's eyes narrowed with hatred.

Aegeus leapt to his feet. "That's my sword!" he exclaimed. "Is it true then? Are you my son? Is your mother Aethra?"

"Yes," said Theseus, smiling as brightly as the sun. "I am your son. You left this sword for me under a massive rock. These are the sandals that were once yours," he said, pointing at his feet.

It looked like Aegeus was about to cry. He embraced his long lost son. The two of them hugged and cried together, unwittingly splashing about in the puddle created by Theseus's spilled wine, destroying Medea's dreams with their clumsy feet. Whether it was poisoned or not, only the gods now know. I suspect it was because I saw a dog lapping at the puddle of wine later that night. That same dog I later found dead in the palace gardens.

Aegeus, wiping the tears from his face, disentangled himself from his newly acquired son. He turned to face his wife.

"Medea," he said, his eyes shining with wondrous hope and love for his wife. "Medea, isn't this magnificent news?

Now I have not one, but two sons. Has a man ever been so blessed by the gods as I?"

A strange thing happened then. The whole feasting chamber, one that was usually filled with raucous laughter and sounds of merriment, suddenly went eerily silent. Everyone seemed to be holding their breath, waiting to hear Medea's response to the news of Aegeas's new addition to his family.

"And you expect me to stand placidly like a cow lead to slaughter while you replace my son with this ... boy here," she spat, gesturing furiously toward Theseus. Her eyes had narrowed with pure hatred, and I half expected lightning to shoot from them and strike Theseus and Aegeas down.

"No, it's not like that," pleaded Aegeas, moving toward her, holding a hand out in an attempt to placate her. "Our son will always have a place of great honor at my table. He will never be overlooked. But can't you see that Theseus is also my son? My eldest son and heir?"

Medea drew herself up straight and adopted a haughty expression, her anger now colder and more desolate than the bleakest of winter winds. "To Tartarus with you both, then," she said. "May the crows feast on your eyes."

Hardly an original insult, but the words had the desired effect. King Aegeas staggered as if he had been struck. Theseus rushed to his side and supported him as Medea suddenly spun around and swept from the chamber.

I later learnt that Medea did indeed choose to flee Athens, taking her young son with her. I'm still confounded by her actions. Presumably, it was only her that was privy to the knowledge of the poisoned goblet. There was absolutely no evidence to corroborate her crime. Regardless of whether her own son became King or not, she could have lived a long and happy life in the palace. Theseus later confided to me that King Aegeus did love her and missed her, as confused as I about her departure.

As for the stories passed down over time—I still chuckle when I hear them. She didn't just flee; she fled in a chariot pulled by dragons. Apparently. Now, I have seen many strange things in my time. I have experienced more than any mortal. This is no exaggeration; this is fact. I am more than a thousand years old now. Some of the creatures I have seen or fought no longer exist, their memories sustained only by legend. But I will tell you one thing—I have never seen a dragon. There certainly weren't any in the palace of King Aegeus.

I'm not so arrogant to suggest that dragons don't or have never existed. I could be wrong. Medea was a witch after all. Perhaps she summoned them from a part of Tartarus I have never seen?

Not that it matters. Medea fled into the night, and King Aegeus was reunited with his son and true heir.

Over the next two weeks, Athens was filled with rejoicing and feasting on a scale never seen before. Athens had a new prince. And not just any prince either. A true hero. One that had almost single-handedly killed thousands of bandits, several monsters, and possibly a titan or two. His actions rivaled that of the gods. The tales seemed to have a life of their own, growing daily. I was hardly mentioned.

If I was honest with myself, it did bother me slightly. How was I ever going to build a reputation so I could rescue Phaedra and possibly confront Minos? I had enough wealth, certainly, but I needed a heroic profile sufficient to make me untouchable by Minos. If I was consistently left out of stories or relegated to a minor role, this wasn't going to happen.

I had a chance to brood about it during those two weeks. I was largely left to my own devices. Theseus spent most of his time becoming acquainted with his father. I was invited to all the banquets of course, but almost ignored by others falling over me in their haste to get to Theseus. Most of them wouldn't have pissed on me if I was on fire. I realize now that if Theseus hadn't been so handsome and charming, things might have gone differently. I was impressive enough in terms of stature. My helmet was certainly a talking point. It's just that I didn't have the charm or charisma Theseus possessed. Did I resent him for it? Possibly. For a time at least. Even though I was in love with Phaedra and would never have betrayed her, it was hard for me to watch beautiful young maidens fall all over Theseus without a single glance in my direction.

I felt depressed. I was lonely. I missed Phaedra and Androgeus. Part of me even wanted to go home, to Crete, to my family, regardless of whether Minos lived or not. A traitorous part of my mind tried to convince me with imagined promises of forgiveness from Minos. That he might even embrace me as his adopted son. In saner moments, I realized that was pure folly, but I confess, I was tempted.

The boredom eventually got to me, and despite my earlier protestations that I wanted to live a quiet life for a while, I realized that excitement and adventure were now a part of me. It was in my blood.

I spent the next few months travelling into the wild lands around Athens. I defeated several bandits and even a couple of monsters. Sadly, unlike the stories of Theseus, my feats went largely unnoticed, probably because I spared many of my enemies, preferring to bring them back to Athens to face trial. This, I suspected, made me appear weak in front of the Athenians. Ironically, many of the bandits I captured were later sentenced to death.

Theseus joined me on a few adventures when he wasn't otherwise occupied. Unlike my exploits, everything he did was recorded. There's no need to go into them in great detail here, as you've probably heard them before. For a change, there was no great embellishment, only my name was not mentioned. Suffice to say that Theseus beat a hero known as Cercyon at wrestling. Together we defeated a giant boar the size of an ox with eyes like coals of fire. I suspect it came from Hades. Theseus killed both Cercyon and the giant boar without mercy.

We travelled to Marathon and captured a bull to rival any other I had previously seen. That was a challenge, but working together, we were successful.

Our bond grew. I had come to accept Theseus for who he was, and he respected me for it. I grew to care for him. It wasn't like the love I felt for my brother, Androgeus, but I did love him in a way.

We faced our greatest challenge when some of Aegeus's nephews, known as the Pallantides, decided to do away with Theseus and myself. They were jealous of Theseus's status amongst the people and wanted one of their own to sit on the throne after Aegeus.

Accordingly, they tried to assassinate him. As his closest companion, I too had to die. They ambushed us one night. We were outnumbered almost ten to one, but our father, Poseidon, must have been watching over us. Not only that, but our adventures in the wild lands outside Athens had taught us well. We were experienced warriors now, not the soft pampered palace boys we had once been. The men we fought were much like ourselves months earlier. And they were not demi-gods.

We slew many of them, and the others fled Athens, never to return.

Killing hadn't come easier to me—it's just that I had come to the realization that it was necessary at times. Even though I still thought about the men I had killed, my dreams were not as troubled as they'd once been.

Theseus, always proud, became more so. He seemed to think he was invincible and became slightly arrogant with the knowledge. It didn't help that he was often surrounded by sycophants who worshipped him, hanging on his every word. I tried to keep him grounded, but as I had learnt by now, Theseus was not the easiest man to change. He was still fiercely loyal though. Friendship for Theseus was also about equality. I had saved his life more than once. He owed me and would never forget the debt.

Before I knew it, the time of the Panathenaic games had come once more. It had been four years since the last one. Soon, athletes and heroes from all across Greece and the islands of the Aegean would be making their way toward Athens.

I couldn't wait. My brother, Androgeus, would be among them. I counted down the days to his arrival.

Ω

I watched the ships glide into the harbor at Piraeus, their sails filled with the strong breeze blowing into the Saronic Gulf, their swift pace aided by the single layer of rowers toiling away. There were six of them, all marked with the bull's head of Crete. I felt a strong mix of emotions seeing them again. Nostalgia, sadness, and, I confess, quite a bit of excitement. The ships carried my brother Androgeus.

Minos was making a statement. He hadn't needed to send six ships when one would have sufficed. He was letting Athens know how strong Crete was; that they were a power to be feared.

In those days, Crete still had a larger fleet than any other city in Greece, including Athens. Not only that but Minos, insecure in his rule, had spent large sums from the palace treasury building up his armed forces.

"Are you nervous, brother?" asked Theseus at my side. We stood on the cliff top directly above the harbor that served Athens. It reminded me of the time when Theseus and I had stood looking out across the Saronic Gulf. Before Theseus had become Prince of Athens. When life was far simpler.

"A little," I confessed. "My brother is on one of those ships. I have not seen him in many months."

"What about King Minos?" he asked.

"I'll face him when the time comes," I said, my face hardening.

"I understand your reasons," said Theseus, referring to my flight from Crete. "You are a wanted man." He placed one hand reassuringly on my shoulder. "I probably would've done the same thing in your position."

His words were comforting, but I still felt unsure. "I don't know what to do," I confessed. "I want to see Androgeus but ... " I trailed off. I'd heard that Minos was also aboard one of those ships. I didn't know why Minos had come to Athens. It was unusual. Normally, Minos never accompanied the athletes to the games. I could not see Androgeus without coming in contact with Minos. I dreaded that encounter.

"Fear not," said Theseus. "You are under my protection and that of my father. You are an honored guest of Athens. Even Minos cannot move against you here. You will see your brother again. In fact, I look forward to seeing your brother too. I have heard much about him."

"You're still going to enter, then?"

Theseus smiled. "Yes, of course. Not the marathon but certainly the wrestling. I think I have an excellent chance. Most of the others I've heard about couldn't wrestle their way out of a wine skin."

I wasn't so sure. Theseus was an excellent wrestler, but he was no match for Androgeus. Androgeus had defeated me on several occasions, just like I had beaten Theseus. Theseus might be strong, agile, and fast, but Androgeus was more so.

The thought had obviously occurred to Theseus. "Why don't you enter? With your great strength, you would have just as much chance as I."

Which was exactly why Theseus didn't want me to enter and risk stealing the glory from him. He knew I had already made my decision. He was just going through the motions in an effort to appear the bigger man.

I shook my head. "Now that you know my past, you know why I can't enter. It would only serve to antagonize Minos. I'd rather not draw his attention any more than I need to."

Theseus didn't push it further. He seemed satisfied by my response. Out of the corner of my eye, I saw him smiling.

Ω

Early that evening, Theseus and I had arranged for a message to be passed to Androgeus.

Theseus sat, calmly polishing the breastplate of his new armor while I paced impatiently about his spacious and richly appointed chamber.

"What's taking him so long?" I grumbled.

"He's probably training," said Theseus without looking up from his work. "It's what I should be doing."

I heard resentment in his voice, but I suspected that it was contrived. Theseus was as keen to see Androgeus as I, more to assess his opponent than anything else.

I heard the door open. I turned swiftly, excitement fluttering in my breast. A familiar figure I had longed to see for the last few months stood there. My brother, Androgeus.

His handsome face lit up. We rushed into each other's arms and embraced warmly.

Eventually, after much patting of backs, we separated.

"It's good to see you, my brother," said Androgeus. "You are looking well. Stronger than ever. I see you've gained a few scars. They've improved your looks."

We both laughed. It was true that my battles during the last few months had left their mark.

"Androgeus," I said at last. "This is Theseus."

The two men clasped hands in a warrior's grip. Looking at them, it was hard to tell them apart. They were roughly the same size, both with slim, athletic builds. Both incredibly handsome. Androgeus was perhaps built a little more strongly, with thicker arms and legs. I felt a sudden surge of jealousy. Androgeus and Theseus could almost pass as brothers. I was the odd one out here.

With an effort of will, I buried the emotion and forced a smile.

I could see that the two men were sizing each other up. Androgeus was four years older but Theseus, thanks to his recent adventures, was a more experienced fighter. Their battle would be closer than I expected.

Androgeus was the reigning champion, having won both the wrestling and the marathon at the previous Panathenaic games. As such, he would not have to enter the competition until much later, unlike Theseus, who would have to battle his way up to earn his place in the finals.

I was eager to catch up on news of my home. The three of us sat down, and Androgeus regaled us with stories of our family and other events from the palace. I discovered that both Androgeus and Phaedra had been punished for their hand in my escape.

Androgeus had been sent away to another island for a couple of months while Minos's anger cooled. Despite being the favored son, Androgeus had risked much by aiding me. Minos got him out of his sight before he did something he regretted.

As for Phaedra, she was also sent away to one of the small fishing villages on Crete, to work and live in poverty, to learn humility and respect for her father. Catreus and Deucalion, both clever and charming, had managed to avoid punishment.

"What of Daedalus and Icarus?" I feared the answer, but I had to know.

"My father may be a little rash at times," answered Androgeus diplomatically. "But he was not so foolish as to kill the two best craftsmen in the known world." I knew Androgeus would've been a little more scathing if it was between the two of us, but there was a rival prince present. One that Androgeus didn't know. He was not about to dishonor his own father in front of a stranger.

"So what did he do to them?" I asked.

"Put them both to work on a major building project underneath the palace. As punishment, they are forced to work night and day. I never see either of them anymore. We've even got a new tutor now."

"What are they building?" I asked. It was a strange thing for Minos to do. The palace was already immense. Why did he need extra room?

"I don't know," confessed Androgeus. "It's very secret though. And large. The amount of rocks and dirt they have already excavated could fill the palace several times over."

Very odd. But the madness of my father did not concern me unduly. I was more interested in my family. And one person in particular.

"How is Phaedra?" I asked. I silently prayed to Poseidon that she hadn't been married off yet.

Androgeus raised his eyebrows at me, trying not to grin. "Wondered when you were going to get to her. Why don't you ask her yourself? You know the whole family is here, don't you?" he asked.

I didn't. Even sitting, I suddenly felt a little unsteady. "You mean Phaedra is here?" I asked, breathlessly.

Androgeus smiled. "She certainly is. She wants to see you."

And I wanted to see her. Desperately.

"How? When?" I asked, my face alive with excitement.

"Easy brother. Don't injure yourself," said Androgeus, laughing easily. "You'll get your chance."

"There's a feast planned for tonight," said Theseus. "To welcome our new guests. King Minos and all his family have been invited, of course."

"I don't think it would be wise for me to attend," I said doubtfully.

"Why not?" asked Theseus. "I told you before. You are under my protection and that of my father. King Minos will not risk offending either of us by pursuing his revenge here. You will be safe."

"Besides," said Androgeus. "Your other brothers and sisters will want to see you too." He reflected for a moment. "Perhaps not Ariadne and Glaucus but Catreus and Deucalion certainly." He laughed again.

"Good," said Theseus, clapping his hands. "It's agreed. We will see you tonight, Androgeus. At the feast."

If I thought the anticipation of seeing Androgeus was almost unbearable, it was nothing to what I felt at that moment. Phaedra. My Phaedra. Very soon, we would be reunited. I had thought about this moment almost constantly, wishing that we would soon be in each other's arms again.

My stomach churned with a mixture of nervousness and

longing, each vying for supremacy, their conflict only serving to make me nauseous. When the time came, I prayed to the gods that I would not embarrass myself in front of her.

Ω

The feast was an elaborate affair as befitted the arrival of King Minos. Hundreds of boar, deer, fish, and birds were roasted, boiled, fried, and baked. The palace kitchens churned out bread and cakes in such quantities to make even the sturdiest table sag under their prodigious weight. Wine flowed, enough to put a small river to shame.

King Minos sat in the place of honor next to King Aegeus. Theseus sat next to his father, and I, being Theseus's closest companion, sat only one seat away from my friend, even though I was not part of the Athenian royal family. I only found out later that Theseus had to use his considerable powers of persuasion to convince his father to allow me to sit at the table. Aegeus, by now, knew who I was and daren't risk offending Minos with my presence. Theseus made him think otherwise. In hindsight, it was a foolish and rash move, but Theseus very rarely listened to the advice of others, including his royal father.

Minos, being the most powerful monarch in the world those days, was not someone you wished to antagonize. I suspect that Theseus did it deliberately. He was not someone who avoided confrontation, and I think that he really did want to embarrass Minos for what he had done to me.

To my disgust, it was Ariadne who got to sit between Theseus and me. It was not exactly a happy family reunion. Ariadne basically ignored me the whole evening, and I had no interest in speaking to her. Just looking at her made me think of Kyon. Even if she had wanted to talk to me, she probably wouldn't have, given that her attention was riveted on Theseus. I have never seen someone so smitten before.

Aegeus and Minos were clearly trying to join their great cities by a marriage between Theseus and Ariadne. Her position at the table was obviously premeditated.

If I was disgusted by Ariadne's close proximity, I felt almost sick due to the lack of another. Phaedra was seated on the far side of Minos, next to my other brothers, so distant I couldn't talk to her unless I actually stood and walked to her side. Or shouted. But that would've been embarrassing. I couldn't move as it meant I would have to pass Minos. Minos was determined to keep her as far from me as possible.

If Minos was offended by my presence, he didn't show it. He didn't even look at me. It was almost like I didn't exist. I spent the evening staring at Phaedra. We exchanged several glances, and she smiled at me so warmly I kept expecting my heart to melt.

I managed to pass a note to one of the servants, asking her to meet me in my room later that evening. I saw her read it and glance up at me. She nodded but the expression on her beautiful face confused me. She looked uncertain.

I couldn't even talk to Androgeus, who was seated next to Minos. My mother wasn't there either. Androgeus told me that she had stayed behind in Crete, claiming that her health was poor. Everyone knew that was an excuse. There was probably nothing wrong with her other than having a desire to stay away from Minos, but her absence pained me. My mother had no idea that I was in Athens. No matter. I would've loved to have seen her again, but I comforted myself with the knowledge that I would soon.

What was important was that Androgeus and Phaedra were here. The two people I most wanted to see in the world.

The evening passed quickly, hastened onward by a great deal of drinking and toasts. Theseus told stories, which entertained and thrilled his audience. Especially Ariadne. She never took her shining eyes off him. I don't think Theseus favored her with any special attention. I think that given he only had his father and her to talk to, he was often forced to make conversation with her by default. He didn't seem particularly enamored with her, despite the fact that she was very beautiful. Theseus had met many beautiful girls in his time. He often slept with them too, discarding them quickly after he became bored. Ariadne was simply another potential bedmate, regardless of the fact that she was the daughter of a King.

Theseus was charming and polite. He was a prince and a hero. How could Ariadne not fall instantly in love with him? Many women did—to their eternal regret and humiliation.

I drank sparingly, only sipping from my goblet during toasts, my mind on Phaedra. I toyed with my food, looking for the first opportunity to slip away.

When it came later that night, I bolted with as much dignity as I could muster and hastened to my room.

My room in the palace was much less grand than that of Theseus's, as you can probably imagine. It was well appointed enough and comfortable. I waited impatiently for about an hour before Phaedra finally made an appearance.

We stood looking at each other for a long moment, which seemed to stretch out for longer than I could bear. She was so beautiful. I wanted desperately to take her into my arms, but I was scared to move, wracked with doubt. I was just an ugly brute of a man. What did she possibly see in me? Perhaps her feelings for me had changed?

I needn't have worried. She suddenly rushed at me, and I gathered her into an embrace. She felt tiny and fragile against me, and I was conscious of not hurting her with my great strength. We kissed and caressed for a long time. If we spoke, I can't remember what we said.

Finally, she broke away from me. She looked sad, and tears rolled down her cheeks.

"What's wrong, my love?" I asked. I tried to wipe her tears away, but she pushed my hand away impatiently.

"Nothing ... Everything," she said.

She sat down on a stool, and I picked up another one and sat down facing her.

"I have missed you, Asterion. More than you know."

"I've missed you too, Phaedra. Why the tears then?"

"Because," she cried, gulping back another bout of sobs, "I have to marry another."

"No you don't," I said firmly. "We can run away together. I have wealth now. Enough for a lifetime. We'll be happy. We'll find a place where your father can never find us."

"It isn't that simple," she said miserably, drying her eyes on the sleeve of her dress. "Minos has my mother guarded by many men. He said that unless I marry, he'll kill her. I can't run away with you."

"Then I will kill Minos," I declared angrily, raising my bulk from the stool. "Tonight. I will go to his room and crush him with my club." I would do it. Although burning with rage, I felt a strange calm settling over me. I could kill him. It didn't matter how many guards he had; I would see him dead. For Phaedra.

She placed her delicate hand on my arm. "Sit, Asterion. Let's talk about this. I don't want you doing something hasty."

Reluctantly, I slowly settled back into my seat.

"Minos has some loyal followers," said Phaedra. "He has already told me that if something happens to him, one of those followers will return to Crete immediately and have my mother killed. You can't kill him. If you do, you also kill my mother."

"Then," I said, thinking quickly, "I will kill your husband to be. Without a prospective husband, Minos cannot protest. Besides, this would-be suitor probably deserves death if he is prepared to align himself with Minos."

Phaedra looked slightly stunned by the remark. "You have changed, Asterion. You never used to talk so lightly of killing and death. Everything you have suggested so far has involved killing."

"Sometimes, a man is forced to do what he has to do. To do what is right." The words of Theseus came to me unbidden. "I am a hero now. And heroes find their own path in life. We do not always do what others tell us to do."

"You sound arrogant, Asterion," said Phaedra. "Those are not the words of the man I love. Those are the words of someone else."

"It doesn't matter," I said, angry now. "I will kill this suitor, and then you and I will be free to pursue our love. Free from Minos forever. When the time is right, we'll return to Crete and rescue your mother. Now, tell me who this suitor is."

"It is Theseus," she said, and the words were like a sword in my heart.

CHAPTER 12

I'd be the first to admit that I wasn't good company in the days that followed. I thought long and hard about Phaedra and the position she was in.

I couldn't figure it out at first. Why Theseus? Minos had placed Ariadne next to him at the feast, a clear indication that she would be the one to marry him. Not Phaedra.

I puzzled it out eventually. It wasn't too difficult. Minos's hatred for me went far deeper than I would've thought possible. He knew that Phaedra and I were in love. He knew that I wanted to marry her. He was marrying her off to Theseus to spite me, particularly now that he knew Theseus and I were friends. If he couldn't kill me then he would harm me in other ways. As long as he had his alliance, Minos couldn't care less who married Theseus.

Minos was a truly despicable man.

What to do? I couldn't, no, wouldn't kill Theseus. Not even for Phaedra. In fact, if I killed any suitor of Phaedra's, I would probably lose her forever. I could go to Theseus and ask him not to marry Phaedra. He'd probably been pressured by his own father but, knowing Theseus, he would easily be able to convince Aegeus that it would be better to marry Ariadne. What did Theseus care? For him, one beautiful woman was no different than another.

Other doubts resurfaced of course. Theseus was much more handsome than I. He was a prince—the rightful heir to one of the greatest cities in the world. I owned only a few sets of clothing and my weapons. He was charming. He was famous. I was none of those things. Not only that, but my horns made me a deformed freak. Why would any woman want to marry such a creature? Perhaps Phaedra really did want to marry Theseus? No one would blame her. He was a much more attractive proposition than I. Maybe Phaedra was just pretending, her reluctance to marry another just a sham?

And then I realized that frustration and my feelings for Phaedra were starting to make me a little insane. The Phaedra I knew wouldn't do that. She was simply not that sort of person. I on the other hand was a mess, riddled with jealously and petty insecurities. A sixteen-year-old boy in other words.

It was Phaedra's mother that was really the problem. I needed to get her off Crete and away from Minos. But how? I didn't know. I considered and discarded several ideas as foolishness.

The Panathenaic games had already begun. Androgeus, as predicted, once again won what would later become the marathon—the run that traversed the hills between Athens and the small village that was its namesake. He was still the favorite for the wrestling, which was getting into the final rounds. I was extremely proud and pleased for him. Phaedra, Catreus, Deucalion, and I celebrated with him. Even Ariadne and Glaucus shared in his victory, although neither made any effort to talk to me. It was like I no longer existed. After my escape from Crete, I had effectively been disowned by them. They gave me as much attention as they would have a servant. In their eyes at least, I was beneath them. A stray dog probably had more status than I.

I tried to mend the rift I felt had grown between myself and Phaedra and succeeded to a certain degree. Both of us were a little miserable, knowing we were trapped by Minos's schemes, but we made the best of it, trying to spend as much time together as possible, despite Minos's efforts to the contrary. Neither of us could see a way out.

Finally, I approached Theseus. He was somewhat distracted by his involvement in the wrestling. He had reached the final rounds and didn't really have time for my problems, but I was at my wits end.

"You can't marry Phaedra," I said. "You know I love her."

"I know," said Theseus, sounding a little exasperated. "But my father and King Minos have already agreed to it."

"Well, get your father to change his mind then."

"I have already tried. I said I would be happy to marry Ariadne, but Minos insists that it be Phaedra."

"What are you going to do then?" I insisted.

Theseus shrugged helplessly. "I don't know. Let me get through the wrestling, and then we'll come up with a plan together. Rest assured, my brother, I have no intention of marrying the woman you love. We will work something out."

I felt a little better after that. Reassured. I still worried, but I was confident that between the two of us, we'd think of something.

Ω

Theseus made it to the final of the wrestling where he faced Androgeus. To no one's surprise other than Theseus, Androgeus won. Though reasonably well matched, Androgeus was the best wrestler I had ever seen. I don't think any man, demi-god or otherwise, could've bested him. There was no shame in losing to him.

Theseus thought otherwise. His pride was damaged. And for Theseus, that was unforgiveable. I tried to comfort him, but he wouldn't let it go.

"He cheated," raged Theseus, two nights after Androgeus's victory. The night before, I had celebrated with my brother. Theseus had been conspicuous by his absence.

"No, he didn't," I said, defending my brother. Androgeus would never cheat. I had watched the bout and knew without doubt that he hadn't. Androgeus had won fairly.

"What do you know?" said Theseus angrily. "You didn't fight him. You didn't see. Motherless dog! He attacked me when I wasn't ready."

That wasn't true at all. I had seen Theseus nod when the referee had asked him if he was ready.

Theseus was already a little drunk, having consumed at

least three goblets of unwatered wine. His eyes had that slight look of madness that they did when he fought. Suddenly, he seemed to come to a decision.

"I'll fight him again," he said firmly. "This time fairly. I'll win this time. I know I will."

I shook my head. "I don't think that's a good idea," I said.

"You doubt me?" said Theseus, his eyes going wide. "You don't think I can beat that Hades born brother of yours, do you? To the crows with you!"

"I don't doubt your skills at all, my friend," I said, trying to placate him. "You're an excellent wrestler. One of the best in the world. But my brother is the best wrestler I have ever seen. He beat me far more times than I beat him. Even with my strength. But strength is not everything."

"And you think just because you beat me as well, that I am no match for either of you?"

"I didn't say that," I said, suddenly fearful that this conversation was getting out of hand. Normally, I avoided Theseus when he was in one of his irrational moods.

"Fight me now!" challenged Theseus. "I will prove to you that I am a match for you or your brother."

"No, Theseus. I don't want to fight you." I stood and made to leave his chambers. But Theseus had other ideas. He tackled me to the floor and soon we were wrestling in earnest.

Theseus, as I said, had been drinking. I probably would've beaten him anyway, but the drink made him slow, sluggish. Eventually, I got him in a hold from which he couldn't escape. I was forced to release him though as I feared his violent struggles would lead to something else.

We both staggered to our feet, breathless from our exertions.

Theseus glared at me. "You freak," he spat. "Bull's spawn. You only won because you aren't human."

Theseus had never spoken to me like that. He knew I was sensitive about this issue. It was unforgiveable.

I stood there, swaying slightly with shock. I think even Theseus, deranged as he was, knew he had gone too far. I could see it in his eyes. But Theseus did have trouble setting his pride aside. He had been humiliated twice, and it was more than he could bear.

He stormed from the room in a rage. Normally I would've let him be, given him time to calm down, to see reason. But this time I couldn't. I knew where he was going.

Ω

I raced after Theseus. Even sober, I was much slower than him. By the time I reached Androgeus's room, they were already wrestling.

It was clear that Androgeus was winning. Theseus was out of control, roaring in fury as they struggled together on the tiled floor. I couldn't stand idly by and watch. I had to do something. This was my friend and my brother.

I bent down and attempted to separate them. I finally pried Theseus's fingers away from Androgeus.

The events that followed are still a blur. Perhaps time has blunted my memories. Perhaps I just don't want to remember, unwilling to deal with the pain. Theseus, deranged at the time, has no clear recollection either.

What I think happened is this. I bent down in order to drag them apart. Just as I did so, Theseus gave Androgeus a final push. Rage gave him strength. My head was down.

Androgeus impaled himself on my horns. They slid into his body easily, almost as if they were welcomed. Despite my unreliable memories, I can distinctly remember the terrible soft, wet sound as horn met the flesh of my brother.

Androgeus cried once and sagged against me. Horrified, I lowered him to the ground and withdrew my terrible spikes. His life's blood gushed forth.

I held Androgeus in my arms. He smiled at me. "It's not your fault, brother," he said and died.

I lowered my head and cried like I have never cried before or since, completely overcome with grief and self-loathing. My horrible deformity had cost my brother his life. I loved Androgeus deeply. He was a far better man than I and a wonderful brother. I miss him still.

I don't know how long I held the dead body of my brother. I was vaguely aware of people coming and going, of the sound of crying, and of voices raised in anger. It meant nothing to me. All I could think was that my brother was dead.

Eventually, rough hands pried my fingers away from him. Despite my struggles, my arms were forced behind my back, and I was shackled. I was dragged roughly to my feet. I howled with despair and anger as the body of my brother was carried from the room.

The chamber was now packed with people. I recognized several faces. Theseus, of course, was still present, his rage subsided, white with shock. King Aegeus was there as was Minos. The rest of my family had gathered, but I only had eyes for Phaedra. She regarded me with a terrible sadness. My heart broke when I saw her look. I can only imagine what she thought at the time. That somehow I had deliberately killed my brother. I desperately wanted to explain, to tell her that it was all a misunderstanding, that Androgeus had died by accident.

I never got a chance. Guards dragged me away. I still remember the pained look on Theseus's face.

I was taken to one of Minos's ships bobbing in the harbor and chained within a darkened recess of the hold. And there I stayed. I can't be sure how long I was in there, but I was given neither food nor water. Not that I would've accepted either, deep in the embrace of my private hell.

Finally, Phaedra came to see me. I was a little surprised that Minos had allowed it, but I guess he realized that it would be another form of torture for me. Her face was a picture of sorrow. I wept when I saw her, saddened beyond belief that I had caused such pain.

She regarded me for a long moment before speaking. "Did you really kill our brother, Asterion?"

For a moment, I couldn't believe that she had asked that. That she had needed to ask that. Did she really think so little of me?

"It was an accident," I sobbed, overcome with grief. "Theseus pushed him, and he stumbled onto my horns. It was an accident."

She looked me in the eyes and saw truth there. She did, after all, know me better than perhaps anyone.

"That's what Theseus said, but no one believes him," she said. "I spoke to him in private, and he told me the whole story. It doesn't matter though. It's much better to believe that a monster killed him."

"Is that what people are saying?" I asked in disbelief. "That I'm a monster?"

"Yes. The whole city is talking about it. They say that you killed Androgeus in a jealous rage because he sided with Theseus over his marriage to me."

"Is that what you think?" I asked.

"I … I don't know what to think any longer. The thought, I confess, crossed my mind. You have changed, Asterion. I know how you loved Androgeus, I know how much he meant to you, but rage does appalling things to a man."

A terrible sadness filled me. Sadness that even Phaedra, my Phaedra, doubted me. Angrily, I pushed aside the feeling.

"What's going to happen to me?" I asked. I didn't really care at that moment, too busy dwelling on the death of my brother and Phaedra's words, but I felt like I had to ask.

"Minos is taking you back to Crete. You will be imprisoned for your crimes."

"But I haven't done anything wrong!" I pleaded.

Phaedra nodded sadly. "Regardless of what happened, Father was waiting for an opportunity like this. He came to Athens for you, and you, it seems, have played into his hands. He may have lost his favorite son, but he has his revenge."

"And what about Theseus? What's going to happen to him?"

"Nothing. I think he has been punished enough. He grieves as much as you. Androgeus meant nothing to him, but he knows the pain his death has caused you."

I wanted to blame Theseus. It was all his fault. It was his injured pride that had caused this. His push had caused

PHILLIP W. SIMPSON

Androgeus's death. But I couldn't. I knew it was hard to blame Theseus for his actions. His rage controlled him. He wasn't himself when he was like that.

"And the marriage?" I asked. It was a selfish thing to ask, especially in light of my brother's death, but I felt compelled.

Phaedra shook her head. "I don't know. I guess that it will be called off. My father now has another goal—I suspect he always did. He would rather dominate Athens than forge an alliance. You've done him a favor. Androgeus's death has put him in a far greater position of power. Androgeus was under Athenian protection during the games. Minos blames King Aegeus for Androgeus's death and demands they pay the price. He has issued a threat saying he will destroy Athens unless tribute is paid."

"So," I said bitterly. "Androgeus's death will only make Minos richer."

"No," said Phaedra slowly, unable to meet my eye. "The tribute will take another form."

It was not until we had returned to the island of my birth that I began to understand exactly what the tribute was, when the terrible nature of it was finally revealed.

Ω

We sailed back to Crete, Minos having settled the terms of the tribute with King Aegeus.

Minos ventured down into the hold once during the voyage. It was almost a repeat of my boyhood encounter with

200

the man. He said nothing, just glared at me with his cold eyes. This time, he didn't bother hitting me. He got his guards to do it instead. They beat me so badly I almost died. But the god in me made me very difficult to kill.

Besides, Minos didn't want me dead. He had other plans for me, plans that involved the tribute from Athens. You, Ovid, a poet and scholar, are of course aware of what the tribute was. Many stories have been told about it, and for a change, they are, for the most part, truthful. But for any who read this recount of my life and have not heard or can't quite remember, indulge me for a moment.

King Minos, as I have explained on several occasions, was a stupid man, weak and mean, despite his power. He could've demanded any amount of gold from Athens to compensate him for Androgeus's death. Instead, he chose to do something dreadful.

He demanded that seven young men and seven maidens were to be sent each year from King Aegeus to Crete as tribute. There, they would be fed to a terrible half bull, half man creature. The creature later known as the Minotaur. Me.

I later discovered that Minos had planned this for some time. He was obsessed with me. He would stop at nothing to get his revenge. Rumors and his spy network ensured that he had known I was in Athens. He'd planned to capture me there and imprison me underneath the palace at Knossos. Then, he was going to prove to the world what a beast I was by feeding me the unfortunate human victims. A starving man, it was said, would resort to cannibalism eventually. If he fed me nothing else, then I wouldn't have a choice.

By the time of the Panathenaic games, the prison he

had specially built for me was almost complete. Daedalus and Icarus had worked on it for months. Minos had spared no expense, importing thousands of slaves to ensure it was completed on time.

It was called the labyrinth. It was to become my home for many years.

Of course, the death of Androgeus had been completely unseen. But it did serve Minos's ends. He had planned to conquer Athens at some point; the death of his son had merely served to hasten his plans slightly. I believe that Minos had originally intended to throw me other prisoners to feed on. Athens subjugation made him rethink. He had always hated Athens and King Aegeus. Gleefully, he decided that the tribute should take human form.

And thus it was shortly after our arrival on Crete that I was taken, bloody and bruised, and forced to kneel before Daedalus. My helm, the helm created for me by Icarus, was thrust back on my head. Daedalus, with his son hostage, was required to make a number of alterations against his will. All of them painful.

Daedalus only once met my eye during the whole procedure. I knew how he felt: trapped and helpless. Toward the end, I saw him mouth the words "I'm sorry."

And then I was thrown into the labyrinth.

CHAPTER 13

Ovid put down his quill and stretched. He felt his back click. The fingers of his writing hand ached terribly. He felt old—much older than his fifty years, almost like the span of time he was writing about was pressing down on him—and exhausted. It was difficult to listen to a story that seemed to be one tragedy after another. Depressing. Outside, the day was fading fast. They'd have to light the lamps again soon.

"So, that's the truth of it then?" he asked. "Minos put you in the labyrinth for killing Androgeus, not because you were some beast?"

Ast nodded his great head. "It happened exactly as I've told you. It may have been a long time ago, but certain events I will never forget. Minos would've found some excuse to put me in there eventually—the death of Androgeus just gave him a convenient excuse."

"I can see how the legend of a half bull started now," confessed Ovid. "It makes sense. The helmet, the mask." He paused to gather his thoughts. "How did you get it off?"

"Not very easily," said Ast drily.

Ovid suspected that the huge man was joking with him but it was hard to tell. If Ast had a sense of humor, it was well disguised.

"And so the Athenian youths demanded in tribute were because of an accident caused by you and Theseus?" asked Ovid.

"It pains me to say it, but yes," said Ast. "Androgeus's death was unnecessary and unfortunate, and it broke my heart. Not a day goes by when I don't think of him. Over the years, I have only drawn comfort from the fact that one day, I will see him again."

This, Ovid assumed, was some reference to the afterlife, but he let it pass. "And what became of Theseus? Clearly, he didn't kill you. Did he actually come to the labyrinth at all, or is that another myth?"

Ast paused, deep in thought. "He came. Eventually. But it did not go the way the legends say. I think you will be surprised."

"I think," said Ovid slowly, "that I will. Few things surprise me these days, but I believe this will be one of them." He reflected for a moment. "Just so I've got the story straight so far, allow me to reiterate," he said, ticking the points off on his fingers. "You aren't half bull, merely have the horns of one, and you were put into the labyrinth because of an accident involving your brother, which Theseus was partially responsible. Is any of the legend actually true?"

"Some of it is based on fact, but there is much that isn't," said Ast.

"What about you eating people? Is that part true?" Ovid, if he was being honest with himself, was not looking forward to that aspect of the story. If it turned out that it was true, what then? Had he been sleeping under the roof of a cannibal? Perhaps Ast was planning on killing and eating him once they were finished here? Maybe while he slept. It was certainly possible. How else could someone survive in the labyrinth for the amount of time Ast apparently had? This sudden surge of fear gave Ovid a remarkable insight. Any lingering doubts as to this man's true identity evaporated. The realization was startling.

"Ah," said Ast, evidentially savoring Ovid's obvious discomfort. "I see that you finally believe. But you will just have to wait now, won't you? Ready?"

Ovid nodded nervously. Steeling himself with another gulp of wine, he picked up his quill once again.

For some reason, his hand trembled ever so slightly.

Ω

Thus began my imprisonment in that place. The labyrinth, like many other aspects of my story, was not exactly what others would have you believe.

Shortly after Daedalus made certain necessary adjustments to my helmet, I was dumped unceremoniously through a trapdoor on the lowest level of the palace into the very center of the labyrinth.

I fell into darkness. The fall wasn't great, perhaps twice the height of a man, but it was sufficient for me to sprain my ankle. The trapdoor above me slammed shut.

I despaired then and huddled on the ground sobbing, clad only in a loincloth and my helmet. Not exactly the actions of a monster. The darkness seemed absolute at first, especially with the trapdoor now closed. I had thought it the only source of light, but as my eyes slowly adjusted to the darkness, I began to realize that was not the case.

Daedalus and Icarus built the labyrinth. They must have had some idea about what it was going to be used for. Even if I hadn't been placed inside, both men had obviously given some thought to the fate of those unfortunate enough to be imprisoned. Renowned craftsmen like those two can't have been supervised throughout the entire construction period. Even if they had, their guards and overseers would have little comprehension of what they were seeing.

Limestone was a common enough building material, much like it is today. It was readily available in Greece and the islands around Crete. As a result, Daedalus and Icarus used it extensively when constructing the labyrinth. Other than being a useful material, limestone has another, more interesting property. It glows in the dark.

Well, I wouldn't say glow exactly, but it certainly emitted some light. Enough light that I wasn't trapped in complete darkness. When I saw the light, my spirits rose slightly. The two craftsmen had also seen fit to embed a few semi-precious gems in the walls, which also glowed slightly. The occasional green or ruby glow provided much welcomed variety and even gave me a little perspective.

Although I couldn't see clearly, the slightly glowing walls enabled me to move around and explore my new home more easily than you would've expected. Humans do have an ability to adapt quickly. Especially when circumstances demand nothing less.

Eventually, I regained my composure and began my exploration, limping slowly about on my sprained ankle. The labyrinth, as you would expect, was huge. The palace under which it sits is massive, but the labyrinth was larger still. Even now, looking at the ruins nearby, it is still difficult to grasp the true extent.

The trapdoor was always my reference point, my marker. Once my eyes became adjusted, I could see tiny slivers of natural light seeping from cracks in the wood. It wasn't just that. The trapdoor was where my food and water was initially lowered, so it was vital that I didn't become lost.

Of course, in the near darkness, eventually that's exactly what happened.

Using the dim glow of the walls, I felt my way around the place. I began to find the touch of limestone soothing, the feel of the stone under my fingers telling me I was still alive. But of course, even limestone walls look almost identical to each other.

I began to feel more confident in my surroundings, venturing further and further away from the reassuring presence of the trapdoor. That was a mistake. Once, I lost my way for three days. I eventually found the trapdoor, starving and seriously dehydrated, sobbing with relief.

It didn't take me long to work out a way to navigate the labyrinth. Using my horns, I sawed grooves into the corner of each wall at the height where I would normally place my hand. If the depression was greater on the left, I knew to turn left. If it was right, then that was the direction I went. A uniform depression indicated that I was to travel straight ahead. The effort caused me some discomfort, but it was little different to the times I had tried to file the points off my horns.

After what was probably weeks, I was reasonably confident that I had explored the entire maze. My exploration revealed one depressing fact. The labyrinth only had one entrance or exit: the trapdoor. There was no door at ground level on either side of the maze as other poets and scholars have insisted.

I was indeed imprisoned.

I lost track of days; the dim, unchanging uniform light emitting from the walls gave no indication of the passage of time. My only clue was the trapdoor. Sometimes the light seeping through the cracks was slightly brighter than at other times. I took that for a sign that it was daytime in the world above.

It was always a little cold. Caves and other places underground are extremely constant in terms of temperature, given how insulated they are. It never got colder or hotter, which was small consolation. Sometimes, my shivering got so intense it would wake me up.

When I was tired, I slept. When I was hungry or thirsty, I ate or drank. I made myself as comfortable as possible on the cold stone floor, but my sleep was restless and uncomfortable. Many parts of the labyrinth flooded at times, and the floor was often wet. I ended up making my uncomfortable bed almost directly under the trapdoor, curled into a fetal position in a vain attempt to keep warm.

My dreams were haunted by images of my beloved brother Androgeus dead in my arms. I dreamt of my mother, her face blackened by Minos's fists. Phaedra also came to me in my dreams, and the memory of her provided some comfort. Even so, I often cried myself to sleep. Eventually, after some time, I began to doubt the existence of Phaedra. Perhaps she was even a product of my overactive imagination? Why would such a beautiful creature ever have anything to do with me?

My madness waxed and waned. Some days, I firmly believed that I had been sent to the underworld for killing my brother. I kept expecting to encounter Hades himself. I imagined that the puddles of water were the river Styx and that Charon, the boatman, would sail along and take me aboard. I think I dipped my head into the water a few times, hoping that the waters of the Styx would banish my memories.

I spent several hours or possibly days trying to remove my helmet without success. During the months that I had worn the helmet during my travels to Greece and my adventures with Theseus, I had grown accustomed to wearing it. It was almost a part of me. But now, due to the craftsmanship of Daedalus, it truly was.

The faceplate was now firmly latched in place by strong, clever metalwork that was beyond my strength or skill to remove. The mouth slit had only been designed for breathing. Fortunately, there was just enough room under the plate to shovel scraps of food. I had to tilt my head back almost completely in order to drip water into my mouth.

That in itself was not enough to prevent me from removing the helmet. Forced by Minos, Daedalus had been thorough. By drilling holes through my horns, he had attached the helmet to me with bronze wires that had been heated to seal them. Even now, I still believe that was almost the worst pain I have suffered. Almost.

Like the faceplate, Daedalus's work was so cunningly wrought and well made that, despite my best efforts, I couldn't remove it. Not only that, but each try brought intense pain. My bellows of pain served to enhance my legend. Servants and visitors to the palace probably wondered about the manner of beast imprisoned beneath their feet. Especially one that made such tormented sounds.

I was bored, lonely, and cold, wallowing in my own guilt and sadness. I gathered the darkness to me and wrapped myself in it like a blanket. I tried to remember the light of the sun, the wind on my face, but the memories were fleeting. After a time, I gave up trying to chase them. It was like I had always been in this place.

I did try to mark the passage of time. At first, I did it as a matter of necessity, a way to keep me sane, my only connection to the world above. On a wall near the trapdoor, I used my horns to scrape marks, one for each day. I really didn't know for sure. I suspect that I might've slept and missed a few but I did my best.

Later, it became a game. Something to do. I started to toy with the marks, embellishing and changing them. In my growing insanity, I thought that I was creating fabulous works of art. Much later, when I was able to examine them properly, I saw them for what they really were. Random marks and scratches. The work of a madman. Or a beast.

As a result, I really had no idea how long the first part of my imprisonment was. At the time, I believed it might have been weeks or months, even years.

I did other things to try and keep me sane and occupied. I exercised, wrestling imaginary opponents. I tried to climb the walls. Sometimes, in utter rage and despair, I attacked the limestone, knowing the feeling of wetness on my knuckles was blood but not caring.

I assumed that food and water came once a day, but perhaps it was every second, lowered down in a basket from above. There wasn't much of it—sometimes a bit of broth or soup, occasionally a chunk of stale bread. The water tasted sour, but I always drank it.

I only caught glimpses of my guards. At first, I yelled at them, pleading, begging. Later, my pleas turned into rants. They threw rocks at me and I swiftly got the message.

It was at this time I discovered the second of my animal friends. I would've preferred the companionship of another dog like Kyon, but dogs were in short supply in the labyrinth. It was a rat.

Like Kyon, we initially bonded over food, sharing my meager scraps together. I named him Glaucus and laughed about my cleverness for days. Glaucus was my only friend in that place. He had much in common with the real Glaucus. He was sneaky and had a nasty streak. He bit me on a few occasions, but I always forgave him. Unlike the real Glaucus, he was nowhere near as fat. That, in part, probably saved his life. I was always hungry and was tempted several times to eat him. Thankfully, I never gave into the demands of my stomach. To do so would have been to eat my only companion.

I told Glaucus stories. I talked and he listened. He was an excellent listener. I told him of my childhood. I told him about my adventures with Theseus. Most of all, I spoke of Phaedra and Androgeus. I cried a lot. If Glaucus became bored or frustrated with me, he never gave any sign. He was a good friend.

Time passed. I started to become accustomed to my new life, but the reality was that I had probably passed into madness.

The amount or perhaps frequency of food and water lowered to me declined. I was even hungrier than before. Often I lacked the energy to move. It was almost too much effort to suck water puddling on the floor nearby. Glaucus became a more and more attractive option.

I contemplated suicide but lacked the means. I couldn't even beat my head against the walls. All I succeeded in doing was wedging my horns into the limestone.

In my saner moments, I thought about simply starving myself to death. It wouldn't have been hard. Hades beckoned and his call was becoming harder and harder to refuse.

Ω

At first, I thought I was imagining the light. I realized that I had gone completely mad and began laughing uproariously.

The flickering light got closer as I lay huddling on the ground, watching it, mesmerized. It burnt my eyes, but I didn't care. Imaginary light couldn't hurt me. I stopped laughing, listening to the footsteps as they got closer.

Eventually, I became aware that someone was carrying the light. Whoever it was stood above me.

"Asterion," said a voice. A voice I seemed to recognize.

"Go away," I said, shielding my eyes from the hurtful light.

"Asterion, it's me," said the voice. A strangely familiar voice. It sounded like Phaedra. But it couldn't be. My mind was playing tricks on me.

"Phaedra? Is that you?" I asked with a sudden surge of hope.

"Yes," she said. "It's me. I'm here, Asterion. I'm here for you."

It wasn't possible. But I wanted to believe. I needed to believe. I began to sob hysterically. I felt gentle hands touching me. They wrapped me in a soft embrace, and it was only with that actual physical contact did I finally believe that I wasn't alone. Phaedra was here.

"How? Why?" I blurted in a voice that sounded startlingly loud.

She shushed me. "Soon, my love. I will tell you all you need to know soon."

She helped me to my feet, staggering under my weight, even though I probably weighed a fraction of what I had before. Phaedra rummaged in a satchel slung over her shoulder. She gave me some bread, which at first I eyed disbelievingly, then devoured hungrily, shoveling it under my faceplate. I looked around for Glaucus, but the light and the presence of another human had scared him off.

"Can you walk?" she asked.

I nodded slowly, not trusting myself to speak.

"Here," she said, thrusting something into my numb hands. "Hold this."

It was a ball of thread.

We walked slowly, me winding the thread up as we followed its path through the labyrinth. Phaedra supported my weight and guided us with the light from a small oil lamp she carried with her free hand.

I wanted to explain to her that I could've navigated that place by using my wall scrapings but for a moment, I was just content having her by my side. I was also terrified that if I spoke, I might offend her somehow and she would disappear.

In silence, we journeyed through the labyrinth. I basked in her presence. I kept looking at her and touching her with my free hand, just to ensure she was real. By the time we reached our destination, I was finally convinced she was.

She led me to a dead end. An indent in the wall assured me that I'd been there before. In the flickering lamplight, I could just make out a large pile of items that certainly hadn't been there last time.

She told me to sit and then lowered herself to the ground, setting the lamp on the damp rocky floor between us.

She looked at me properly then, and the anguish on her face told me everything I needed to know about my appearance. I was filthy, emaciated, and disheveled. She stroked my mask with one hand and began to cry. I saw her flinch when she first laid hands on the cold metal that was now my face, but she quickly repressed any feelings of revulsion. If the mask surprised her, she didn't show it. Presumably, she had already been told what had been done to me.

For my part, I drank her up. She was just as beautiful as I remembered. I had missed her so. It was almost too much to bear. I felt tears welling up and began to sob again.

"Oh, Asterion. My poor Asterion," she said, taking me into

her arms again. "I'm here now. It's going to be alright."

"But … but how are you here?" I croaked. "You can't be. There's no way to get in. There's only the trapdoor. The trapdoor …" I trailed off, my eyes glazing over.

"Asterion," said Phaedra, taking my masked face into both her hands. Tears were still running down her cheeks, but she had regained her composure. Phaedra was always stronger than me. "I know it's hard. I can't even begin to understand what you have been through. But you need to concentrate now. I have much to tell you."

"How … ?" I stammered.

"Peace," she said, releasing me and settling back onto her haunches. I wanted to grab her and make her put her hands back on me. I needed her touch.

"First, you probably want to know how long? You need to steady yourself, Asterion. It has been three months."

I was actually a little surprised. If Phaedra thought I would be dismayed, she was wrong. I thought it had been much longer. I had started to believe that I had always dwelt in the labyrinth, that the outside world was pure fiction created by my overactive imagination.

Phaedra watched me digest this news in silence, although my faceplate meant she couldn't see my expression. She did, however, know me well enough to read my body language. Phaedra had probably thought I would break down, but when I seemed able to handle this revelation, she continued.

"Listen to me, Asterion. I know you have many questions. I will tell you everything you need to know." She breathed deep, steadying herself. "Firstly, my love. I am sorry. I am sorry for so many things. I am sorry that Androgeus died by accident. I am sorry that you had a hand in it. I am sorry that I doubted you. I am sorry that you were put in this terrible place. Most of all, I am sorry that it took me so long to reach you."

My mind was whirling. Yes. Phaedra was here, but why hadn't she come for me sooner? Why did I have to suffer for three months that may as well have been three years?

As if reading my mind, she reached out and took my hand. "Daedalus and Icarus hold the key to this place. They built it. They know its secrets. Unfortunately, Father has had them imprisoned. When they disappeared, I assumed that Father had either had them killed or imprisoned them with you. I despaired of ever helping you. But Father was not foolish enough to kill them. Perhaps also, he knew that Daedalus and Icarus may have built an escape for themselves within the labyrinth, suspecting rightly that he would never let them leave Crete.

"Minos displayed uncharacteristic wisdom. The craftsmen did indeed plan ahead. They thought they would be imprisoned here and had created a secret way out. Unfortunately, my father did not put them here. I eventually discovered that they have been imprisoned in a tower on a remote part of this island, heavily guarded.

"Thankfully, the guards have become a bit complacent over time. With the help of our brothers, Catreus and Deucalion, I managed to get into the tower and talk to Daedalus. Icarus was held in a separate chamber. Daedalus was the one who told me about the secrets of the labyrinth. He drew me a map and showed me how to use the thread to mark my route. Yes, Asterion. That is how I am here. There is a secret way in and out of the labyrinth."

Hope flushed through me. My heart began to beat wildly.

Was it possible? Was there a way out of this dungeon?

"Why are we still here then?" I asked, my voice rising. "Let's get out of here! Now! This instant!" I surged to my feet, intent on leaving then and there. And then I noticed Phaedra wasn't moving. Something was wrong. "What is it?" I asked, feeling the hope drain away as quickly as it had arrived.

She took my hand again and gently forced me to sit. "There is a way out. But not for you," she said sadly. "Daedalus and Icarus, like myself, are slim and slightly built. They built a secret tunnel for themselves that was only large enough to accommodate a normal sized person. Even in your state, there is no way you would fit."

I knew that I had lost a great deal of weight. Even looking at my arms in the uncertain light of the lamp, I could see that my body had shrunk. Even so, I was much wider at the shoulders and hips than the two craftsmen. No amount of weight loss would change that. Then there was the matter of my horns.

Phaedra read my mind. "You are too big, Asterion. I know what you are thinking though. That I could bring you tools. Yes, that is possible, but it would take a great deal of time. The secret passage is long."

"What then?" I asked, feeling my frustration spill over into anger. "Am I trapped here forever?"

Phaedra shook her head. "No, my love. I will think of something. But for now, at least, you will be comfortable. I will visit as often as I can, even though I am constantly watched. The ports are all guarded. Father has become paranoid. Spies are everywhere. Every boat, even the smallest fishing boat, is searched before it leaves the island. Father suspects that I am planning something. Outside, it is after midnight. My guards, drunk from the wine supplied by Catreus and Deucalion, are asleep. But we won't get away with that very often. Here, I have brought you food, drink, light, and a blanket. You will not be in the darkness again. Next time, I will bring you parchments to read and some straw for a bed."

Even though I was desperately disappointed, I realized that my predicament was much better than before. It was something. I had that to be thankful for.

"And are you still going to marry Theseus?" I asked a little more sharply than I had intended. It was a question I had wanted to ask as soon as I saw her.

Phaedra shook her head. "Of course not. The marriage was only necessary before the death of Androgeus. Now, Father has power over Athens. Far more useful than an alliance."

I felt a huge surge of relief hearing those words. The thought of Phaedra marrying someone else—especially my friend—was almost unbearable.

"There is more I need to tell you, Asterion," she said. "First, have you noticed your guards have been feeding you less?"

I nodded. This was certainly the case. I just assumed that Minos had finally decided to starve me to death.

"Soon, they will feed you nothing."

"I guessed as much," I said.

"It's not what you think," said Phaedra, her lips pursed into a grim line. "Within a month, the first tribute from Athens will arrive. That was the catalyst that finally forced me to risk the secret passage. I had to tell you what Father plans. Seven youths and seven maidens will be dropped into the labyrinth from the trapdoor."

"Yes," I said, unsure what Phaedra was getting at.

"Don't you see?" she pleaded. "Minos means to starve you. Starve you to the point that you will eat anything. *Anything.*"

I suddenly realized what she was saying. My stomach, unaccustomed to such a large meal, lurched. I staggered into the corner and vomited, emptying the contents. Minos had intended me to become a cannibal. To get his revenge. To make the world realize that I was just a beast.

I felt Phaedra's hands on my shoulders. She tore a strip of linen from her dress and used it to wipe the vomit from under my mask.

"That's not going to happen, Asterion. I will make sure you always have enough food. You will never have to resort to such a thing."

"But ... but what will happen to these tributes from Athens?" I asked.

Phaedra smiled at me. "You will show them the way out. Lead them to the secret passage, and I will help them from there. They will fit, unless of course they are as massive as you. Which is unlikely. I know of no man as large as you."

"It's too dangerous," I said. "Minos is watching you. In any case, how will you possibly get fourteen people off this island without him noticing?"

"Leave that to me," said Phaedra firmly. "You just have to get them out."

"Won't the guards notice that I haven't eaten them?" I asked.

"That's the clever part," said Phaedra, smiling again, this time a little smugly. "Your reputation is beginning to aid you here. The guards are starting to believe the rumors, despite what they know to the contrary. They've heard the noises. Their imaginations have done the rest. Some really believe that you have become part bull. A beast. They are terrified, and I doubt whether they will risk entering the labyrinth themselves to investigate. For all they know, you will have killed and eaten the Athenians, discarding their bones somewhere in the dark."

I sucked in a deep breath and blew it out. It was a dangerous plan. So much could go wrong. Phaedra could get caught. Even if she didn't, what about the Athenian tributes? How would Phaedra get them off the island when every ship was watched and searched? They could hardly swim back to Athens.

But that was Phaedra's problem, not mine. I had a part to play, just like she did. Phaedra was a truly exceptional woman in many ways. That is why I loved her so. I love her still.

But for now, I had to concentrate on the present, and there was something I needed to see.

"I suppose you'd better show me this secret passage then," I said.

CHAPTER 14

Life became so much better then. Phaedra saved me. She dragged me out of the dark abyss of insanity. If I'd spent a little longer in the darkness, there was a very real possibility that I would've become permanently insane. Phaedra came to me at just the right moment. Sometimes, I think perhaps Poseidon helped her, not that Phaedra really needed anyone's help. I guess I just like to think that my father was watching over me in some way.

As promised, Phaedra brought me more food and fresh water. I quickly learnt not to stuff it under my mask and into my mouth as hastily as possible. The three months of my imprisonment had taken their toll on my stomach. It had shrunk and cramped unless I ate in small amounts. I gradually increased the amount of food I could tolerate. Soon, I regained my ability to eat normally. My strength also returned.

My pet rat, Glaucus, seemed smug and quite pleased with the changes in my—and by default—his fate. His coat became glossy with his improved diet. He even started to get fat, taking on the appearance of his namesake, which I found funnier than it probably was.

Before she departed, Phaedra showed me the secret entrance to the labyrinth. It was an extraordinary piece of craftsmanship, as I would've expected from Daedalus and Icarus. It looked exactly the same as the rest of the limestone wall it was hidden within. Even though I knew where it was, I often failed to find it. Eventually, I marked the wall opposite to avoid any confusion.

It opened by a cunning latch that appeared as a normal outcropping of rock. You had to twist it, which meant it couldn't be opened by accident. Even if I had brushed against it in the dark, it would've failed to open.

As Phaedra had assured me, it was much too small for someone of my stature. A normal person, as long as they weren't too broad, would manage, even though it was still a tight squeeze. I hoped that none of the Athenians were terribly large.

It doglegged. I couldn't see any indication of the outside world from glancing within. I watched Phaedra leave, and the glow from her lamp followed her for some time, giving me a clearer indication of its true length.

The length of the escape tunnel was intimidating. It would take months to widen. But that didn't deter Phaedra. On her next visit about a week later, she brought me a bronze chisel that I began to use, slowly chipping away at the tunnel. I only chiseled as far as I could comfortably reach. Then, I had to make a troubling decision. I couldn't reach any further into the secret passage unless I widened the entrance itself. To do so would be to destroy the clever latch plate and cover. What if it needed to remain a secret? What if Minos and his guards decided to investigate? From what Phaedra had told me, it was unlikely, but I was loath to take the chance.

I decided to wait and see what happened. If I got the first tribute of Athenians out without incident, I would begin to tunnel further.

As promised, Phaedra brought me some straw. To me, it was like sleeping in a palace bed again. After three months of sleeping on cold, damp rock, straw was bliss. Not only that, but she brought me parchments to read and light. Light! An oil lamp with tinder and flint to strike a spark. It took me a long time to adjust once more to having light. I often just lay on my bed of straw looking at the lamp sitting next to me, watching the tiny flame flicker with the occasional eddy of air circulating around the maze.

For a long time, I considered the light and my ability to make it nothing short of amazing.

I set up my bedroom some way from the secret entrance, in another dead end of the labyrinth. Even if by chance Minos's guards did investigate the maze, I didn't want to make finding the entrance any easier than I had to. They would no doubt wonder how I came to have food, a bed, and a lamp, but I had already concocted a simple explanation. My father, Poseidon, had appeared and given them to me. Let them wonder over that.

Phaedra had said they would soon start to starve me. To keep up appearances, I journeyed in darkness to the trapdoor every day, relying on my marks incised on the walls to guide me. Sure enough, a few days after her first visit, they stopped lowering food. I still received the same bowl of muddy water, but no food.

It didn't matter of course. I had more than enough food by now. Phaedra had even supplied me with some fresh clothing and warm blankets. For the first time during my imprisonment within the labyrinth, I was warm and comfortable.

I had companionship too. Glaucus would snuggle under my blankets, and we slept together in cozy contentment. Phaedra visited twice more. I looked forward to seeing her like a flower looks for the sun. She brought light and happiness into my world. Thanks to her, even in that terrible place, I was almost as happy as I'd ever been.

Her last visit, however, brought news that I both dreaded and hoped for.

"The Athenians will arrive in two days," she said, as we lay on my straw bed, caressing each other. We could no longer kiss of course, but at least I could touch her. "Are you ready, Asterion?"

I shrugged casually. "Of course. I don't have to do much now, do I?"

She laughed and swatted at me playfully. "Take this seriously, Asterion. You cannot afford to make a mistake; otherwise, all is lost. Tell me what you plan to do."

"I will meet them at the trapdoor and escort them to the secret passage."

"It's not that easy, you dullard. You'll have to appear as a beast; otherwise, the guards will suspect something is wrong. Roar at the tributes. Make them scared. Look hungry and deranged. Do not take the light. Remember, the guards will be watching closely."

"But what happens if I scare the Athenians?" I asked.

"Better that than to have our ruse uncovered," said Phaedra. "You have a part to play. Play it well."

"As do you," I countered. "Have you decided how you are going to get them out?"

"I have," said Phaedra. "But I won't tell you just yet. A woman is entitled to her little secrets."

I laughed. It felt good to produce a happy sound in such a dreadful place used to the sounds of misery and despair. I had spent far too long wallowing in misery and madness. "Shall I wait for you or just send them through?"

"I will try to meet you at the entrance. Otherwise, you may accidentally send them outside during broad daylight. I will wait for the cover of darkness. If I cannot sneak away—which is likely—I will send someone else in my place."

"Who?" I asked, trying to think of someone who Phaedra could trust.

"Who else but our brothers?" asked Phaedra.

Of course. I hadn't thought of that. From what Phaedra had told me, it would probably have been safer to send them in the first place. Catreus and Deucalion were not guarded or watched as closely as Phaedra.

"I will watch for them," I promised.

"Make sure you do," said Phaedra. "Now, come lie down with me and hold me in your arms. We don't have much time. I may not see you again for some time."

I hardly needed to be told again. I did what I was told without protest. Phaedra was right. We had to make the most of our time.

"Did you know you are called Minotaur now?" asked

Phaedra suddenly, breaking the comfortable silence.

No I didn't. "What?" I said, sitting up.

"In Greece they are calling you Minotaur. The bull of Minos. I thought you should know."

"So I'm not Asterion anymore?" I asked, feeling my anger rise.

Phaedra pulled me down to her again. "You will always be my Asterion. I guess that people need to put a name to their fears. Asterion just wasn't that name. I quite like it. Minotaur," she said, savoring the word. "It's got a nice ring to it."

"I'm not sure I agree with you," I replied, trying to let go of my anger. "It makes me a beast, which I'm clearly not."

"Of course you're not," said Phaedra soothingly. "But that reputation will keep you safe down here. Even the people of Crete have started using it."

I was still unconvinced. I knew Minos had probably come up with the name and encouraged its use. I resented any association with him.

"I have something for you," said Phaedra suddenly, trying to change the subject, extracting herself from my embrace and sitting up. She opened up her satchel and brought forth some flowers. They were slightly crushed, but I knew what they were as soon as she brought them forth.

They were sea daffodils, a beautiful white flower found all along the coast of Crete. The damp earth smell of the labyrinth was suddenly overwhelmed by their sweet, heady perfume.

"Happy birthday," she said simply.

My birthday? Was it my birthday? I had no idea. Phaedra obviously had a much better grasp of time than I. That meant I was now seventeen. I would never have guessed that I would spend my birthday in such a place. Who would've?

My initial reaction was to try and kiss Phaedra, but that was impossible. I had to settle for several birthday kisses Phaedra planted on my neck.

"Thank you," I said finally. The flowers were the most beautiful gift anyone had given me. They reminded me of the happy times Phaedra and I had spent on the shores of Crete. Now, every time I smell the perfume of the sea daffodil, I think of that moment Phaedra and I shared deep in the labyrinth.

I felt so happy then which is why I always keep sea daffodils on my window sill. To remind me of Phaedra and the love and comfort she brought me when I needed them the most.

Ω

The Athenians arrived two days later. I positioned myself with some care, two twists of the maze away from the trapdoor.

I decided not to wait directly under the trapdoor for a variety of reasons. The first—I didn't want the guards to get a good look at me. If they did, they'd quickly realize that I wasn't starving. Secondly, I didn't want the Athenians to panic. I could imagine the bedlam. If the unfortunate tributes caught sight of me too soon, anything could happen. I was all too conscious of my appearance, especially with the bull mask fixed permanently in place. It would be best to give them a little time to adjust to their predicament and let their initial terror diminish.

Finally, I wasn't sure how I felt about all this. Other than

Phaedra, I had been all alone for three months. I couldn't really predict how I was going to react. I wanted to observe the intruders and become comfortable with their presence first.

Looking back now, it was a little comical to think that I regarded others coming into my labyrinth as intruders. I guess I felt slightly possessive of the place. It had become my home, and I was about to have unwelcome guests. Slightly irrational I know, but there you have it.

I heard their screams long before they reached the trapdoor. Shortly after that, the thud of flesh hitting rock echoed about the labyrinth. More cries. More sounds of bodies being thrown down the trapdoor. It sounded like the guards were fairly ruthless, barely allowing any time for each victim to get out of the way before another body toppled down.

Then, I heard the sounds of the trapdoor being shut and the click as the bolt was drawn across. More screams. Pleading. I wondered if I had sounded like that and realized that I probably had.

Eventually, the screams became sobs, the sobs gradually turning into whispered conversation. I gathered from the fragmented voices I heard that they were trying to decide what to do. Most sounded like they wanted to stay put. A few brave souls voted for exploration.

Now that they had settled a little, it was time to put on a show. I didn't relish this, but Phaedra had insisted. I needed to be convincing. Even though the trapdoor was closed, I knew the guards would be watching and listening. Probably Minos as well, relishing each moment.

I opened my mouth and bellowed. The noise echoed away into the labyrinth and was met by complete silence. I could imagine the fourteen Athenian tributes, shocked and frozen, their imaginations running wild. Fated to be eaten by Minotaur, the bull of Minos. I can't even begin to imagine how terrified they must have felt.

Very few, if any, remembered the name Asterion. It was around this time, I believe, that any mention of my previous association with Theseus was stricken from the historical record. The adventures we had together were changed. Theseus had triumphed alone. He never had help from his good friend Asterion.

I liked to think Theseus had no hand in this, and I suspect that I was probably right. The legend of Minotaur had taken on a life of its own, much like the adventures of Theseus before he arrived in Athens. Once people started obsessing over the stories, facts become almost obsolete. Oddly enough, the truth was actually stranger than fiction. But people didn't want the truth. They wanted to believe in heroes and monsters. Theseus was the hero and I the monster. It made their simple, uneventful lives easier to understand, easier to bear.

I understood how they felt. I just didn't like it.

I waited a few more moments, listening as the hysterical cries started up once more. And then I made my move.

I emerged from behind one of the walls in the maze. By now, the young tributes' eyes had adjusted sufficiently for them to make out that someone or something was standing there. The limestone walls glowed with enough luminescence for them to see that much at least. They knew that Minotaur had come for them. The beast of the labyrinth. They were convinced I was going to eat them.

Almost all did exactly what I thought they would. These

were the ones that had resigned themselves to death. They huddled together on the cold stone floor, wretched, frozen in terror. At least four ran for their lives as I'd intended. That wasn't a problem. Actually, I'd hoped that all would do that. For our ruse to work, I could hardly eat the Athenians in plain sight of the guards. Better for them to run away. The guards' imaginations would do the rest.

I had planned to just get closer and closer and force them to move, to flee before me. I knew they would eventually, and then it would be a relatively simple matter of rounding them up.

Unfortunately, they had two heroes amongst them. I, being a hero myself, fully understood their drives and motives. I respected them, I could relate. I also hated them for their stupidity.

It was just light enough for them to attack me without the risk of running into one of the walls. They didn't have weapons of course, but fear lent them strength. The two youths charged at me without tactics.

My eyes were much more accustomed to the darkness than theirs. It gave me an advantage. Combined with my newly returned strength, they stood no chance. To their credit, it didn't deter them at all. They must have been scared. Who wouldn't be? I stood head and shoulders above them, and my helmet and bull mask, only barely visible, must have been terrible to behold.

Both tried to close with me, instinctively realizing that it was their only hope. I punched the first one who reached me. Boxing, like wrestling, had always been one of my stronger skills. I wasn't very fast, but I was immensely powerful with a reach greater than any other man. My fist hammered into his face, throwing him off his feet. He bounced off a nearby wall and slumped to the ground, absolutely still. I was a little dismayed by this, hoping that I hadn't killed him. I really shouldn't have hit him so hard.

In hindsight, I should've tried to do something else. Wrestle him perhaps? But then again, wrestling was only effective against one man. When fighting multiple opponents, especially unarmed, it was better to strike hard and fast, removing them from the fight as soon as possible. Paris told me that.

Distracted, I turned my attention to my second attacker.

As I've mentioned several times already, I was not the fastest of fighters. My time in the labyrinth had not served to hone my reflexes either. I was sluggish. My attacker, as young as, or perhaps younger, than I, was much fleeter of foot, even hampered by the darkness. He was also driven by the will to survive, which makes any man a dangerous animal.

I had intended to stop his attack with another punch, but I was too late for that. He was already inside my swing. He punched low, connecting with my naked stomach. I reacted completely normally, doing what any other person would do in that situation. I stooped suddenly in pain. The movement forced my head downwards.

One of my horns plunged straight into my attacker's eye. Horrified, I picked him up off the ground with both hands, intending to remove the horn as gently as possible. To any onlooker, it must have been a terrible sight. A young man impaled and lifted into the air by a great beast. Of course, he struggled mightily, his struggles only driving the horn even deeper. By the time I set him on the ground, he was already dead. I was absolutely devastated. Not only had I killed a man by accident, but I had done it in almost the same manner as I had killed Androgeus.

Feeling sick, I turned to those Athenians still huddled before me. I put my hands out, placating, grasping for the words to reassure them. Nothing came out of my mouth. There was nothing I could have said. They had just witnessed me smashing one of their friends into a wall and then skewering the other. They were probably expecting me to immediately start feasting on the bodies.

It was the catalyst required to finally make them move, eventually doing what I had intended for them to do all along. The irony didn't escape me.

They fled, screaming, into the cold dark embrace of the labyrinth.

CHAPTER 15

"I see," said Ovid, nodding his head slowly. "I understand." He did—with absolute certainty. As Ast had related the events, Ovid had pictured them in his mind, even as he furiously scribbled. He understood exactly how everything had unfolded—and why. Human nature being what it was, it couldn't have happened differently.

Ovid was experienced enough to know that people acted unpredictably when scared. Imagined terrors are often worse that actual ones. How terrible for this man to have killed—entirely by accident—one of the people he was trying to save. It was enough to haunt you for the rest of your days. He couldn't begin to imagine what Ast had gone through. If he was being honest with himself though, he realized that he was quite relieved that Ast had never eaten people. If that were the case, Ovid probably would've fled.

"Don't blame yourself," said Ovid, in what he hoped were reassuring tones. "It's not your fault."

Ast sighed wearily. "I know that, but it's poor consolation. I think that if I had somehow acted differently, it wouldn't have ended in tragedy."

"I hardly see what you could've done differently," said Ovid, eyeing the man with growing sympathy. He took a sip of wine. There wasn't much left now. He was even considering rationing himself, which was almost unthinkable. A thought suddenly occurred to him.

"Couldn't you have somehow got out the trapdoor?" he asked.

"Don't you think I tried that?" said Ast, a note of irritation in his voice. "Several times I waited in the shadows for the rope to be lowered with my water. Once, I even managed to grab it. They simply cut it before I could climb. There was no other way to reach the trapdoor."

"What about levering some of the stone blocks out of the walls, stacking them and using them as a ladder?" asked Ovid. He knew it as soon as the words emerged out of his mouth that it was a foolish question, but he was tired and drunk. That combination made him incautious.

"Would you like me to finish my story, or are you just going to keep bombarding me with stupid questions all night?" snapped Ast.

"Please," said Ovid, making a gracious gesture. "Be my guest. I am sorry if my quest for the truth irritates you."

Ast stared at him. Many men would've flinched from that stare, but not Ovid. He was feeling brave now. Reckless. Ovid met the stare and then smiled. To his surprise, Ast smiled back.

"I believe I have chosen wisely," said Ast. "If anyone has the courage to reveal the truth, it is you. Would you like to hear more?"

Suppressing a sudden desire to laugh hysterically, Ovid nodded and bent his head, quill poised.

Ω

"So what are we supposed to do now?" asked Catreus.

"Don't ask me," I said shrugging wearily. "I suppose we could herd them like cattle." I was tired, having spent the last few hours unsuccessfully trying to round up the Athenians. It was like trying to corner scared cats. Not that I blamed them. I was feeling frustrated and more than a little horrified by the turn of events.

"We'll have to light both … " said Deucalion.

" … lamps, obviously," said Catreus. The twins exchanged knowing glances.

Which was fine. My half-brothers had seen fit to bring only one lamp with them, to guide the Athenians through the passage. Phaedra had given them explicit instructions, instructions that now were completely irrelevant.

We sat in my small bedchamber in the maze, discussing our options around the light of my own precious lamp. They had appeared an hour earlier, explaining that they had come in Phaedra's stead. I had been waiting at the entrance to the secret passage for at least double that time, pacing impatiently. I had a rough idea when it was night outside, but my calculations were often a few hours out.

My own efforts to round up the Athenians had come to nothing. Every time they saw me, they screamed and fled in terror. On a couple of occasions, I'd had an opportunity to corner one or two of them but hadn't, dreading a repeat of the earlier encounter. Thankfully, when I'd returned to the place below the trapdoor, the body of the one I had punched was gone. I assumed he still lived. The dead youth was still there, lying in a cooling pool of his own blood.

Phaedra was now too carefully watched to chance another venture into the maze. Although disappointed, it was nice to see my younger brothers. The twins had become men during my absence. From recollection, they might have been fifteen or perhaps sixteen at the time.

"I don't know if you should ... " said Catreus.

" ... come. Perhaps you should stay right here," continued Deucalion. "They'll only run again if they see you. Probably can't ... "

" ... blame them. And we only have two lamps," finished Catreus.

"Fine," I muttered. I knew it made sense, but I wanted to help, to fix this debacle. "Make sure you stay away from the trapdoor. If the guards see your light, they'll know something is wrong. Remember, use the scratches on the walls to guide you."

In the two days prior to the arrival of the Athenian tributes, I had extended my scratch system. In theory, Catreus and Deucalion could use it to guide them to the secret passage from anywhere in the maze. In practice, I knew they would probably get lost. It worked for me, but I was much more familiar with the maze than anyone else.

It didn't matter that much though. Even if they got completely lost, hopefully by then they would have the Athenians in tow. Then I could guide everyone out, with Catreus and Deucalion at my side to reassure the prisoners that I wasn't about to eat them.

"Right ... " said Catreus, standing.

"What are we waiting for?" asked Deucalion, finishing his sentence for him.

I left them to it, having to content myself with sitting patiently in the relative darkness. Of course, I couldn't sit still. I heard all sorts of commotion within the labyrinth as Catreus and Deucalion attempted to corner the terrified tributes. The gods only know what the labyrinth guards thought was happening below their feet.

Eventually, I could bear it no longer. I reasoned that as long as I stayed outside of the light, no one would be the wiser. I could even help, driving any stragglers toward my half-brothers. I just prayed to Poseidon that I wouldn't encounter any more heroes.

Fortunately, the survivors were too scared to risk confronting me again. If they caught any glimpse of me, they immediately fled. I did my best, trying to herd them in the direction of my brothers or toward the escape tunnel. I was only partially successful.

Our plan had been relatively simple, and on the face of it, it should have worked. But, what I have discovered over the centuries is that few things go to plan. What should have been over in a matter of hours actually took several days.

Catreus and Deucalion had to return to the outside world

on a number of occasions during the operation. They would arouse too much suspicion if they weren't seen around the palace for all that time. Not only that, but they ran out of food, water, and oil for the lamps and had to return for supplies.

Catreus got lost twice. Deucalion three times. On one occasion, he even dropped his oil lamp and couldn't relight it. Where possible, I tried to guide them with my voice rather than risk frightening their charges with my presence.

They brought the tributes back to the escape tunnel in ones or twos. It became impossible to try and bring back more than that at a time. Once either of them had one or two Athenians, they would guide them through the escape tunnel and out into the world. The rescued youths often had to wait until it was dark enough to venture outside. I don't know what my brothers did with them and never got an opportunity to ask. Fortunately, none of the Athenians were of heroic proportions, and all managed to fit through the tunnel.

I tried to remain hidden all that time. It just became too difficult otherwise. I didn't have a light, and I resented this, but I was much more accustomed to the darkness than any of the others.

It was a simple matter to know how many remained in the labyrinth. Fourteen had arrived, one was dead, so thirteen remained. When Catreus and Deucalion had eventually found twelve, we knew we were close to the finish line. All three of us were exhausted by that point, having had very little sleep during the entire process.

The last youth proved almost impossible to track down. I suspected it was the heroic tribute who had attacked me. The one I had punched. Given that none of the others sported a bruised face, it made sense that it was him.

The three of us eventually cornered him. Catreus and Deucalion tried to reason with him, but he was past that point. The look in his eyes was feral. Once again, he displayed his heroic tendencies, attacking me with great ferocity even though he must have been more exhausted than the three of us, not to mention hungry. We subdued him and carried him kicking and screaming to the escape tunnel. It wasn't until we actually forced him into the tunnel that he began to calm down.

I wished I'd learnt his name. It is not very often you encounter such bravery, even as foolish and misplaced as his was.

Catreus and Deucalion followed him out but not before both my brothers hugged me.

"It will be your turn … " said Catreus.

" … one day. Not too far distant," said Deucalion.

I thanked them, and then, finally, I was once again alone in the labyrinth. I almost experienced a sense of relief that I had the place to myself once more. I realized that I was becoming comfortable being by myself. That I liked my own company. That I liked being alone.

I retired to my bed of straw. I must have slept for many hours or possibly even days. Eventually, noise intruded into my consciousness. Through my foggy, sleep filled head, the noise finally registered. It was the sound of footsteps and voices.

Once again, the labyrinth had intruders.

Ω

I didn't dare light my lamp. As silently as possible, I moved toward the sounds. It sounded like several people but it was hard to pinpoint their location due to the echoes that bounced and rebounded off the walls.

Eventually, I realized where the noises were coming from. In the direction of the trapdoor. Cautiously, I made my way toward them. At first, I thought perhaps my brothers and I must have miscounted. One or two of the Athenians were still in the maze. And then I remembered how thorough we were. With all our checking and rechecking, there was no way we could've made a mistake. It wasn't Phaedra either. Couldn't be Phaedra. If it were her, she would have found me in my bedchamber. She knew where it was almost as well as I did. I ruled out my brothers for the same reason.

And then there was the feeling I got from the labyrinth. I have never spoken of this, and probably will never speak of it again, but I feel this is the right time to mention it. I was the labyrinth's first and only true prisoner. We were connected. It was part of me, and I was part of it, especially given the length of time I spent within its confines. Somehow, I knew when I was alone within it, just as I knew when there were intruders. Just like now.

If they weren't the tributes, then there was only one other possibility: guards. Minos's guards.

As I got closer to the location of the trapdoor, I knew I was right. Despite Phaedra's certainty that they would never enter the labyrinth, they were here. I knew why they were here too. They were looking for me.

Minos wanted confirmation of my descent into madness and cannibalism. He'd probably had to threaten or bribe the guards, but regardless of how he'd done it, guards were now in my home, and they were unwelcome.

There were four of them, all holding oil lamps that they waved fearfully about the place, expecting the shadows to come alive at any moment. In their free hands, three carried drawn swords. One had a club grasped firmly in both hands. Clearly, they weren't about to take any chances.

I kept far back in the shadows, knowing the labyrinth well enough to find places where I could observe them easily without being observed in turn.

"Here," shouted one of the guards excitedly.

The three other guards hastened over to examine what he had found. It was the dead body of the Athenian youth I had killed. I don't know why they didn't find him straight away. They must have explored in a different direction first.

"He did for him alright," said one of the men. "You can see the where the horn went right into his eye. Nasty."

"What's that moving?" said one of the others in a voice that had gone high with fear, pointing toward the corpse.

All four guards bent down, bringing their lamps closer to better inspect the body. Unable to restrain my curiosity, I edged toward them.

"Just a rat," said one of them disgustedly. "A fat one too."

He bent down and grasped a squealing black shape in one hand.

Even in the uncertain flickering light, I recognized the rat immediately. Only one rat I had encountered in the maze was that fat. Only one rat I had seen had a coat that glistened with good health.

It was Glaucus.

My heart skipped a beat. I felt fear. Fear for my friend. I knew why Glaucus was on the corpse. Sometimes, Glaucus would accompany me on my wanderings about the labyrinth, usually perched on my shoulder. These wanderings would often take hours so occasionally I would take a snack for both of us. With nowhere else to put it, I would tuck scraps of food into the top of my loincloth. Glaucus knew that I kept my food there. He'd been ransacking the corpse looking for treats.

The guard held Glaucus up for the others to see. They laughed as he squirmed desperately, trying to win his freedom. The guard grasped Glaucus in both hands and twisted viciously. I heard a sharp crack, and then Glaucus's body went limp. The guard tossed him casually to the ground. All four guards laughed again.

The sound of Glaucus's spine snapping also severed my links to sanity. The bond between my rational intelligent mind and my animal instincts was gone. For a moment, only the beast remained. I truly became the Minotaur.

With a bestial roar that shook the walls, I charged. All tactics forgotten. There was only my rage. It was the only time in my life that I lost complete control, and I am still ashamed of it.

Heedless of their swords, I waded into them. My roar had frozen the guards in terror. For a moment, they were too shaken to move. I picked the one who had killed Glaucus. I grabbed him and slung him over my shoulders, snapping his back much the same way as he had done to Glaucus.

The death provided an incentive for the others. Motivated by survival, they attacked, slashing, swinging, and stabbing at me with their weapons. I didn't care. Several times, the blades bit home, but I hardly felt them. The wielder of the club aimed for my head, but the blow bounced off my helmet. I didn't even feel it. It was almost like my body belonged to someone or something else.

I picked up one of the other guards and broke his neck. The third, I punched so hard he was dead before he hit the ground. The fourth, well the fourth did the only thing he could. He ran.

I charged after him but fear had given him wings. A rope, the same rope the guards had once used to lower my food, was still dangling from the trapdoor. The guard reached it and scrambled up it faster than I would've believed. The rope was quickly pulled up before I could reach it.

I stood underneath the trapdoor and vented my rage, screaming and roaring. I have no idea how long I stood there. Eventually, some semblance of sanity returned, and I was overwhelmed with sudden fatigue and loss. I returned to where the bodies of the three guards and the poor Athenian youth lay. Gently, reverently, I gathered the tiny dead body of my friend Glaucus to my breast.

I knelt there for a long time, gently rocking back and forth, crooning to Glaucus, telling him over and over again that I was sorry. That I would never forget him. It seems absurd, I know, to be so grief stricken over a rat of all things. You have to remember that Glaucus was my only companion and friend for months while I was trapped in the darkness. I loved him unconditionally.

Cradling his tiny broken body, I returned to my bedchamber. I lay down and curled into a fetal position, tucking his slowly cooling corpse next to mine and closed my eyes, suddenly overcome with exhaustion. It was just like the way we used to huddle together before we had blankets to warm us.

Several days later, that was how Phaedra found me.

Ω

Phaedra told me later that I almost died. She nursed me for two weeks. When she wasn't able to, she sent my brothers. I don't remember any of it, wracked as I was with feverish dreams, coated in sweat.

I dreamt of Androgeus lying dead in my arms. My rat Glaucus was there too, drowned in Androgeus's blood. Kyon, dead on the sacrificial altar. The faces of the Athenian youth, and the guards I had killed haunted me. There were other faces too. It seemed that every man I had killed decided to pay me a visit.

The wounds I had suffered were deep, almost beyond anyone's ability to heal. Phaedra did her best to sew the worst of them up with catgut, but she confessed later that she despaired and had resigned herself to my inevitable death. I suspect it was only my innate strength and perhaps the favor of Poseidon himself that saved me.

Eventually, I recovered from the fever and woke to find myself alone in the darkness. I fumbled around and managed to light my lamp after several failed attempts. The sudden light stung my eyes, but I finally oriented myself. I realized where I was. I found some food and water that Phaedra had set beside me. My stomach gurgled alarmingly, so I contented myself with the water only.

By the time Phaedra returned three days later, I was on my feet, weak as a newly weaned baby but well on the road to recovery.

"What did you do with Glaucus?" I asked as she fussed around me.

I could tell she was confused. "Glaucus? Oh, your rat. I took him outside and buried him."

At first, I was angry that she had touched him, but I knew I was being irrational. Phaedra knew of my attachment to my rat. She hadn't meant any offense. I suppose I had wanted to be the one to bury him, but I knew that was impossible here in the labyrinth.

"I thought you'd squashed him. You did thrash around a lot," she said.

"No," I said sadly. "I didn't squash him."

She looked at me strangely but didn't ask how Glaucus had died, and I was in no mood to explain.

She told me to sit so she could examine my wounds. "Do you want to tell me what happened?" she asked gently.

I thought about telling her, but I couldn't bring myself. I doubt whether she or anyone else would understand my actions. That I had killed three men over a rat.

"The guards attacked me," I said finally.

"But why?" asked Phaedra, evidently confused.

"Out of fear," I lied.

"Strange," said Phaedra. "I wonder why they were in the labyrinth in the first place?"

"They wanted to see the body," I said.

"The body? You mean the poor Athenian boy?" She nodded slowly as understanding dawned. "They wanted to know whether you had eaten him. Well, they are destined to be disappointed. You will never become like that, Asterion. I know you won't."

I had my doubts. I had experienced full-blown madness. I wasn't sure exactly what I was capable of at that moment.

"Everyone's talking about it, though," said Phaedra.

"What? About how the beast of the labyrinth killed some poor innocent guards?" I asked angrily. "Trust me, they weren't innocent."

"I'm not sure why you're getting angry, Asterion. It seems simple enough. They attacked you. You defended yourself. I understand."

"No, I don't think you understand," I said, beginning to feel more sad than angry. I think my sadness stemmed from the fact that Phaedra didn't know me as well as she used to. The old Phaedra would've known something else was wrong and questioned me until she got to the bottom of it. But then it wasn't Phaedra who had changed, was it? It was me.

Phaedra shook her head, frustrated. "Regardless of whether I understand or not. Regardless of what really happened, you know I love you, Asterion. I will always love you, no matter what." She crept toward me as if I was some animal she didn't want to startle and wrapped her arms around my waist.

I flinched as her hands touched some of my wounds. I didn't know what to do at first. I felt somehow unworthy of her affections and kept my hands at my side. Slowly though, her arms began to tighten around my waist. I couldn't resist. I wrapped her in an embrace and began to cry, letting out the grief I felt over the death of Glaucus.

If my tears confused Phaedra, she didn't show it. She

didn't speak, content to stay in my arms. We held each other for a long time, but all good things, as they say, must end.

Change, blown by the winds of the Aegean and the Cretan sea, was coming.

CHAPTER 16

A new phase of my life began. I had almost everything I needed in the labyrinth. Everything but companionship. I missed Glaucus terribly. In some ways, I almost missed him more than Kyon or even Androgeus, but I think that is probably understandable. Glaucus was there for me during the most trying period of my life. I felt his absence like a part of me had been severed. It was especially difficult during the periods where I slept. I often woke up expecting him to be there and cried when he wasn't. I thought about befriending another rat but I didn't want to betray Glaucus's memory.

Phaedra visited as often as she could, which of course wasn't often enough for my liking. Catreus and Deucalion came too, often making me laugh with tales of their adventures. Phaedra brought more flowers, and my brothers brought papyrus, quill, and ink, which I used to write down some of my thoughts and experiences.

Months passed. The seasons, unremarked upon in that dark place, flowed from one into the next. My bedchamber became almost cluttered. Phaedra and my brothers had even managed to bring furniture into the labyrinth, breaking it down and then reassembling it once it was through the secret passage. I now had two stools and several shelves that were lined with my writing implements, wads of papyrus covered with the scrawl of mine and other's thoughts, vases filled with wild flowers, and other oddments that were brought below to remind me that the world still existed above.

Minos must have calculated that my food sources would have been depleted. He reinstated my feeding program, and I was careful to remove every scrap lowered from the basket, even though I did not touch the disgusting food offered.

Gradually, the pain of Glaucus's death diminished. My love and bond with Phaedra grew as if to compensate. So much so that her absence brought almost physical pain. I took to counting the days until we were together. If she returned later than she had promised, I began to fret.

This prompted me to continue work on widening the tunnel. I began to obsess, believing that Phaedra would never return. I had to widen the tunnel, not necessarily to escape, but to ensure that I would be able to see her again. If Phaedra didn't return, I would venture outside and bring her to me. This, I realize, sounds like madness. If I widened the tunnel sufficiently for me to get out to see her, it was obviously enough for me to escape the labyrinth altogether.

I didn't really see it like that though. Despite my earlier brush with madness, I suspect that my mind had still been deeply affected by my experiences. I began to view the labyrinth as my home. I didn't really want to leave. I was safe within its embrace.

The tunneling itself was conducted with a great deal of caution. I was only too conscious of the noise of my chisel against rock. I had no real fear of the guards once again entering the maze. The surviving guard had ensured that, telling everyone who would listen of the horrendous monster that now dwelt inside. But I had no illusions that the sound of tunneling would not bring some form of armed response. It would have to. Now that I was such a fearsome monster, they would not risk the chance that I might escape.

As a result, my labors were incredibly slow. I would gently chisel a small piece of limestone away and then stop to listen. Of course, in order to dig further, I had to destroy the cleverly concealed hatch, but I no longer cared a fig about that. I actually welcomed the task. It gave me something to do. There was only so much exercising, reading, and writing I could do. I still wandered the labyrinth at times, pretending that Glaucus was still with me. I talked to him, often emitting noises that were probably more like grunts or roars than actual words. If Glaucus's ghost could have spoken, he would've told me I was mad.

Then came the day when Phaedra brought more unexpected news.

"Asterion," she said softly. "I have to go away for a few weeks." Phaedra often spoke to me softly now. I think she realized that my mental state was a little fragile.

"Why?" I demanded. "You can't. Who's going to keep me company? What about my food?"

She took my hand and stroked it, trying to soothe me. "Catreus and Deucalion will still be here. They will look after your needs."

"But where are you going?" I asked, unsuccessfully trying not to sound too pitiful.

"To Athens. Father and Ariadne are going with me."

"Why?" I asked, confused. Perhaps Phaedra had decided to marry Theseus after all? I felt an irrational surge of betrayal and anger.

"Hush, Asterion. It's all right. We are going to escort the new tributes here." If Phaedra had been able to see my face, she would've known how shocked I was by this news. But Phaedra did know me well, despite my doubts. She knew I was wrestling with the knowledge that it had been another year. Another year in the labyrinth.

"Yes," she said, as if reading my mind. "It has almost been a year since the last tributes were sent. But this year, there will be one amongst them who is special."

"Special?" I asked. "How?"

"This one is the prince of Athens. Your friend, Theseus, has insisted that he be among the tributes."

I was absolutely stunned by this news. If I hadn't already been sitting down, I would've staggered.

"Why would Theseus willingly volunteer?" I asked shakily.

"For you," said Phaedra simply.

"How do you know this?" I asked hotly. "What makes you think Theseus isn't coming for my blood?"

"Answer you own question, Asterion," said Phaedra, choosing her words carefully. "You know him better than any.

251

Do you really think Theseus is coming to kill you?"

I thought about this. Theseus and I had been through a lot together. We had had our disagreements, sure, but we were friends, comrades. Brothers in arms. Possibly brothers in the real sense too if it were true that Poseidon was our father. I knew in my heart that even though Theseus could be a cold-hearted killer, he only killed those who warranted death. Even at my lowest, wallowing in self-doubt and loathing, I knew I didn't deserve to die by his hand. I also knew that Theseus could never bring himself to kill me, unless he truly believed that I had become a monster.

"No," I said finally, knowing that it was true.

"Then," said Phaedra, "the only other solution is that he is coming to rescue you. Don't worry, Asterion. I will talk to him during the voyage. Together we will find a solution."

I trusted Phaedra, just as I trusted Theseus. I had no doubt that they would come up with a plan. Theseus was a man of action—not of thought—but Phaedra amply made up for his shortcomings. They would make a good combination, something that once again began to churn my feelings of jealousy.

Even reassured by Phaedra, I still had my doubts. Perhaps Theseus was coming to kill me. Maybe his father had forced him to do it. What then? I guess I would have to face him when the time came. And that time was coming soon. Theseus was coming to Crete.

He was coming, so everyone else believed, to slay the dreaded Minotaur. To kill the beast. To kill me.

Oddly, despite these thoughts, I was looking forward to seeing him again.

Ω

Phaedra, Minos, and Ariadne left on their fateful trip to Athens. I remained in the Labyrinth. Where else would I be? It's not like I could go anywhere.

The weeks passed slowly, agonizingly slowly. My birthday passed without notice. Phaedra was not around to celebrate the occasion with me, and I was unaware in any case. I was eighteen now, not that I knew it.

Catreus and Deucalion kept me company whenever possible. I continued work on the escape tunnel, more to keep myself occupied than for any other reason. I felt confident that the tunnel would no longer be needed once Theseus arrived. Somehow, Theseus would defeat Minos and his guards and pull me out through the trapdoor. I doubted whether any of the tributes would even be lowered into the labyrinth. Theseus would have the palace under his control long before then. He was, after all, a hero.

Years later, Phaedra told me of their journey back from Athens. How Ariadne fawned over Theseus, and how he basically ignored her advances. Phaedra and Theseus spent as much time as they could together without arousing suspicion. Time they used to finalize their plans. She would take water to him where he was chained in the hold of the ship and loiter for as long as she dared.

Other than that, the voyage was largely uneventful. Some poets decided embellishment was necessary, that the sea voyage can't have been without some adventure. I've read stories of how Theseus encountered one of the Nereids, the daughters of the sea god Nereus. The only thing Phaedra said they encountered was a whale that almost sank the ship.

Then there was the story about Minos making advances toward one of the Athenian maidens and how Theseus took offence. Apparently, Theseus sprang to her defense, claiming it was his right as a son of Poseidon. Just how you spring to someone's defense when you are chained up in the hold is a mystery to me.

Then, so the stories go, Minos asked Theseus to prove his divine origins. He threw his signet ring overboard and challenged Theseus to find it, knowing it was an impossible task without Poseidon's aid. Theseus, of course, emerged triumphant from the water of the Cretan sea. Not only did he have Minos's ring but also a jeweled crown given to him by one of the Nereids.

Phaedra, who was actually there, told me that the only person who went overboard was one of the sailors, who was thrown into the sea on Minos's command for being drunk. And the only thing that came out of the sea was a large chunk of seaweed that had become entangled in the anchor.

But of course the heroic tales surrounding Theseus continued to grow. Much like my growing reputation as a fearsome flesh-eating monster that had to be killed at all costs.

Truth often suffers for the sake of entertainment.

Ω

The noises above told me that the labyrinth was once again about to receive some reluctant guests.

If I had hoped that Theseus might somehow take over the palace, that hope was shattered when the first of the tributes was dropped unceremoniously from the trapdoor.

Alerted by the noise, I had taken the same position as I had when the first tributes arrived a year earlier. The memories of that event still haunted me. I was in no hurry to repeat past mistakes.

This time, I was content to wait. As I watched each body fall into my realm, a plan began to take shape. Theseus would seek me out or I would find him. Together, we would take the other tributes and help them to escape through the secret tunnel. Then Theseus would help me complete the widening of the tunnel. Together, we would emerge into the starlight. I would gather Phaedra in my arms, and the three of us would take over one of the ships nestling in the harbor by force.

Then, we would set sail for Athens and return to that city in triumph. I would marry Phaedra and Theseus could marry Ariadne, if he wanted. I wouldn't have been surprised if he decided not to. Couldn't blame him really. I don't think anyone really wanted to marry Ariadne.

Calmed by these comforting thoughts, I settled down onto my haunches.

Finally, the last of the tributes was thrown into the labyrinth. Events first unfolded exactly as they had done previously. Most of them huddled on the rock floor, weeping uncontrollably. Several of the young men stood, trying unsuccessfully to control their fear.

Even in the darkness, I thought I recognized one of them

by his bearing. Proud, upright, unmoving. He was standing a little apart from the others and, unlike them, seemed unaffected by fear. Even though I couldn't see his face, I knew it must be Theseus.

I didn't dare approach for fear of the reception I'd receive from the others. Other than Theseus, there was probably at least one other hero amongst them, a youth eager to make a name for himself, keen to impress the young women. Possibly even someone who was just brave. Or stupid.

I realized that I would have to bide my time. Even as I watched from the darkness, I saw several other youths begin to gather around Theseus. He was a prince and their leader. Someone they trusted. A hero whose fame had spread all across Greece. If anyone could save them from Minotaur, it was Theseus. I saw him offer comfort, kneeling down to embrace those who were more distraught than others.

This, I realized, would be more difficult than I had anticipated. The other youths would be reluctant to become parted from Theseus. It would not be easy to get him alone.

I thought furiously. If I bellowed and charged, I would probably be attacked by any heroes amongst them. Possibly Theseus himself if he thought I was a threat to the others. But, if all the others decided to flee, Theseus would be left alone, and we would be free to talk.

I decided to abandon that idea as too risky. There was too much that could go wrong, and if anything went wrong in that place, it often led to death. I could call out, asking Theseus to move away from the others and come talk to me. But that too was fraught with risk. His companions would probably not allow Theseus out of their sight. What if Theseus believed it to be a trap and decided to attack me? Perhaps while he was talking to me, the other brave members of the tribute might plan a surprise attack. I know this sounds paranoid but after my long imprisonment, my mind played tricks on me.

I had no option other than to wait. They would fall asleep soon, exhausted by their long journey from Athens and the expense of so many tiring emotions. I would creep up on Theseus, tap him on the shoulder, and lead him back to my bedchamber. Or something like that.

It was a good plan, I thought. I began to feel my spirits rise, confident that things would work out, content to watch and rest. Time for action would come soon, and I would need all my strength for the trials that awaited me.

Ω

Several hours passed before the Athenian tributes actually settled down and slept. Understandably, none of them had decided to investigate the rest of the labyrinth. Knowing Theseus, I suspected that he had cautioned them to stay where they were. This suited me just fine. I actually heard him say to the others that he would stand watch. Even better.

I watched them carefully, especially the one I suspected was Theseus. I noted where he lay down with his back propped against a rock wall. Luckily, he was a little removed from the others, but I had no idea whether he was asleep or not. I decided that it would be foolish to creep up on him. Instead, when I was reasonably confident that everyone was asleep, I picked up a handful of small limestone rocks.

My intention was to hit Theseus with a rock, get his attention, and lure him to where I crouched in the dark. It sounds simple, but I had discovered through experience that the best plans often are.

I threw the first rock. It was a scene reminiscent of my fight with Sinis and his bandits. Not only did it miss Theseus but it clattered against the wall well above his head. It rebounded and hit another sleeping body. Whoever it was woke immediately and sat up with a small cry of alarm. This served to rouse the others.

I had to wait another hour until they all settled down again. Theseus must have been aware that I was out there somewhere and was clearly expecting me to try again.

I aimed carefully and threw. Unfortunately, the throw was almost as bad as the first. Luckily, Theseus was awake and ready. His eyes had become accustomed to the darkness. He was also a superb athlete with supernatural reflexes. He sprung silently to his feet and intercepted the rock before it could hit the wall.

The direction of the rock told him roughly where I was. As silent as death, he crept toward me. I melted back behind another wall and waited.

Moments later, Theseus appeared before me. I knew it was him, even without being able to see his face clearly.

We stood facing each other in silence. Neither of us moved. It was probably the strangest reunion I have ever had. My imprisonment had made me awkward and uncomfortable around others. I really didn't know what to do. Theseus, for his part, was probably a little nervous and possibly frightened—

although I had never seen him so before.

Theseus always saw things in black and white. There was usually no middle ground for him. He let his actions speak for themselves. I realized that he only had two options. He was either going to try and kill me or renew our friendship. I didn't know which one he would choose.

Suddenly, Theseus moved. It startled me, and I threw up my arms as if to defend myself. Before I knew it, his arms were around me. For a moment, I thought perhaps that he was going to wrestle me, and my arms stiffened, prepared for combat. Then I realized what this was. Theseus wasn't attacking me. Theseus was hugging me.

A little confused and feeling a trifle awkward and self-conscious, I eventually returned the embrace, and we held each other for long moments in the dark. I felt my body relax. Theseus was here. My friend was here. Like we had many times before, we would fight together.

We didn't speak; we couldn't for fear of rousing the others. Indicating that Theseus should follow, I led him through the labyrinth. In the first few months of my imprisonment, it would've taken me the best part of an hour to travel from the trapdoor to the place that I considered my bedchamber. Especially in the darkness. Now, we made the same journey in less than half the time. After perhaps a year and a half in that place, I was so confident of my surroundings that I hardly needed to consult the marks on the wall to find my way.

Theseus kept a grip on my shoulder as we walked. I found it comforting. It reminded me of Glaucus sitting there.

Eventually, we made our way to my room. I fumbled around in the darkness and lit my small oil lamp. I bade Theseus sit while I took a stool and sat facing him.

"It's good to see you, my friend," said Theseus, smiling so brightly it would've melted any woman's heart. He looked good. It was hard to imagine that he'd just spent several days imprisoned in the hold of Minos's ship. Even his loincloth looked less stained than mine. He shone with good health and appeared strong and fit. I envied him.

The loincloth was the only thing he wore. He didn't even have sandals. He certainly didn't have a sword or a club like the stories said. Some say that Ariadne had hidden a weapon for him within the labyrinth, but that is laughable. Ariadne had almost nothing to do with Theseus during the voyage from Athens. Not only that, but how was she supposed to enter the labyrinth and conceal a weapon for him? There is also the matter of the ball of thread, but I have already touched on that.

"Take off your mask so I can see your face, my brother," he said.

I shook my head. "I can't. Daedalus made sure of that."

Theseus leant in closer to examine the helmet and the mask itself. "Clever," he said finally. "It's no wonder your legend has grown. I am ... sorry," he said eventually, his smile faltering.

"You have nothing to be sorry for," I said, but I knew it as a lie as soon as the words had left my lips.

"I do," said Theseus. "I'm sorry for what I said to you. I'm sorry about what happened to Androgeus. It was my fault. I lost my temper and your brother died."

The pain of old memories resurfaced. I remembered Theseus pushing Androgeus in his rage and the unfortunate outcome. I thought perhaps I would never be able to forgive Theseus, but seeing him like this, seeing the honest regret on his face, I couldn't hold onto my anger. I knew how great Theseus's pride was, too. For him to apologize was a rare occurrence and something he didn't do lightly.

"We were both to blame," I said, tears starting to roll down my cheeks. I was glad Theseus couldn't see them. "If I hadn't tried to intervene, Androgeus would still live."

Theseus nodded. "I am sorry, too, that you've had to endure this terrible punishment you don't deserve. And I'm sorry it's taken me so long to come for you. But that's all in the past now, brother. Together, we will escape here and end Minos's tyranny."

"How do you plan on doing that, exactly?" I asked.

"Simple," said Theseus, smiling again. "Once we escape, we will kill that whoreson Minos. Crete's power will be broken, and her hold over Athens will be no more. There will be no more tributes."

As I might have mentioned before, Theseus wasn't the brightest ember in the fire. He was all for doing. Thinking usually came afterwards—if at all.

"What did Phaedra tell you?" I asked, choosing not to criticize. Antagonizing Theseus was not a good idea, especially in such a delicate situation.

"She said that I, with your help, would lead the tributes and my fellow Athenians to a secret tunnel. Once there, she and your brothers will help them escape Crete and return to Athens. The rest is up to you and me."

"Did Phaedra say how she planned to get you off the island?" I asked.

Theseus shook his head. "She didn't." Of course, he probably hadn't thought to ask either.

"Did the tributes from last year return?" This was something I had thought long and hard about. Phaedra had never given me details about how she'd liberated the tributes nor what had happened to them after.

"No," said Theseus, shaking his head and looking a little confused. "I confess that at first, I feared the worst."

"The worst? What do you mean?" I asked, already knowing what he was getting at.

"When they didn't return, I thought perhaps you ... that you had become what they said you had," said Theseus, looking a little sheepish.

"And what's that exactly?" I asked, trying to quell the defensiveness in my voice.

"A monster," said Theseus, meeting my eye without flinching. "They said you had become a monster that devoured any human thrown into the labyrinth."

"Did you believe the stories? Do you believe them now?" I asked.

Theseus shook his head. "I was confused at first. I knew you. I *know* you. I couldn't believe what people were saying. But when the tributes didn't return, I didn't know what to think. Now that I've seen you, I know the truth. That you couldn't have done what they say you did."

I thought about this for a moment. "So *what exactly* happened to the tributes?" I asked. "The last I saw of them was my brothers leading them to freedom."

"I told you—I don't know," said Theseus. "But I know you weren't responsible."

"I suppose it doesn't matter," I said finally. "I'm confident that Phaedra and my brothers got them to safety. What matters now is freeing the new tributes."

"Agreed," said Theseus, his smile returning with renewed vigor. "I'll return and guide them back here."

"Not so hasty," I said. "You can't bring them here because this is where I will hide. First, I'll show you the secret passage. Then, I will guide you back to them. You can use the ball of thread that Phaedra used and my lamp."

Theseus nodded. I knew from his reaction that Phaedra had already told him about the thread.

"Be careful," I said, repeating the instructions I had given to my brothers, "not to let the guards see the light. Leave it several turns of the passage away, and then go and get the others. The thread will guide you back to the escape tunnel."

"And what about you, brother?" he asked.

"I can't risk being seen by the other tributes. I will only scare them, and that could lead to … an unfortunate incident." I wanted to tell Theseus about the poor youth I had killed but wasn't sure how he would react. "I'll come with you only to show the way. Then, I'll return here. Once the tributes are out, come for me. Together, we'll finish widening the tunnel."

And then what? I thought. Embark on some foolish plan to kill Minos? As much as I wanted to get my revenge him, it was a fool's errand. He would be heavily guarded. Despite Theseus passion and enthusiasm for bloodshed, we wouldn't stand a chance. Together, we were a formidable force, but even so, against hundreds of guards? Ridiculous. Our best hope would be to get to a ship. Or so I supposed.

Of course, I never mentioned these doubts to Theseus. One step at a time. Get the tributes out first, then think about what to do next.

Ω

I guided Theseus to the entrance of the escape tunnel. Wedging my chisel into a crack in the rock, I tied one end of the thread to it and played it out as we walked back toward the center of the labyrinth.

When we were close, I set the lamp down on the ground.

"See these marks on the rock?" I asked Theseus, pointing to the scratches I had made months earlier. He nodded, and I explained their use.

"They will guide you to the trapdoor. If you get lost or lose the thread, use them to return back the way you came."

"I will," Theseus promised. He clapped me on the shoulder. "I will see you soon. Luck to us both."

Ω

I returned to my bedchamber to wait. I didn't have to wait long.

I heard the sounds of commotion long before their cause became apparent. I was about to charge off into the labyrinth to investigate and almost crashed into Theseus on my way out.

"What is it?" I asked.

"Trouble," panted Theseus breathlessly.

"Tell me," I demanded.

"Guards have entered the labyrinth," he said, his eyes wide with excitement. "Sons of maggots. I will send them all to Tartarus."

"What?" At first, I didn't think I'd heard him correctly. Why would guards be in the labyrinth? After our last confrontation, I didn't think they'd dare. I was clearly wrong.

"They descended down the rope just as I was leading the last tribute away from the trapdoor. There were many of them," said Theseus. "I thought about staying to fight, but I was unarmed, and I had to get the others to safety."

"Are they out yet?" I asked, meaning the tributes. Thankfully, Theseus understood.

"That's the other bad news," said Theseus. The glint in his eye told me he was almost enjoying this. "The far end of the escape tunnel is blocked. It looks like someone has put a huge boulder against it. No one is getting out of there. There was no sign of Phaedra or your brothers."

I shook my head in confusion. I didn't understand what had gone wrong but it was clear that Minos had discovered our plot. He was not about to risk either myself or the tributes escaping, especially when he had Theseus in his grasp. Like most Kings of that age, Minos relied on one simple rule: when in doubt, kill everyone. From experience, King's tend to rely on this type of plan all too often.

I thought quickly. "Did you wind up the thread?" If I understood correctly, all the tributes would now be gathered at the entrance to the escape tunnel. The thread would lead the guards directly to them.

I saw realization dawn on Theseus's face. I almost felt sorry for him.

"No," he said finally. "I must have dropped it when I saw the guards."

"Then, I guess we'll have to stop them," I said.

A lesser man—or perhaps a wiser one—would have immediately argued against this plan. Theseus and I were heavily outnumbered. We couldn't hope to defeat them all. But this was Theseus. He was a hero and not very bright to boot. He took this news in his stride.

"You haven't got any weapons by chance?" he asked hopefully. "If I am going to feed some men to the crows today, I'll need more than just my fists."

"I think, my brother, that I can help you in that regard," I answered, smiling grimly.

CHAPTER 17

We crouched in the darkness, waiting. I gripped the handle of my club nervously. It had been a long time since I'd held a weapon in my hands. I began to fidget.

"Stop that," hissed Theseus. "They'll hear you." Theseus, of course, was completely composed. In contrast to me, he was absolutely still. Like a statue. His sword rested lightly in his palm, as naturally as an extension of his arm.

The waiting was getting to me, but I could hear the guards getting closer. It wouldn't be long now.

At least we were armed. The weapons I'd taken from the guards who had killed Glaucus had finally found a use. I'd stored them in my room on a whim. I didn't think I'd actually get to use them, but I was comforted by their presence. It was fortunate that I had them at all.

Weeks after I'd killed the guards, I finally got around to

disposing of their corpses. Although they didn't decompose like a body would have in the open air, they were still starting to smell. Not only that, but I tripped over one of them once, falling onto the body. I guess I was so used to the labyrinth that I didn't expect to encounter a foreign object. I'd almost forgotten they were there. For anyone who has ever touched a decaying corpse, you know how unpleasant the experience could be. I don't recommend it.

I dragged the bodies into a recess far removed from the trapdoor or my own chamber. I threw them into an untidy heap, unwilling to give them any sort of dignified rest, especially after what they'd done to Glaucus. The body of the Athenian youth I put elsewhere, adjusting his arms and legs in a dignified manner so he appeared to be sleeping. I would've preferred to give him a proper burial, but I lacked the means. It was the best I could do.

I almost left the weapons of the guards with their bodies. Common sense prevailed, and I eventually put them in my bedchamber. Now I was glad I had.

Flickering yellow light appeared around the corner. I could clearly hear the voices of the guards now. They sounded scared, as well they should be. They had entered the labyrinth—in all likelihood unwillingly—to face the monster. And they got something else in the bargain. They had to contend with Theseus as well, and he was not to be taken lightly.

They certainly hadn't expected us to be armed. Whether they'd forgotten about the demise of the last guards to enter or had just overlooked that fact, it certainly gave us an advantage. There were other factors in our favor too. The corridors of the maze were relatively narrow—only the width of an average sized man stretched end to end, just enough room for two men to stand abreast. That meant they could only attack two at a time. Not only that, but I knew the labyrinth intimately. They did not. Fear also had a hand to play. Their fears threatened to unman them.

Theseus and I had just enough time to come up with a strategy of sorts. It wasn't much of one, but it was all we had. The guards thought that the ball of thread would lead them to where the tributes would be huddling in fear. That was no longer the case.

Theseus and I had returned to the secret passage. Cries of terror from the tributes had welcomed me, but the presence of Theseus and his hurried explanation managed to settle them to a degree. They still eyed me with a combination of fear, loathing, and disgust, but I was used to that by then.

Quickly, we gathered up the thread and laid a path far removed from the Athenians. And there we lay in wait.

The first two guards, carrying torches and spears, appeared from behind a wall. Theseus and I leapt up and were onto them before they realized what was happening. Their cries and screams must have unnerved those behind because the corridor was suddenly filled with confused shouting.

Normally, their spears would've been a problem. They had a much longer reach than the sword and club wielded by Theseus and I. With the first two, it didn't matter. It was over so quickly, they didn't have time to utilize their advantage.

Even now, I was reluctant to kill. These guards were only guilty of obeying orders. Unlike the others, they had not killed my pet rat. I was not motivated by vengeance. I blocked the clumsy spear thrust and brained the guard in front of me without using unnecessary force. It was enough to knock him out, but I felt confident that I hadn't killed him.

Theseus had no such compulsion. Unhampered by conscience, he attacked with a will, yelling and swearing, intending to kill with each thrust. He skewered the first guard and then knelt down to finish off the one I had incapacitated.

"Don't," I warned, knowing what he was about to do. Theseus ignored me and slit the guard's throat.

"Go feed the crows, maggot eyes," he said with something approaching glee.

I had no time to contemplate this though, the next two guards were upon us, and I was busy trying to save my own life.

Theseus fought with the same fury I remembered. If anything, he was a better swordsman than ever. He dispatched both guards while all I could do was keep their spears at bay. His eyes had taken on that familiar cold, furious glint. I knew better than to get in his way.

The rest of the guards retreated in confusion that was part real and part ruse. They needed to give themselves some space. I saw what the next two guards were carrying.

"Bows!" I warned.

Theseus charged anyway. His blood was up, and there was no way he was about to retreat. You have to admire that in a man.

"Come join me in Tartarus!" he roared, brandishing his sword. "You calf brained sons of dogs!"

The first arrow struck him in the lower leg. It didn't slow him down at all. In the time it takes me to say this, two more guards were down. The rest retreated in disarray.

"Theseus!" I was shouting now. When Theseus was like this, he became almost impossible to control. "Theseus," I said again, grabbing him by the arm.

He turned to me and raised his sword. I saw death in his eyes.

"Theseus, it's me, Asterion. We'll retreat and set another ambush for them."

He narrowed his eyes and then realized what was happening. I finally saw recognition there. He nodded curtly.

I helped him down the corridor, following the thread. He was limping slightly. I heard the twang of bows behind me and felt a hot surge of pain as an arrow penetrated my back. I grunted and gritted my teeth, trying to ignore it. I had suffered worse.

I knew the other guards would be more wary now. They would not pursue us in haste. It gave us time and advantage. But we were both wounded, and there were many more guards to deal with. The labyrinth was probably filling up with more guards even as we retreated. For everyone we killed, two more joined them.

It was hopeless, but Theseus and I were both committed to fighting to our last breath. We had to protect the innocent tributes. I began to question my reluctance to kill. If I left the guards alive, they would only return to try and kill me again. I didn't really have an option.

This place, as I had long suspected, would become my tomb. It saddened me to think it would be Theseus's too. There was no way out of the labyrinth now. Or was there? Of course there was—the trapdoor! We just had to reach it. I felt a sudden surge of hope. If the guards were spread throughout the labyrinth looking for us and the other tributes, then perhaps the trapdoor wouldn't be well guarded. But how to lead all the tributes there without being discovered? I gritted my teeth in frustration.

Theseus and I retreated into the darkness. After several minutes, we stopped to catch our breath and examine our wounds. The arrow had only grazed Theseus, but the wound was bleeding heavily. He staunched the bleeding with a strip torn from his loincloth. The wound on my back was a different story. The arrow was wedged firmly below my shoulder blade. I knew it hadn't penetrated my lung or any other organ. If it had, I would have been unable to breathe. Or just plain dead.

"I have to take it out," said Theseus, examining the wound.

"No, leave it," I said. It hurt, but Theseus would only make it worse if he took it out. There was a chance he could cause more damage as it exited the wound. Not only that, but there was another consideration. I doubted a puncture like that would be easy to plug. I ran the risk of bleeding to death.

"Break it off instead," I said.

"You have changed, Asterion," said Theseus laughing happily, grabbing the arrow shaft and snapping it with a quick twist of his hands. "You have become as soft as a hag's breasts," He threw the arrow shaft away. If it had been him, Theseus would have insisted I take the arrow out. But that was Theseus. I, at least, tried to consider consequences. I also suspected that Theseus liked pain.

"We'll move further into the labyrinth and ambush the sons of brainless goats again," said Theseus firmly.

"It's pointless," I said wearily. "We won't be able to defeat them all."

"Then we will sacrifice our lives at great cost to them. We will take many to Hades with us. The crows will feast on their eyes tonight!"

Typical Theseus. You couldn't help but admire his enthusiasm, and I certainly didn't blame him for it. Theseus really took the expression *charmei gethosunoi*—Greek for "rejoicing in battle"—quite literally. I didn't have the heart to point out that there were no crows down here either. He was a hero after all and a product of his own legend. He firmly believed that a hero should die in battle, taking as many enemies with him as possible. I had a more pragmatic approach—one that wouldn't result in my own untimely and unnecessary death. I knew we were unlikely to escape the labyrinth alive, but I wasn't prepared to throw my life away. Not when a tiny hope remained.

"There is another way," I said.

Theseus shook his head. "No, there's not, brother." He touched me on the arm. "Be brave. This is our time to die. I am with you. Let's embrace our fates together." He laughed.

And I thought I was the crazy one.

I shook his hand off. I was beginning to get a little frustrated with Theseus's battle lust. "The guards will follow the thread, right?" Theseus nodded. "Then," I continued, "we won't. We go back to the tributes and lead them to the trapdoor. They won't be expecting that." Or would they? Probably, but it was the only plan I had. The labyrinth, you have to remember, was huge. Even with tens or even hundreds of guards, it was unlikely we would be discovered. Until we reached the trapdoor, that is.

Grudgingly, Theseus agreed, reluctantly putting his suicide

attempt on hold for the moment.

We left the path of the thread and headed back to where the tributes waited. Unfortunately, a group of guards had already found the tributes. Theseus and I knew something was wrong as soon as we neared the escape tunnel. Voices lifted in fear. Confused shouting.

We ran into the corridor where we had left the tributes. A palace guard loomed in front of us. Theseus cut him down without hesitation. Another sprang up to replace him and received the point of Theseus's sword as his reward.

The corridor was a claustrophobic mess of bodies. Most of the tributes were kneeling. Several guards were down the far end carrying torches. Some had bows. I could see a few dead bodies lying on the ground. One of the Athenian youths was wrestling with the guards.

I was at a momentary loss as to what to do. Theseus, much more a man of action than myself, felt no such confusion.

"Go," he commanded. "Take as many as you can and get to the trapdoor. I will hold the guards off."

I didn't have time to argue. I wanted to stay and help, but this was the only option. Theseus couldn't lead them to the trapdoor. He didn't know the way.

Using shouts and kicks, Theseus urged the nearby tributes to stand and told them to follow me. Under normal circumstances, I doubt they would have, but this wasn't a normal circumstance.

He pushed his way through them, and I lost him in the chaotic corridor clogged with human bodies. I heard the twang of bowstrings and cries of pain.

"Follow me," I yelled to any of the tributes who were

within earshot and hurried off back the way we had come. I didn't turn to see if they followed. If they did, they had a chance to live. If they chose to stay, they would probably die. I didn't have time to convince them of the merits of either option.

Reassured by the sounds of hurried footsteps behind me, I slowed and let them catch up. Luckily, one of them still carried the lamp I had left. I counted eight frightened tributes. Behind them, I heard the sounds of battle as Theseus guarded our retreat with his life.

I moved as swiftly as I could. Not nearly swiftly enough but I was hampered by two factors. One, the arrow in my back was beginning to take its inevitable toll, and two, the tributes were reluctant to get too close to me. I had to constantly stop and urge them on.

A guard suddenly sprang out before me, thrusting with his spear. I was taken completely by surprise and grunted heavily as the spear tip entered my side. The guard tried to withdraw it and thrust again, but I stopped him by the simple expedient of grasping the haft of the weapon with my free hand. I pulled him toward me and brought my club down. He was wearing a helmet, but even so, I heard his skull crack like an egg.

The wound to my side was fortunately not deep. Only the tip had penetrated. I pulled it out, heedless of the blood that ran down my side and along the inside of my leg.

Perhaps my actions had convinced the tributes that I was now trustworthy. Maybe they just realized that if I hadn't eaten them by now, I was probably not hungry. Whatever the reason, they started to follow me with greater enthusiasm.

We reached the trapdoor without further incident. If I had

hoped that it would be relatively unguarded, I was disappointed. Minos may have been a cruel and often unwise ruler, but he wasn't foolish. The floor space directly under the trapdoor was crowded with guards. I could clearly see how hopeless our situation was by the several torches that now lit the space. Even as I watched, more descended the rope.

I clenched my teeth together in frustration and anger. So close! To have come this far and be denied now was almost unbearable. I resigned myself to die, knowing the wounds I'd suffered would kill me inevitably if they weren't treated soon. Perhaps Theseus inspired me. I would take as many as I could with me before I died.

I heard sounds of commotion behind me and turned by head. My great height enabled me to see over the heads of the tributes. I saw Theseus rush up behind us, panting and bleeding. He was smiling. Several guards trailed behind him, blocking our path.

I met his eye, and for some reason I grinned back. His expression was infectious. I felt a little comforted knowing I would die with my friend.

I turned my attention back to the guards in front of me and hefted my club menacingly. They hadn't moved, reluctant to be the first to die. Time seemed to slow for a moment. One of the faces of the guards seemed to be familiar for some reason. My eye was drawn instinctively toward him, even though he was close to the rear of the clustered guards.

Now, I confess I didn't know every one of the guards. Many I recognized from my time spent in the palace, but I had no doubt that there were many, many others I had never encountered. There were hundreds or possibly thousands of guards and soldiers on Crete in those days. There was no reason why I would've recognized one of them. But I did.

Perhaps it was because he was larger than the others. Perhaps it was because of his noble bearing. He had long dark hair that flowed down his shoulders and a full beard. This was not unusual amongst the guards. What set him apart mostly was his clothing. He wore a rich tunic instead of a loincloth and armor. And he wasn't carrying a sword or spear. In one hand, he grasped a trident.

It was the trident that did it. The trident was the symbol of Poseidon. I had no doubts at all that my father had come to me in my hour of greatest need. We locked gazes for a fleeting moment. His expression was unreadable, and then his mouth quirked into the briefest of smiles, and he nodded at me.

Time resumed its normal languid pace.

And then the earth shifted.

The walls of the labyrinth shook. Many were thrown off their feet, but I managed to stay upright. Chunks of rock began raining down upon everyone gathered there. Screams and dust filled the air. Several of the guards were crushed by falling rock. I received a glancing blow from a large rock falling from the roof of the labyrinth. I staggered and fell to my knees. One more step to the left and it would have flattened me.

Many have said that this was a natural earthquake. Crete was prone to them after all. But I know better. My last thousand years upon this earth has taught me wisdom. There are those who attribute natural events like earthquakes to nothing other than what they are—a natural occurrence. Often that is the case. Experience and my interaction with the gods in the centuries since have taught me to recognize the difference.

This earthquake was not natural. Poseidon had merely bided his time and waited for the perfect opportunity to bring about his final revenge on Minos. To make him pay for what he had done to the sons of Poseidon. I know this because Poseidon himself told me, many, many years later. You may choose to believe me or not. I don't care. I know it is the truth.

The guards, understandably, were in disarray, confused and disheartened by this turn of events. Many had been killed. Some had fled in terror. Most had forgotten about us. I got to my feet and looked around. The earthquake was over. Rocks continued to fall from the ceiling and walls. The ceiling of the labyrinth had been torn asunder as if by the hand of a titan. A jumbled pile of rocks lay before me, reaching well above even my head height. Of Poseidon, there was no sign. I saw Theseus trying to pull one of the tributes to their feet. He was dusty and shaken but thankfully otherwise unharmed.

"Did you see him? I asked after I'd gingerly picked my way to Theseus. I felt weak. Blood leaked in a constant stream from the wound in my side. The arrow in my back was a source of constant, throbbing pain.

"Who?" asked Theseus, helping another one of his fellow Athenians up.

"Never mind," I said.

A couple of guards moved as if to attack us. Both Theseus and I raised our weapons, faces grim. The guards fled rather than face our cold wrath.

"It seems we have a way out after all," said Theseus, looking above us.

We did indeed. The labyrinth, once my prison and home, was now shattered and broken. Never again would it serve to imprison the unwilling.

As for the willing, that is another matter entirely.

Ω

Of the fourteen Athenian tributes, only six—including Theseus—clambered out of that dreadful place alive.

We emerged into a palace that had fared little better than the labyrinth itself. Much of it was in ruins. Walls and ceilings had crumbled, tumbling broken remains of frescoes to the cracked mosaic floor. Fire had broken out and was clearly out of control. There were dead or dying bodies everywhere, many crushed by falling pillars and other debris.

It was a scene of unbridled chaos and confusion. Guards ran everywhere. None paid Theseus or the surviving tributes any attention. Several however glanced fearfully at me. Thankfully, none moved to attack. The earthquake had drained whatever fight was left in them.

We helped the tributes outside, moving away from the palace. As soon as I set foot outside, I stopped dead. It was the first time I had been in the open air for well over a year. It was early evening. I looked up. Even though smoke from the burning palace obscured my vision, I still caught glimpses of glittering stars. This night sky was one of the most beautiful sights I had ever seen.

Other sensations impinged on my awareness. The wind moving through the trees, the same wind that was even now caressing the faceplate of my helmet. The smell of flowers, redolent with the sweet scent of spring. I felt suddenly alive, free. But also curiously exposed, as if my soul had been bared for everyone to see.

It was strange to experience such a rush of emotions all at once. I was a little overcome. I think if Theseus hadn't physically kept me moving, I would've stayed there for hours.

Eventually we found an open space in the palace gardens that appeared relatively safe. I sat down and tore a piece off my loincloth, using it to bind the wound in my side. At least it stopped the bleeding.

"We have unfinished business here," said Theseus, grasping the hilt of his weapon. If his wounds affected him, he certainly didn't show it. "I came to kill Minos. I'm not leaving without first separating his head from his shoulders."

"I need to find Phaedra," I said, groaning as I got to my feet.

Theseus shook his head. "Minos first. Then Phaedra."

I agreed reluctantly. I was in no condition to attempt a rescue mission by myself and needed his help. Phaedra would have to wait until Theseus's thirst for vengeance was satisfied. I'd learnt that once Theseus got an idea in his head, there was no point trying to change his mind.

What's more, Theseus needed me. The palace at Knossos was vast. Strangers had been known to get lost for days inside. Now that it was in ruins, it would be even harder to find his way around. He wouldn't be able to find Minos without me.

We picked our way through the ruins slowly. I knew, of course, where Minos's chambers were, but there were no guarantees that he would be there. For all I knew, he had been near the trapdoor, gloating as his guards flooded into the labyrinth.

We eventually found what had once been Minos's extensive

and lavish royal chambers. They weren't so lavish anymore. The earthquake had left very little intact. Smoke clouded the room, rising up from the now out of control fires below. I watched it spiral into the sky through the smashed roof. In hindsight, it was probably foolish to attempt to climb up to his chambers given the state of the palace. I was still surprised that parts of it remained standing. But much of what Theseus and I did was foolish. And Theseus was not to be denied.

Minos was there. Three guards were with him. Theseus brandished his sword, and that was enough for them. Evidentially, their lives were more valuable than that of their king. They edged around us under the watchful gaze of Theseus. Once they reached the door now hanging partially off its hinges, they took to their heels and ran. It was only this action that saved their lives. Theseus wouldn't have spared them otherwise. I think he was a little disappointed that he didn't get to kill them.

Minos only vaguely resembled the man I remembered. It had been over a year since I had last seen him, and time had not been kind to him. I had thought him a huge man with a size to rival my own, but that was an image painted by a boy. His presence suddenly rekindled memories of him hitting me. His cold manner toward me. The way he'd studied me from afar. I felt the old fear resurface for a moment, but then I remembered who I was now and what I had become. I was a boy no longer. What I saw before me now was an old man, possibly of average height, slightly stooped about the shoulders. He appeared a shriveled shell of his former self. The price of his revenge against me was a weight not easily borne.

He stood before us, clearly a little shocked by recent events. His hair was disheveled, and there was a wild look in his eyes.

He spared Theseus only the briefest of glances. Then, he fixed his cold eyes on me. They widened, and his face twisted into something far more intense than plain anger. Anger could not even begin to describe the look on his face. "You!" he screamed. "Hades born creature. You are responsible for this." He drew his sword and charged.

I'm not sure how Theseus managed to restrain himself. I knew he desperately wanted to kill Minos himself for the humiliation Athens had suffered. But I think he knew that this was between my stepfather and myself. Theseus could have easily stepped in and cut Minos down. Maybe that's what stopped him. It was too easy. Perhaps he thought Minos was not a worthy opponent even though he deserved Theseus's special brand of justice. Pick a reason. It hardly matters now.

I doubt whether the old man was conscious of anyone else in the room other than myself. For that reason, it would've been a simple matter for anyone else to have killed him. One stroke of his sword, one severed King's head. In the long run, it probably would've been the kindest thing to do. I wish sometimes that Theseus had done it.

As it was, I didn't even bother using my club. It was unnecessary. Minos swung at me with such wild abandon even I was fast enough to avoid his attack. I stepped to the side and smashed my fist into his face.

To say that I hit him and he fell to the ground would be a gross understatement. I hit him with a force nurtured by years of physical and emotional abuse. A force channeled into furious action. I'm actually surprised that I didn't kill him, but, according to some accounts, he was a son of Zeus. Demi-gods, as I may have mentioned, don't die easily.

Theseus told me that as I struck, I roared so loudly that he was forced to cover his ears. I don't remember. I do, however, remember the outcome. Minos actually flew off my fist. His robes fluttered around him as he sailed through the air. He hit the floor with bone breaking force and skidded along the broken tiles.

Minos was the cause of everything bad that happened in my life. The flaws that exist within me exist because of him. The insecurities, the fears, the remarkable lack of self-worth. I spent over a year locked in a labyrinth because of his pride, arrogance, and desire for vengeance.

If he had accepted me as I was, I have no doubts I would've been a much greater man than I am today. My life would've been completely different. Better.

Hitting him went some way to sooth my traumatized soul. To be honest, nothing I have done before or after has ever felt so good.

Perhaps as a testimony to his semi-divine heritage, Minos sat up moments after his body came to a halt. If I hadn't seen it for myself, I probably wouldn't have believed it. I know first-hand what happens to a normal human when I hit them with my not inconsiderable strength. And not one of them ever sat up afterwards like he did.

"Where is my mother?" I roared. I knew where Phaedra was and hoped my brothers were imprisoned with her. I hoped that my mother still lived.

Minos flinched at the sound. His nose was broken, blood dribbled from the corner of his mouth.

"A place where you will never find her," he spat. A gobbet of blood splattered on the floor.

I stepped toward him threateningly and raised my club. "Tell me," I demanded.

He laughed at me, the sound gradually rising in pitch. I realized that Minos was probably mad. His madness possibly exceeding my own. Unlike mine, his was entirely of his own making.

"Never," he said and laughed again. I think I probably could've killed him then, but Theseus intervened, for once setting aside his own rage filled desires.

He joined us and knelt down next to Minos, whispering in his ear words that I couldn't catch, but I could guess at. Minos's eyes went wide. Theseus stood and looked down at the King of Crete. Something passed between them. Minos saw something in Theseus's cold, dispassionate look that he feared even more than I. I had seen the form that Theseus's vengeance took in the past. I knew what he was capable of. Minos had just been enlightened.

"With the others," stammered Minos. I took this to mean that he had imprisoned her along with Phaedra, my brothers, and the two craftsmen.

With this admission, Theseus raised his sword, his intent clear.

Minos threw up warding hands. "Please don't," he pleaded. He began to snivel and raised himself to his hands and knees. He clutched Theseus's ankle. "Please don't kill me. I'll give you anything. Athens is now free. That's what you wanted, isn't it? No more tributes. I will pay you gold. Enough gold to make Athens the richest city in Greece. In the world. Just don't kill me."

I saw the disgust on Theseus's face. The loathing. Suddenly,

I felt a wave of pity for Minos even though I knew he didn't deserve it. He was just a sad, bitter old man. He wasn't worthy of a quick death, especially a noble one at the hands of a hero like Theseus. He deserved to die alone and in poverty.

Theseus shook him off. "Shall we kill him, Asterion?" he asked. I wanted to say yes, but that would make me worse than Minos. I wasn't like him. I would never be like him. It was also Theseus's way to seek revenge, to do to others what they had forced upon their victims. I suspect that if the labyrinth had still been intact, Theseus would've forced Minos to live out the rest of his days there. As it was, he didn't have that option. As much as Theseus was my friend, I didn't want to become like him either.

After long moments of consideration, moments where Minos looked fearfully from me to Theseus, I finally made up my mind.

"No," I said. "His hold over Athens is now broken. His death will serve no purpose other than to satisfy my thirst for revenge. Death will not change anything. He has nothing now. No kingdom, no crown. His children have deserted him. I can't think of a worst fate. Leave him with his madness."

I locked gazes with Theseus for a moment. Suddenly, he shrugged. "As you will, Asterion. He is your stepfather after all." He smiled brightly. That was the thing about Theseus. He could be cold and rage filled in one moment, relaxed and carefree in the next. He was not a forgiving man, but he believed that a punishment should fit the crime. Evidentially, he thought that Minos had gotten what he deserved. And that was enough for him.

"Come," he said. "Let's go rescue your family."

CHAPTER 18

That was the last time I saw King Minos. If you think perhaps I was too gentle with him, have no fear that he got his just desserts in time. Now I am glad I didn't kill him. If I had, I believe I would have deserved to join him in Tartarus. Because that's where he is now.

The earthquake marked the end of Crete as a power. Most of the towns and cities in Crete were destroyed. Many soldiers were killed and her navy smashed by a huge wave that could have only been the rage of Poseidon.

Minos eventually left the island to pursue his vengeance against Daedalus. It was Daedalus who had betrayed him, who had given up the secrets of the labyrinth to Phaedra. You may wonder why he switched his attention from me to Daedalus. There is a simple reason for that. As far as Minos was concerned, I was dead.

As for the King of Crete, he eventually met his end rather ignominiously at the hand of the daughter of Cocalus, the King of Agrigentum. She poured boiling water over him while he was taking a bath. When I heard this news, I remember feeling nothing at all. No grim satisfaction, no joy. Nothing. When all is said and done, Minos was nothing to me.

His remains were sent back to Crete. The few loyal Cretans who remained built him a sarcophagus and inscribed it with "the tomb of Minos, the son of Zeus." I would've preferred something else. Maybe "Minos, bitter tyrant. Petty seeker of vengeance."

I actually remember his tomb being built. At the time, I had to wrestle with an impulse not to deface it but managed to resist mostly because it would've been beneath me. I sometimes go there still. Seeing it helps me remember. The memories are painful but they are a part of me. For good or ill, they have made me what I am.

$$\Omega$$

Hurrying as quickly as our injuries would allow, Theseus and I made our way to the tower where Phaedra and the others were imprisoned. It would've been quicker and far more efficient to take horses but any that had been housed in or around the palace had been scattered by the earthquake.

I'd been to the tower a few times before when I was younger, more out of curiosity than anything else. It was a large stone structure Minos used to imprison those he particularly despised. I remember being a little scared by the place. It was on an isolated part of the island, a league or two from the palace. Windswept and desolate, it had always seemed an appropriate place for misery and suffering.

It took longer than expected to get there. It must have been almost midnight by the time we reached our destination. I was completely shattered, feeling weaker by the minute. The events of the last few hours had also taken their toll emotionally. In addition, I knew that if the arrow in my back wasn't seen to shortly, it might well kill me.

The tower, although still largely intact, had not escaped unscathed from the destruction wrought by the earthquake. Large blocks had toppled from its battlements to lie scattered around the base. As we approached, I could see a group of figures clustered around the entrance, carrying torches. In the darkness, it was difficult to make out who they were.

I had hoped it might be Phaedra and the other prisoners already making their escape. It wasn't. As we neared the base of the tower, I could see that it was four guards.

They challenged us as we strode up.

"Who are you, and what is your business?" asked the oldest of the guards, a grizzled veteran in his middle years. He recognized me of course and probably suspected that I'd escaped from the labyrinth rather than being released. He may well have known who Theseus was too, which was probably why he didn't give the order to attack straight away. The years had given him wisdom. Even with the odds in his favor, the fight could go either way.

"Our business is our own," said Theseus in a tone that brooked no argument. "Stand aside or face the consequences." He laid a hand on his sword hilt and grinned.

"Have a care with that tongue," said the guard. "Lest you lose it."

I saw Theseus stiffen and his grin widen. I placed a cautionary hand on his arm to forestall his predictable reaction.

"Your work is done here," I said to the guard. "The palace is destroyed, Minos is dead." The lies came easily and were much preferable to the alternative. Theseus may still have had a desire for battle, but I was all but spent. It was unlikely that the guards knew exactly what had taken place at the palace.

"Your loyalty now lies with those inside this tower. Catreus and Deucalion are now the rightful rulers of Crete. Before he died, Minos commanded us to free them." At this point, I wasn't even sure that Catreus and Deucalion were inside, but the guard's reaction confirmed that was the case.

The guard looked me up and down in disbelief. "He commanded you? Minotaur? King Minos sent the creature he most despises in the world on an errand? I don't think so. Go back the way you came or blood will be spilt." His lip curled disdainfully, and he placed a hand on the hilt of his sword.

I gambled and lost. Perhaps if the words had come from someone other than myself, it might have worked. It had been a bad idea for me to go there. I should have sent Theseus alone. Or perhaps not.

I believe that the situation would certainly have degenerated into bloodshed. But then a voice rang out from the darkness. A woman's voice.

"He speaks the truth. Do what he says."

Two figures emerged on horseback. As they trotted up, I finally saw who was riding them. Ariadne and Glaucus. My mouth fell open in amazement.

"What?" said Ariadne defensively, catching my eye. "I'm allowed to help."

I knew immediately that she was up to something, and it troubled me. Ariadne never did anything that didn't serve her own interests. She wanted something. Suddenly, I knew what. Crete as a power was finished. Minos was finished. Ariadne was no longer in a privileged position. But she knew someone who was. Theseus, Prince of Athens. And Theseus and I knew nothing of her betrayal at that point. How it had been her who had revealed the secret entrance to the labyrinth.

I think she realized that Theseus was her only option. Even though he clearly didn't want her, once back in Athens, she would be in a position to start her power play. I wasn't worried about Glaucus though. Although fifteen now and almost a man, he was overweight and certainly no warrior. Besides, he followed Ariadne's lead in almost everything.

"Your father did say that no one was to enter," said the guard hesitantly.

"That was before," said Ariadne curtly. "His last command before he died was to free those in the tower."

"Well, if you say so, Princess," said the guard. He shrugged and stepped aside. If Crete's power had just been destroyed, then it was probably a good time to seek employment elsewhere. Become a mercenary. Blocking access to the tower was no longer in the guards' best interests.

Ariadne and Glaucus dismounted, and we followed as Theseus led the way inside. The interior was a shambolic mess. A table had fallen over, spilling the remains of the guard's meal onto the floor. A weapons rack had buckled and loosed its contents.

Thinking back now, the guards were lucky Theseus didn't

290

kill them. They had obviously fled outside, rightly believing the tower to be no longer safe. They had given no thought to their prisoners, unconcerned that they were being left to their fate. More humane guards would've released them. At least that way, the prisoners would have some hope if the tower collapsed.

A minor tremor shook the building. Dust floated down in gentle eddies. We steadied ourselves against the walls, and I was appalled to find that the blocks were shifting alarmingly beneath my hands. The tower was indeed unsafe. It probably wouldn't be long until it broke apart altogether.

"Phaedra!" I shouted. No answer. Stone steps spiraled upward. Given that there were no other doors, it was clear that the prisoners were held above us. "Wait here," I said to Ariadne and Glaucus.

I raced up the stairs, Theseus at my heels. We found ourselves in a circular tunnel, punctuated by a series of doors. They were all unlocked. Each one concealed a cell. Frantically, we searched, but all the cells were empty. We raced up the next flight of stairs and found ourselves in a corridor that was almost identical to the one below. I tried one of the doors and found that it was locked.

"In here," I heard a voice say.

Theseus and I put our shoulders into it and broke it down. We found ourselves in a large chamber almost completely filled with tables cluttered with all manner of tools and instruments.

Daedalus stood there, looking a little shaken but otherwise none the worst for his experience. I was not at all surprised that Daedalus had been imprisoned with the tools of his trade. His knowledge and intelligence was too valuable to Minos to have him sitting idle.

When he saw my masked face, his expression was that of sadness. Regret. At first, I thought he was like all the others and had started to believe the tales. But that wasn't it at all.

"Asterion," he said his voice faltering. "It's good to see you."

"And you, Daedalus," I said. "Where are the others?"

"In the cells nearby, I think."

"Get outside. It's not safe in here."

Without waiting, Theseus and I raced to the next adjacent cell. We were about to break down the door when Daedalus stopped us.

"It might help if you have this," he said, handing us a large bronze key. "I made it by examining the lock. I couldn't access it from my side, but it will save your shoulders unnecessary punishment."

I thanked him and inserted the key into the lock. Like everything Daedalus made, it worked perfectly. We still had to force the door though. The earthquake had moved everything out of alignment, and the door was jammed.

Eventually we got it open. This cell was much smaller than Daedalus's. There were no tables or equipment, just a straw bed. It had one occupant: Phaedra. She rushed into my arms.

"I was so worried about you," I said.

"And I you," she replied, hugging me tightly. "Especially with the earthquake." Her questing hands found the arrow in my back, and she gave a small cry of dismay. "You're hurt."

"I know," I said simply. "We'll deal with it later."

"No," she said firmly in a tone that brooked no argument. "We'll deal with it now. Daedalus has tools and instruments that can remove it. We'll just get you outside."

"I can't. I have to get the others out."

"Theseus can take care of that." She turned to the man in question. "Isn't that right, Theseus?"

Theseus nodded, smiling crookedly. He obviously knew Phaedra well enough now not to argue with her. In this, he was smarter than me.

We clasped each other and made our way out of the tower. Outside, we found Daedalus sitting on the grass, gazing up at the stars. Ariadne and Glaucus were sitting several paces away, engrossed in conversation. The guards had disappeared.

Phaedra seemed surprised to see her half brother and sister. Her eyes narrowed, and she pursed her lips in distaste. "What are they doing here?"

"Ariadne helped us get into the tower."

Phaedra said nothing, but I knew she would have a reckoning with them eventually.

"Daedalus," she said, turning to the old craftsman. "I need your help. Asterion has an arrow in his back."

"Yes," said Daedalus. "But that is not the only thing he needs to have removed." He met my eye. "I am sorry, Asterion. Minos forced me to do it. He threatened my son." I knew what he was referring to, of course: my helmet.

I nodded. "I know, Daedalus. Don't blame yourself. I don't."

"We must return to my cell above," he said. "It has everything I need."

"It's not safe," I said, shaking my head.

"Regardless," said Daedalus. "I cannot work here. If that arrow isn't removed, it will kill you. The helmet, well that is another story, but the sooner you are rid of it, the better."

I was about to argue, but at that moment, Theseus returned with several other figures in tow: Icarus, Catreus, and

Deucalion. And the person I most wanted to see other than Phaedra: my mother.

When she saw me, she gave a tiny cry and threw herself into my arms.

"Asterion, my son," she sobbed. It had been well over a year since she had seen me last. "Take off your helmet so I can kiss you."

"That," said Daedalus, turning away from the embrace he was sharing with his son, "is what we were just discussing. Icarus, I will need you. You too, Phaedra. You will need to sew up his wound while Icarus and I deal with the helmet. You," he said, pointing at Theseus. "You look strong. I will need that strength."

"Catreus. Deucalion. Stay here and keep a look out," said Phaedra. There was probably no need. She wanted our brothers to keep an eye on Ariadne and Glaucus.

I wanted to argue, but Phaedra was having none of it. They were prepared to risk their lives in a building that could collapse at any moment. For me.

The five of us returned to the tower and marched up the two flights of stairs to Daedalus's cell. The tower continued to shift dangerously. I knew it was only a matter of time until it collapsed.

Daedalus cleared one of his tables and told me to sit. I did what I was told. Phaedra and Theseus, working with instructions and tools from Daedalus, began extracting the broken shaft of the arrow from my back. The pain was terrible but I gritted my teeth against it stoically.

"The horns will have to be removed," said Daedalus finally. "There is no other way."

"No," I said. I remembered the almost unbelievable pain I had suffered when Daedalus had drilled holes in them.

"The mask must come off," said Icarus. "You cannot wear it for the rest of your life. To do that, we must remove your horns."

"Is it safe?" grunted Phaedra. She and Theseus had almost worked the arrow out of my back.

"I don't know," said Daedalus. "There is a chance it could kill him."

"Then don't do it," she said with a note of finality in her voice.

I knew what this cost her. To go through the rest of her life without being able to look on the face of the man she loved. To never be able to kiss me again. It was a terrible price to pay, and my heart surged with love for her then. She would rather deal with that than risk my life.

Her sacrifice made my mind up.

"Do it," I said, gritting my teeth as Theseus and Phaedra finally plucked the arrow out. I suddenly felt a little dizzy feeling the flow of something warm running down my back. I knew it was my blood.

"You can't," said Phaedra behind me. "You might die. I won't risk that."

"I will," I said. "And it's my life to risk."

"Now is as good a time as any," said Daedalus. "The blood loss will make it likely that he will pass out. Icarus and I will be able to work unhampered."

Phaedra said nothing. She sewed up my back with catgut in silence. I could tell she was angry, her hands a little rougher than strictly necessary.

It seemed that Daedalus had been supplied with all manner of items. I did wonder at the time why he had catgut. I discovered later that he had been experimenting with it for reasons associated with flight.

Eventually, Phaedra finished. Daedalus and Icarus helped me lie down. It hurt my back dreadfully but both craftsmen weren't about to take the risk of me fainting on them. Phaedra held my hand. I smiled at her reassuringly, forgetting for a moment that she couldn't see the expression. Perhaps, when this was all over, she would.

The tower shook again as another tremor passed through it. No one moved for a moment.

"I think you should hurry," said Theseus. He took my other hand and clasped it firmly, grinning at me. "This will be nothing, brother. You've suffered worse." He was wrong. So completely wrong. I have remarked earlier that the worst pain I had endured up to this point in my life was when Daedalus drilled holes into my horns. That was nothing compared to what I went through next.

Daedalus bustled about gathering tools and instruments. I eyed the files, pliers, and saws with growing alarm. Finally, he declared himself ready.

"If he moves," he said to Theseus, "hold him. If he continues to struggle, strike him hard and fast."

Theseus nodded and smiled. He clenched his fist and winked at me. I knew he wouldn't have a problem doing that.

It turned out he didn't need to.

Daedalus began sawing through the first of my horns. As I suspected, the pain was so terrible my mind instantly shut down, instinctively knowing it was too much to bear. It seared my body and soul.

My stomach churns to think of what I suffered, even though it was only for a moment.

CHAPTER 19

"Ah, the sleeping giant awakes from his slumber."

I opened my eyes to see Phaedra sitting on the pallet next to me. She lent in close and kissed me. Kissed me! I didn't realize the import of this at first, and then it hit home so hard my heart stopped for a moment.

I tried to sit up but was too weak. The blazing sun beat down, forcing me to squint uncomfortably. You have to remember that I was still unaccustomed to such bright light. It would be a long time before I adjusted. I began to look around and was initially confused by a number of odd sensations. The first was movement. We were rocking slowly from side to side. I thought perhaps I was still dreaming or hadn't recovered properly from my ordeal, but after a few moments, I realized that we were indeed rocking. We were on a ship! Actually, I was on the deck of a ship. All around me, I could hear the slap of oars against the sea.

The mast soared above me. Gulls floated and squawked above. I could smell the salt water and taste it on my lips. All sensations I had not experienced for a long, long time. It was a heady experience.

There was something wrong with my vision though.

I couldn't quite put my finger on it at first, and then I realized. It was my peripheral vision. I had gone so long without it, it was a stunning revelation to have it suddenly returned to me. I could see clearly without turning my head for the first time in almost two years.

You have to remember that I wore that helmet for a long time, rarely taking it off. During my adventures with Theseus, I only removed it to eat, bathe, and sleep. After my imprisonment in the labyrinth, the helmet—and especially the mask—took on a much greater significance. At first, I raged against it. Gradually, I began to accept it. Eventually, I became almost indifferent. It was a part of me and I it. We were two objects that had melded seamlessly to become one.

Gingerly, I reached up and felt my face and head. My face was no great revelation. Smooth. Someone had shaved me whilst I slept. Even with the mask on, I could still poke my fingers under to scratch or force food through the gap. But my horns. For the first time in my life, all I felt was … nothing. No horns. It was hard to make a thorough inspection because my head was fully bandaged in linen, but the absence was strange. Uplifting, joyous, exciting, but still strange.

My horns were something entirely different. I had been born with them. They were an innate part of me, not something forced upon me that I gradually came to accept. I hated them of course. They made me stand out; they made me different. People feared me because of my horns. But, I had thought it was impossible to remove them without killing me. I had suspected it would be like removing a perfectly good arm or leg.

I was fortunate that I had the most skilled craftsmen of the age available. I think I would've died if someone else had made the attempt. Not only that, but Daedalus had studied the healing arts extensively in his travels—all in the interests of being a holistic craftsman. He was fascinated by every subject and applied his great intellect to its utmost extent—no matter what the task. He was the sort of man that would have excelled in any intellectual pursuit.

The mask and my horns are what made me the Minotaur of course. Without them, I was just a man. A huge man perhaps, but a man nonetheless. I wanted nothing other than to live a normal life. To be a good husband and eventually a father for the children I hoped to have with Phaedra.

"How ... how did it go?" I asked.

Phaedra smiled at me sweetly and stroked my face. "Well, you're alive aren't you? That means it went well. You almost died. Again. I think it was probably the blood loss and shock. Then, right at a crucial moment—when Daedalus was almost through your first horn—there was another earthquake."

"So, what did you do?" I asked weakly.

"Daedalus wanted to stay. He said it was too dangerous to move you, but Theseus disagreed. He said that Poseidon had just appeared to him and told him we had to move." She shrugged. "So we moved. Theseus is a hard man to argue with."

I laughed softly. "He is that. Where is he?"

"He's onboard somewhere. I'll find him later. He'll want to

know you're awake. He has something to show you."

"What happened next?" I asked.

"We carried you outside. Daedalus and Icarus finished sawing through your horns. There was blood. A lot of it. I didn't know that horns bled like that. You were so pale; I thought you couldn't possibly have any blood left in your body."

"And how did we get on this ship?"

"It was the only intact ship left in the harbor. The wave created by the earthquake destroyed the others. Theseus got us all aboard by threatening the crew and promising to reward them richly when we reach Athens."

"And what of the tributes?" I asked.

"Safe," said Phaedra. "Theseus collected the survivors before we set sail."

I felt myself relax. It seemed that Phaedra and Theseus had everything organized. I had a few nagging doubts and many more questions, but I was still absolutely exhausted.

Phaedra saw my eyes droop. She kissed me lightly on the cheek. "Get some more rest. I'll come and check on you later."

The sounds of shipboard life faded around me. My eyes closed of their own accord, and I slept.

Ω

When I awoke again, I felt much stronger. I tried to sit up, and this time succeeded although I had to wait several moments for my head to stop swimming. I could hear the steady thud of oars. The wind had picked up, billowing the sail.

Sailors bustled around the deck, for the most part ignoring me. I looked around for familiar faces. I hadn't really been aware when I last awoke just how crowded the ship was. The deck was filled with people, some lying on makeshift pallets like myself or just making do on the hard wooden deck. Several passengers moved around listlessly, talking or looking out at the sea. I recognized a couple of the Athenian tributes. Some others were dressed in loincloths or dresses that marked them as Cretan. I suspected that the disaster that had befallen Crete had created many refugees.

Through the crowd, I saw two faces I recognized. Theseus and Phaedra. They smiled when they saw me sitting and joined me.

"My brother," said Theseus, smiling broadly. "It's good to see you up."

I smiled back tiredly. "I'm not up yet. Help me."

Theseus threw my arm around his shoulders and helped me to my feet. I sagged against him, feeling as weak as a baby. Phaedra tucked herself into my side, content to hold me. I didn't lean on her for fear of my weight squashing her.

"Are you up for a walk around the deck?" asked Phaedra.

I nodded, and the three of us shuffled slowly across the wooden deck.

"Where's my mother?" I asked finally. "My brothers?"

"Your mother is resting below deck," said Theseus. "As for your brothers, probably getting up to mischief. Last I saw of them, they were having a go on the oars."

I nodded. "And what of Icarus and Daedalus?" I asked.

"Ah," said Phaedra. "They chose not to come."

We rested against the rail of the ship. The short walk had

drained my limited supply of energy. I looked out over the shifting waves. White caps had been whipped up by the wind, although the swells were rather small, perhaps exhausted by the energy taken to destroy the harbor at Knossos. I wondered for a moment what my father, Poseidon, was doing at that moment. Was he under those white caps, staring up at me? Perhaps he was in the depths, doing whatever it was that sea gods did to pass the time.

There was an island looming on the horizon. It was still some distance away, and I didn't recognize it despite having spent some time in these waters. The ship appeared to be heading toward it.

"Where are they then?" I asked.

"They decided to escape Crete in a different manner entirely," said Phaedra.

I could've guessed but I wanted to hear Phaedra tell the story.

"They used the wings," she continued. "While you were imprisoned, Daedalus and Icarus perfected them. I think both of them couldn't wait to try."

"Did they work?" I asked hopefully.

Phaedra smiled. "Oh yes. It didn't hurt that they've had a lot of volunteers to trial them."

"What?" I asked, confused.

"You've asked before how I got the first batch of Athenian tributes off the island. I used the wings. After you escaped the island, Minos had much of Daedalus's equipment transferred to the tower. Minos, however, left several items behind in Daedalus's workshop. I had one set of wings to work with. I copied them and used them to free the Athenians."

I should have guessed.

"And they survived?" I asked. I vividly remembered my own flight. How I had almost died but for the assistance of Poseidon.

"Of course," said Phaedra smugly. "When I finally managed to see Daedalus in the tower, not only did he tell me of the secrets of the labyrinth, but he also suggested changes to the wings. I arranged for a fishing boat to pick them up once they were safely off the island."

A thought occurred to me. I turned to Theseus. "Didn't you say none of the tributes made it back to Athens?"

Theseus nodded. "That's true. We assumed the worst."

"That's because I told them not to go back," said Phaedra. "If they had, news of their escape would've reached Minos's ears. He would've known for certain that there was another way out of the labyrinth. I couldn't risk it."

"So where did they go, then?" I asked.

Phaedra nodded toward the island looming nearby. Even during the short amount of time we had been at the rail, the ship had closed the distance.

"Naxos," said Phaedra.

Ω

You've no doubt heard the tales of what became of Daedalus and Icarus. Much of that is unfortunately true, and it still pains me to this day that I never got to say goodbye to either of them. Especially Icarus who met his end in the surging waters of the Aegean.

The legend says that Icarus chose not to heed his father advice and flew too high, thereby melting the wax on his wings. No one, of course, was there to witness exactly what happened, but I did know how willful Icarus could be, so it doesn't surprise me. Whatever the truth, Icarus did indeed die. Perhaps the wings broke; perhaps Icarus lacked the strength. Who knows? Daedalus flew on without him, and I have never seen the master craftsman since.

As for Ariadne and Glaucus—in the end they got exactly what they deserved. Phaedra knew it was those two who had betrayed her. And Phaedra told Theseus.

Theseus, as I might have mentioned, meted out his own special brand of justice. The punishment should fit the crime. If Ariadne and Glaucus thought they might live out their lives in luxury in the palace at Athens, they were much mistaken.

The ship stopped at Naxos only long enough to pick up the surviving first batch of tributes. And to drop off two passengers. Much to their disgust and accompanied by a great deal of howling, tears, and protests, Ariadne and Glaucus were left on the island.

Some tales report that Theseus abandoned Ariadne while she slept. Let me assure you—she was very much awake at the time. Even now, I can still recall her screams of hatred, using language that would make a sailor blush. From what I gather, she later became the wife of Dionysius, the Greek god of wine. I don't know what he saw in her. He was probably drunk when he married her. I do know that she received a fitting end at the hand of Perseus who killed her at Argos. As for Glaucus, I do not know and do not care. He was never much of a brother to me.

The rest of the journey to Athens passed uneventfully. The winds, perhaps guided by Poseidon's hand, were in our favor. I spent as much time as I could with my mother, Pasiphae, my brothers, Theseus, and of course, Phaedra.

I confess that as we neared Athens, a feeling of disquiet started to grow within me. I went below deck often, mostly to avoid the sun and the open sky. After so long underground, I was distinctly uncomfortable exposed to open air. My uneasiness was so great that Phaedra began to worry about me. I didn't voice my fears because I considered myself weak. I thought it would pass. It did not.

The bandages came off my head. After being covered by a helmet for so long, my scalp was a mess of scabbed and dried skin. My hair was long and patchy. Phaedra attempted to give me a haircut, but it only served to highlight my already mundane looks and draw attention to the areas of flaky skin. Two patches were different though. Daedalus and Icarus had sawn the horns off at the base. What remained were two glossy spots that looked and felt like bone. Hair never grew over them, which is why I have always worn my hair long.

It was, however, the greatest relief to no longer have horns. For the first time in my life, I was normal. Well, as normal as someone could be after experiencing the labyrinth.

We sailed into the Saronic Gulf and edged our way toward the harbor at Piraeus. It was only then that Theseus took me below deck.

"I have something to show you," he said.

Phaedra had told me that Theseus had a surprise for me. Surprising is one word for it. Somewhat disturbing are two others.

He led the way into the hold. The first thing I noticed was the smell. We had been at sea for a few days—long enough for whatever it was to start rotting.

In a darkened recess, there was a bundled shape. Theseus unwrapped it from several cloaks and stood back.

It was a body. Not just a body, but a massive one. And it didn't have a head.

Theseus watched me, trying to gauge my reaction. "Well?" he said finally.

"Well, what?" I said, confused and a little angry. Why on earth would Theseus show me this corpse?

"Perhaps this will give you a clue," he said, darting further into the hold and emerging with a much smaller wrapped package.

He tore off the cloth that bound it. I watched in growing horror and realization.

It was a bull's head. A bull's head wearing my helmet.

"I went back to the palace before we took ship to Athens. I found this body there," explained Theseus. "I had to remove the head of course. Then all I had to do was kill a small bull and put its head in your helmet."

"This was your idea?" I asked, finally finding my voice.

"Mine and Phaedra's. If you're discovered still alive, then other heroes will find you and try to kill you. This was the only way."

I grimaced, feeling a little sick. But I knew they were right. If it was known I was already dead, no one, including my stepfather, would ever seek me out. And then there was Theseus's reputation to consider. I don't doubt for a second that the plan was mostly of Phaedra's devising, but Theseus went along with it. Why wouldn't he? By presenting the body of the Minotaur to the people of Athens, Theseus's reputation would be further enhanced. The hero returns triumphant, displaying the body of the beast for all to see. It was a simple and highly effective strategy.

So, now you know the truth. Theseus, of course, never killed me. He was my friend. A headless corpse and a bull's head enhanced the legend of Minotaur. And who wouldn't believe that? The people of Athens, in fact all of Greece, wanted to believe that Theseus had killed the monster. Why would he stop them?

I know Theseus did it for me. He did it to keep me safe. He was an honest and proud man. It wasn't actually a very heroic thing to do and went against everything he stood for. Phaedra told me later that he did take a considerable amount of convincing. I'm still glad that they didn't tell me—not that they could, given my unconscious state.

If they hadn't done it, I suppose I could've lived out my life in Athens as quietly as possible. Even so, it was only a matter of time until someone worked it out. That Minotaur still lived. Not only that, but lived amongst them.

I guess that was the reason why I did what I did. I knew that despite the precautions that Theseus and Phaedra took, someone would eventually recognize me. My size would always mark me as someone unusual. The stubs of my horns, although disguised under long hair, would inevitably be spotted. Questions would be asked. Theseus's reputation would suffer. My presence put everyone I loved in danger.

I realized that there was only one thing to do. There was only one thing I could do.

Ω

"You don't have to go," said Phaedra. She was crying.

"Yes, I do," I said sadly. "You know I do."

We'd been in Athens for two weeks. Two weeks of constant parties. Two weeks where the city celebrated Theseus's triumphant return. He had killed the Minotaur, freed the tributes, and released Athens from the yoke of Crete. I don't think Athens had ever bore witness to such celebrations.

The celebrations were marred in only one way—by the death of Theseus's father, King Aegeus. Overwhelmed by the excitement caused by his triumphant return to Athens, Theseus had neglected one important detail. More specifically, a task. A task he had promised his father before his departure to Crete. It was this: Theseus was meant to replace the common black sails of the ship with white sails, giving a sign to his father that he had returned alive. Theseus failed to do so, and his failure had tragic consequences.

As our ship was ushered into dock, we heard a cry of despair and a shape, unmistakably that of a man, had hurtled past us from the cliffs above, shattering on nearby rocks.

At the time of course, Theseus had no idea it was his father's body that lay nearby, mangled and lifeless on the rocks. The fact that someone had just fallen to their death wasn't quite the auspicious return that Theseus had wanted, but he wouldn't allow the death to interfere with his celebrations.

He raced off ahead of us, eagerly charging up the stairs

to the palace only to be met with grim faced palace officials burdened with the task of relaying the sad tidings to Aegeas's son.

The rest of us followed more slowly. At first, I believed that the anguished sound rising out of the palace above me must have been the sound of some animal being sacrificed. Approaching the steps leading directly into the palace, I recognized the huddled form of Theseus.

As swiftly as I could manage in my weakened state, I hurried to Theseus's side and embraced him. He responded immediately to my touch, returning the embrace with a painful ferocity. We held each other like that for a long time, and then suddenly Theseus released me and stood.

"It would seem," he said calmly to no one in particular, "that I have both a celebration and a funeral to plan."

And like that, Theseus overcame his grief. As I may have observed before, Theseus's passions ran deep and blazed with the intensity of the sun. But he let things go just as easily. I don't doubt for a second that he loved his father and mourned his death, but, unlike other (or perhaps lesser) men, I believe that one intense outpouring of emotion was enough for Theseus. I often wonder how he would have reacted to news of my demise.

Besides, now that Theseus was King of Athens, he had many other matters of state to attend to.

Theseus was so busy I only saw him rarely. He had his problems, and I had mine. I knew I could delay no longer. But there was another consideration. Something that I hadn't told Phaedra. I found being above ground too disturbing. I stayed indoors as much as possible, but it wasn't the same. I missed the strength and solidness that only being encased by rock walls could offer. The truth was that I missed the labyrinth. I wanted to go home.

The series of parties had been too much for me. After my long confinement, I found that I had no desire for constant companionship and conversation. I preferred my own company. That isn't to say that I didn't want to be around Phaedra, Theseus, or my family; I ... just needed time alone. Time that Athens could not give me.

"But Minos will never find you here. You will be safe, especially now that Theseus is King," pleaded Phaedra.

I shook my head. "People are already starting to look at me strangely. It will only be a matter of time before they discover who or what I am. I put all of you at risk by being here."

"People are looking at you strangely because of the way you act," said Phaedra. It was a mean thing to say, and I knew she immediately regretted it. She ran at me and threw herself into my arms.

"I'm sorry, Asterion. I didn't mean it."

But I think she did. Even Phaedra couldn't help noticing how odd I acted when I was outside. I couldn't help myself though. I suspect I was becoming embarrassing.

"Come with me," I asked, not for the first time.

Phaedra closed her eyes. "You know I cannot, Asterion. Please don't ask me again."

I knew her reasons. Crete was no longer her home. It was in ruins, and she had no desire to return to the labyrinth with me. She also feared for her life, worried that once Minos had dealt with Daedalus, he would return to seek his vengeance on everyone else. I suppose I should have let Theseus kill him. It would've been easier.

I picked up my satchel. "This is it then," I said, determined not to cry. I pushed her gently away.

Phaedra nodded her head sadly. "Come back to me when you are ready."

I nodded, but something told me I never would be.

She walked with me to the harbor. Theseus, my mother, Catreus, and Deucalion were waiting for me. The twins were looking somewhat worse for wear. They had already gathered a reputation in Athens for enthusiastic celebrating.

Theseus embraced me. "Goodbye my friend. I will see you soon. Phaedra and your family will be safe with me. I promise."

I thanked him and embraced my mother and brothers in turn. I saved Phaedra for last.

"Last chance," I said meeting her eye.

She lowered her head, and I knew what her final answer would be. I suppose I always knew.

I walked onto the ship, and we cast off almost immediately. I didn't look back.

CHAPTER 20

True to his word, I did see Theseus again. He came to visit, but I could see he was clearly uncomfortable talking to me in the ruins of the labyrinth. He never came again.

From what I gather, he was rather busy and found another best friend in the form of Pirithous, Prince of the Lapiths. Together, they had a great time, having adventures and abducting women, although how much of this is true is anyone's guess. As he grew older, Theseus seemed to particularly enjoy the latter. He stole Helen away—the same Helen who was the cause of the Trojan War. He and Pirithous kidnapped her. Theseus planned to marry her as soon as she was old enough. He left her at the city of Aphidna where another hero rescued her. Helen seemed to attract such behavior.

Theseus and Pirithous travelled to Tartarus. They spent many months there in darkness. It probably gave Theseus an insight into my own life. Eventually, Heracles rescued him, but Pirithous never escaped. I guess Pirithous suffered a similar fate to myself in the end. Funny how Theseus's friends had a knack for such things.

Theseus abducted an Amazon queen named Hippolyta. This instigated a war between the Amazons and the Athenians. He later married her, and she bore him a son.

But Theseus was always a bit fickle when it came to women. He got rid of Hippolyta in favor of someone else. Someone who for the longest time I couldn't forgive. He married Phaedra.

I don't blame either of them now. That is all in the distant past. I knew Phaedra always loved me, but I had abandoned her. Theseus was King of Athens and was in a position to protect her and keep her safe. I suppose it was inevitable that they would marry.

I know that Phaedra and Theseus never had children. In fact, her relationship with Theseus was largely platonic.

She eventually got tired of Theseus and his womanizing—not to mention his hopelessly immature obsession with abducting women—and left. It's that simple. There was never any love between them. For Phaedra, the marriage was one of convenience.

As for Theseus, I hope to see him again one day. He met his end in a none too glorious manner. The hero, Lycomedes, threw him off a cliff. Knowing Theseus, he was probably trying to abduct his wife at the time.

I'm sure I will find him in Olympus. If not, I will search for him in Tartarus.

After all, he is still my friend.

He will always be my friend.

Ω

"What became of your mother and your brothers?" asked Ovid. Now that the tale was almost complete, he was wracked by conflicting emotions. He'd never written so much so quickly before. He was exhausted, on the verge of collapse, relieved that the story was almost at an end. But also a little resentful that he would hear no more. Even though he was bone tired, several questions remained unanswered.

Night was almost over. The horizon, just visible out the uncovered window, was beginning to glow with the onset of dawn. The ship back to Rome would be leaving in a few hours. Ovid was not looking forward to the journey back to the port, especially on that accursed donkey.

"They visited several times over the years," said Ast. "It has been said that my mother was the daughter of the sun god, Helios. She was a demi-goddess and, as such, an immortal. Pasiphae could have chosen to remain on the earth much like I have, but she decided not to. She had suffered much and was tired of life on this mortal plane. She went to Olympus. Perhaps I will see her there again soon."

"And your brothers?" prompted Ovid. "What of Catreus and Deucalion?"

"They were only mortal, despite their parents being descended from gods," said Ast. "The blood of the gods did not flow as strongly within them. They are long dead. Before they died however, they lived long, happy lives and made much mischief."

Ovid nodded. "I'm glad." And indeed he was. It was satisfying to hear that some of the people in Ast's life had been rewarded for their loyalty.

Ovid had more questions, some he had been dreading for fear of Ast's reaction. To fortify himself, he attempted to fill his goblet from the one remaining wine skin. To his disgust, he found it all but empty. He shook the dregs into his eager mouth. Perhaps it was time to get going. There was plenty more wine where this came from at the port of Iraklion.

"But you returned to the labyrinth," said Ovid. "Why don't you live there now?"

"I did for many years," said Ast. "The earthquake and fire made the palace uninhabitable. Few people visited. After a time, some of it was given over to worship of the goddess Rhea, and a shrine was built in her honor.

"Over time, I managed to get over my fear of open spaces again by spending some time every day outside tending the gardens. Eventually, I made my home here. I didn't really want to leave the labyrinth completely, but it has become too unstable—too dangerous—inside. Subsequent earthquakes have seen to that. You've seen what it is like. Much of it is now filled in with rubble and erosion. Time has not been kind to it. Eventually, there will be little evidence that it existed at all."

Ovid nodded. The place was a death trap. The thought of living there—even over a thousand years earlier—was almost too much to think about. "And ... and what happened to Phaedra?" he asked hesitantly.

Ast said nothing for a long moment, looking at Ovid with an unreadable expression. Finally, he spoke.

"She was the daughter of Minos. Unlike my other siblings,

she was filled with the strength of the gods. Immortal, like me."

"So where is she now?" asked Ovid.

Ast sighed sadly and shrugged his massive shoulders. "I don't know. I haven't seen her for many years. Long after her marriage to Theseus, she returned here, but the memories of this place were too much for her to bear. She wanted to forget, and she couldn't release the past surrounded by the ruins of this place. Besides, I prefer the dark, and her place is in the sun."

"Oh," said Ovid, for once lacking the words. He felt like he should say something comforting, but casting around inside his head, he realized nothing he could say would be suitable or appropriate.

"Now," said Ast, standing suddenly. "You have heard my story. Are you satisfied? Do you believe?"

Ovid nodded his head slowly. "I am. I do." His scholar's instinct told him he had heard nothing but the truth these last two days. As far-fetched as it was, Ast was the embodiment of sincerity. Ovid believed him with his entire being. There was no doubt in his mind that the man before him had once been the fabled Minotaur. It was hard to come to terms with the skeptic he was when he first arrived. That was almost a completely different person.

"What are your plans then?" asked Ast.

"I will return to Rome and write up my notes for publication. *Metamorphoses* is all but finished, so I will concentrate all my attention on your story."

"And what then?"

"Then it is up to the people to believe. They will have to decide what the truth is."

Ast nodded. It was all he'd expected.

Ast helped gather Ovid's possessions into the bags the poet had brought from the port. He carried them outside and loaded them onto the donkey waiting patiently nearby. It was just past dawn, and although early, the sun was already providing a comfortable warmth.

Ovid appeared with his writer's satchel slung over his shoulder. Ast helped him up onto the donkey.

"Do you want me to accompany you?" asked Ast.

"No need, my friend. I know the way now. I will write to you and send you a copy of the manuscript when it is complete."

"Very well," said Ast. "Safe travels."

"And you also," said Ovid. He paused. "Thank you," he said finally.

"For what?" asked Ast, slightly confused.

"For your story. It is a gift. It is not a common thing to tell the truth."

"For me, there is little else left."

Ovid inclined his head but made no comment. Without another word, he turned the donkey and set off.

Ω

Ast, sometimes known as Asterion, the man that had once been known as the Minotaur, watched him depart. When Ovid had disappeared, he returned to his cottage and sat down wearily at the table.

The door opened, and a figure appeared.

"Has he gone?"

Ast nodded. "He has."

"Do you feel better now?"

"A little," he confessed. "It was good to tell the truth. Finally. Theseus is a thousand years dead. I no longer feel like I am betraying his memory."

"I think he'd understand. You and he went through a lot together. It's only fair that your part in it is heard. Besides, you can apologize to him in person one day."

"And what now?" he asked.

"You promised that once this was done, we would finally find our rest in Olympus. You haven't changed your mind, have you?"

"No, of course not. You of all people should know that once my word is given, I do not break it lightly," he replied, somewhat stiffly.

"Oh, don't be like that," she said. She walked over to the table and hugged him tightly. "Just out of interest, was it really necessary for you to lie to him like that?"

"What do you mean?" he asked.

"About me," she said. "Don't be stupid. You know what I'm talking about."

"It was," he said firmly. "Humans struggle with the truth as it is. If I give them a happy ending, there is no chance it would be believed. Happy endings only happen in myths and legends."

"Is that a fact?" said Phaedra, kissing him on the lips. "Then how do you explain us?"

And then she laughed.

THE END

Map of ancient Greece used with permission from greeka.com.

NOTES

Ovid

Publius Ovidius Naso (43 BC – AD 17/18) was commonly known as Ovid to the majority of the English-speaking world. He was one of the more famous Roman poets, best known for his three major collections of poetry: the *Heroides*, *Amores*, and *Ars Amatoria*. The *Metamorphoses* is probably his greatest known work.

By 7 AD, he had almost finished the *Metamorphoses*. The *Metamorphoses* is an epic poem comprised of 15 books that explore Greek and Roman mythology. It tells of the transformations of human beings into new forms.

Ovid embarked on a voyage just before its publication, visiting some of the places where the heroic events had taken place, possibly for inspiration but more likely to check the validity of his stories.

It was around this time that he met Ast on Crete.

In 8 AD, Ovid was banished to Tomis, on the Black Sea, by the Emperor Augustus.

According to Ovid, he was banished for *carmen et error* (a poem and a mistake). No one knows for certain why Ovid was exiled. Many scholars have offered explanations but not one of them guessed at the truth. None of them are credible.

The truth is this: Ovid attempted to publish the true story of the Minotaur. Augustus, long a fan of heroic adventures, especially those of Theseus, refused to believe. When Ovid insisted it was the truth, Augustus exiled him and destroyed one of the two copies in existence.

This recount is based on the remaining copy that was recovered from Ovid's tomb in Tomis.

Knossos and the Labyrinth

Scholars have long agreed that Knossos, Crete, is the site of the labyrinth. Arthur Evans conducted a series of excavations on the palace revealing the true extent of the site. It contained over thirteen hundred rooms, giving rise to the belief that the palace itself was part of the labyrinth. Ruins of the palace still contain many depictions of men leaping over the horns of a bull.

It is unknown whether the labyrinth was actually underneath the palace because of erosion and other natural processes.

According to archaeological evidence, Knossos was abandoned in the late Bronze Age (1380 – 1100 BC) due to damage caused by both a massive earthquake and a fire. It was never occupied again.

Most believe that the earthquake was a natural disaster. You know better.

Acknowledgements

My thanks to all the people who read the initial drafts and offered advice and constructive feedback. Special thanks go to D.C. Grant, Catherine Mayo and Suzy Rutan. My wonderful agent, Vicki Marsdon at Wordlink, has been there for me the whole time, championing *Minotaur* from the outset. Of course this wouldn't have been possible without Georgia at Month9books and her wonderful editing crew— Nichole and Cameron ... My eternal thanks. I am very grateful to the other staff at Month9books including Allie, Jaime, Jennifer ... To Najla Qamber Designs for the wonderful cover ... My eternal thanks. As always, my thanks and love to my wife, Rose, for giving me the time and space to write. Her support and encouragement have always been unconditional. And to my son, Jack, for the inspiration and drive to do better.

PHILLIP W. SIMPSON

Phillip W. Simpson is the author of many novels, chapter books, and other stories for children. His publishers include Macmillan, Penguin, Pearson, Cengage, Raintree, and Oxford University Press.

He received both his undergraduate degree in Ancient History and Archaeology and his Masters (Hons) degree in Archaeology from the University of Auckland. He started, but has yet to complete, his Ph.D. in Archaeology. He has post-graduate diplomas in Museum Studies, Teaching, Education, and Human Resource Management.

Before embarking on his writing career, he joined the army as an officer cadet, owned a comic shop, and worked in recruitment in both the UK and Australia.

His first young adult novel, Rapture (Rapture Trilogy #1), was shortlisted for the Sir Julius Vogel Awards for best Youth novel in 2012.

When not writing, he works as a schoolteacher.

Phillip lives and writes in Auckland, New Zealand with his wife Rose, their son, Jack, and their two border terriers, Whiskey and Raffles. He loves fishing, reading, movies, football (soccer), and single malt Whiskeys.

For more information, go to www.phillipwsimpson.com

OTHER MONTH9BOOKS TITLES YOU MIGHT LIKE

FINGERS IN THE MIST

HORROR BUSINESS

UNDERTAKERS: SECRET OF THE CORPSE EATER

FIND MORE AWESOME TEEN BOOKS AT MONTH9BOOKS.COM

Connect with Month9Books online:

Facebook: www.Facebook.com/Month9Books

Twitter: https://twitter.com/month9books

You Tube: www.youtube.com/user/Month9Books

Blog: www.month9booksblog.com

Request review copies via publicity@month9books.com

HORROR BUSINESS

A NOVEL

RYAN CRAIG BRADFORD

FINGERS IN THE MIST

THE REDEEMERS ARE COMING!

O'DELL HUTCHISON

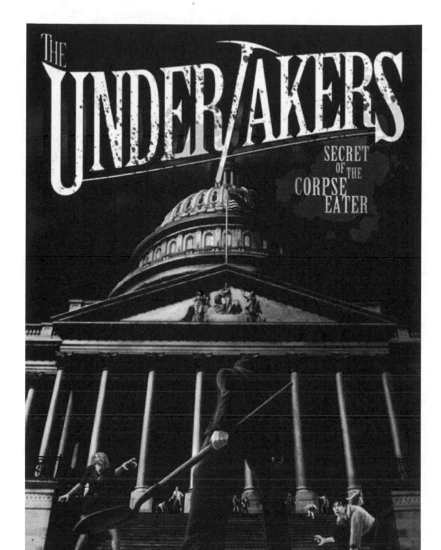

THE UNDER AKERS

SECRET
of THE
CORPSE
EATER

TY DRAGO